On the Downtown Mall

ON THE DOWNTOWN MALL

GARY D. KESSLER

With Contemporary Photographs by
Rick Britton and Stacey Evans

GORGIAS PRESS
2002

First Edition, copyright © 2002 by Gorgias Press LLC.

All rights reserved under International and Pan-American Copyright Conventions. Published in the United States of America by Gorgias Press LLC, New Jersey.

ISBN 1-931956-00-6

GORGIAS PRESS
46 Orris Ave., Piscataway, NJ 08854 USA
www.gorgiaspress.com

Printed in the United States of America
10 9 8 7 6 5 4 3 2 1

To my parents, Velma and George Kessler, and to several unnamed Charlottesville-area personalities, whose stories have been spun into "essences" that then were twisted and skewed to be woven into the fabric of the stories in this book.

Table of Contents

Dedication	iii
Table of Contents	v
Preface	vii
Acknowledgments	x

PART ONE: SOME STORIES — 1

Just Coasting	3
The Edge	13
Where There's a Will, …	17
Good Customer	29
Invisible	35
Just Two More Years	41
War Souvenirs	51
What's Mine Is Mine	62
Readers' Choice: Gordon's Ride	68
The Game: One	76
Just Call Me Rose	83
The Present	96
Sad Eyes	103
The Wedding Plans	108
The Game: Two	113
Decision Point	117
The Feud	123
The Gauntlet	131
Something to Tell You	137
Pork Chops Tonight	146

Hardship	149
Cruel, Cruel Fate	159
The Appointment	164
Honor Violation	169
The Favor	173
A Matter of Weight	179
Save the Children	185
The Game: Three	189
The Chasm between "c" and "C"	192
Perspective	199
He/She/Them	204
The Game: Four	222
Another Day	225
Tug of War	229
Ain't Whistlin Dixie	233
The Spotlight	240

PART TWO: THE HISTORY — 247

Reflection of American Resilience: The Charlottesville Downtown Mall	249
From Three Notch'd Road to Downtown Mall	250
Timberlake's Drug Store	255
The Hardware Store	257
The Paramount Theater	259
Urban Renewing the African-American Community	260
References	262
About the Author	264
About the Photographers	265

Preface

This volume of short stories is anchored in a real place, the Charlottesville, Virginia, Downtown Mall, and in time, a single unseasonably warm day in mid-April in some near-future year. But it is too much of an unruly collection to be limited by the realities of the actual Charlottesville Downtown Mall or of its regular inhabitants, or to be pinned down on a particular date.

Businesses and buildings that are mentioned in the book are not necessarily located where a particular story puts them and are not necessarily real businesses or buildings on the actual Mall. And in all cases, even the real businesses and buildings appearing in the short story section of the book are populated by an entirely different set of characters than those you would find on the real Downtown Mall. The goal of the short story collection is to capture the spirit and essence of the vibrant Charlottesville Downtown Mall, not just to faithfully mirror its actual buildings and people.

The book even wriggles out from underneath a label as fiction as opposed to nonfiction. It includes, in an afterward, an essay on the origin and development of the real, historically significant, Charlottesville Downtown Mall. In addition, the short stories are accompanied by a photo montage by two talented Charlottesville-area photographers that has been inspired by Charlottesville's current center city. The concluding essay includes photographs from the past.

This book is, in fact, meant to be taken as a salute to all of those towns and small cities across the United States that have, as Charlottesville, Virginia, has done, managed to revitalize and beautify their downtown centers as rejuvenated meeting and activity grounds for their citizens of all ages. If there is a general theme for this collection, it is that, in life, things are not always what they seem to be (and the Downtown Mall of the short stories is slightly askew from the actual Mall precisely to add emphasis to this theme). Some of the stories come right out and scream this as their central theme. Some let that theme creep in gently and in subtle tones. Some just play with that theme as a side issue. And some, since this is an unruly bunch, blithely ignore the general theme altogether.

The book structure itself plays with this central theme. While the stories are anchored, to a lesser or greater degree, in the Charlottesville Downtown Mall, many stray far afield from that place and from the established time frame of the book. Both the characters and story lines have refused to stay within bounds of set pieces. Rather, they often break out of their homes and intrude on their neighbors. Some stories insist on being arrayed in integral sets. At least one story doesn't reveal its irony within its own bounds but is illuminated by the stories around it. One story refuses to impose an ending, leaving the choice to the reader. And one story refuses to stay together in one piece and scatters itself around the book, bringing in a story-within-a-story-within-a-story dimension to the work.

I didn't make any of these decisions in putting the book together. The stories just appeared and found their own zones of comfort. From time to time, characters refused to be developed as new characters but, rather, informed me that they really were a character I had used incidentally in an earlier story. And some characters told me that it would be all right if I used them as a minor character in the story I then was writing, but wouldn't I really like to know about, and include, their own fascinating story at a later point?

Even the development of the book defied conventional rules of organization. The stories simply materialized in a poof of realization, in nearly complete form, when and as they saw fit. They popped up when I was trying to sleep, when I was helping the cat make the bed, when I was making the long drives home from visiting my mother. They intruded when I was cleaning up in the garden, when I should have been listening to sermons

Preface

(although it could be argued in these instances that the appearance of the story simply meant that the essential point of the sermon was sinking in), and even when I was working hard to develop a different story idea altogether.

Above all, the collection attempts to be a study of the human condition in all of its fairness, foibles, and follies and of the isolation and connectedness, or both together simultaneously, that bless or plague people, depending on how they are prepared to deal with what life has offered them. I was delighted to find, after the stories had made their own way onto the pages just as they wished, that some favorable traits seem to override all else in the unfolding of daily human activity. These include simple nobility, common decency, a rejection of pomposity and self-indulgence, and an empathetic concern for the well-being of others. I hope this collection will leave you with the same feeling that human civilization is, overall, indeed progressing toward a higher ground. As you may guess in reading the stories, as muddled about as they were in construction to protect both the innocent and the guilty, nearly all of them are grounded in real stories of real people.

Gary D. Kessler
Charlottesville, Virginia

Acknowledgments

This book has developed through an interactive and, I believe, innovative "book building" process that used various forms to involve the reader even before the ink had dried on the book, and thus there are many people who helped bring it into publication.

As with most any book development project, this one was blessed with a group of readers, who read, commented on, and pointed to grammar and structural problems in individual stories during various stages of book construction. For this service, I am very thankful for the thoughtful and open responses of Evelyn Kessler, Margaret Baker, Katie Kessler, and Pamela Roblyer.

The "book building" process included interactive serialization on my Internet website (www.editsbooks.com), with people all over the world making suggestions and comments. Specific invitations went to Charlottesville-area high school- and college-level creative writing programs to make use of this Charlottesville-based collection in their programs. I am grateful for the feedback I received on individual stories from this process.

The stories were also presented and critiqued in a long-term seminar at the Warwick Forest retirement community in Newport News, Virginia, (with thanks to Carole Stockberger, Cindy Seward, and Dawn Roe).

Margaret M. O'Bryant and Howard Newlon Jr. of the Albemarle County Historical Society library, provided valuable help in tracking down information for the background essay.

I offer a special note of appreciation to Teresa Dowell-Vest, whose moving play, *Vinegar Hill,* pointed to background information for one of the stories and for the essay, and, as far

Acknowledgements

as I can determine, may have provided the inspirational seed for the book project. Many thanks also to Nancy Damon, director of The Virginia Festival of the Book, for graciously endeavoring to belatedly include this book in the 2002 book festival events.

The decision to include photographs nearly doubles the time, effort, and expense involved in producing a book. I thank my photographer collaborators, Stacey Evans and Rick Britton, for helping to simplify the process and for making the photograph selection process pleasurable. The contemporary photographs herein are provided with the permission of the respective copyright holders, Ms. Evans and Mr. Britton. Margaret Hrabi and Michael Plunkett of the Albert H. Small Special Collections Library of the University of Virginia's Alderman Library provided invaluable help in assembling the vintage photographs the appear with the concluding essay and in granting permissions for the use of these photographs in this book. My thanks also to Melba Christy for her generous technical support.

A final note of appreciation to the book's copyeditor, Kevin Quirk (www.awriterseye.com), who was both professional and helpful—but most of all, kind—in his edits, and to an extremely helpful and accommodating publisher, George A. Kiraz.

PART ONE

SOME STORIES

The Downtown Mall from the West End. (Photo by Stacey Evans.)

Just Coasting

I always thought of it like the line by Jerry in the Albee play *The Zoo Story*. The one where he says "sometimes a person has to go a very long distance out of his way to come back a short distance correctly." That is, without the suicide angle, of course. But Paul has never agreed with that. And for years, when I'd come up with that excuse, he'd say, "John, you've just pissed your whole friggin life away."

Those are his words, not mine. I haven't used language that strong since we were in the eighth grade and under the thumbs of the Sisters of Mercy. Of course, even then Paul wasn't cowed by either a thumb or a sister.

Up till the day when we couldn't remember what the ocean looked like even though it was stretched before us, Paul and I had been joined at the hip—long beyond when most like us had already gone their separate ways. We were together right through when we finished seminary and then we had to split up to some degree. I guess we always knew they wouldn't put identical twins in the same pulpit. In his more playful moments, Paul thought we should give that a shot. See how long a congregation could take a good minister/bad minister routine before catching on.

But there we stood on the bluff at Brookings, Oregon, trying to pick out the water through the heavy fog. Mom had just died from exhaustion, which meant that Dad had to go into a nursing home and be a burden to a whole new set of folks. And we'd turned over the last of the family's savings to the seminary in exchange for two pieces of parchment. Paul said, "I'm tired of knowing there's an ocean there and not being able to see how big it is. I think I'll try the Atlantic for a while." And then it was just me and the fog—and Dad.

I thought we were real fortunate in the way it worked out. Dad got a semiprivate room. We were able to cover that and my room, with bath privileges, at Mrs. Sutter's in exchange for my working as assistant activities director cum back scrubber, bedpan porter, and bus driver at the home. After the first five years, it became pretty much a routine, and it was always good to see the faces light up when I made my rounds.

All except for Dad's, of course. He'd preferred life when he was running Mom into the grave and didn't have to compete with other invalids. As the years rolled on, he increasingly looked through rather than at me, and the only thing that would bring light to his eyes were those letters from Maryland. I still remember the last one we received from somewhere outside Annapolis a couple of days before Dad died. Dad got a real kick out of the shine on Paul's new Buick. I was more partial to the obvious fun the kids in the photo were having washing the big sedan. Paul's letter explained that this was the confirmation class at his church doing one of their required good deeds. The same letter told me that Paul thought he could get me a pastor's charge in the suburbs of Baltimore. So, Dad's passing and Paul's offer coincided with my boarding a train in Seattle for the long trip east.

☙ ❧

I shouldn't have stepped out on the platform to stretch my legs in Denver. And I *really* shouldn't have gone around that corner to adjust my money belt so it wouldn't feel like my back was trying to swallow a lump of coal for the ride into Kansas.

The kids weren't all that big, but there were just too many of them to handle. The scrawniest of the lot must have been in training, because, while the other four were getting in some pretty good punches, that kid stood off to the side, his sad eyes wide as saucers and tears streaming down his dusty face. He finally mustered up some strength, however, and came into the scrum for his initiation jabs just as the others latched onto the money belt. That was how I came to have a good grip on his already-torn T-shirt just as his buddies lost interest in me and scurried back around the corner. My memory can still raise the squeal of rage from a distance when the grungy little urchins discovered how little there was in that money belt. Still, it was all the money I had to carry me to Annapolis, so there was no use getting back on that train.

Turns out Denver was as nice a divergence from my way as any, and getting Manuel processed through the Colorado legal system pretty much structured my new life at the foot of the Rockies. That lack of vision thing that Paul and Dad always were riding me about was getting in my way again. I had trouble visualizing Manuel as the hardened criminal type that would have put him on the road through the reformatory and to prison. They said they couldn't keep him off the slippery slide without a parent or guardian who would stand up for him and that he could only avoid the reformatory by being accepted in a Big Brother program. I was told the waiting list for that program was longer than Manuel was tall. So, the Denver Big Brother program wound up with its first package deal.

Manuel was at a pretty impressionable age, though. His buddies from the train station seemed to have some sort of case of honor about putting him on the wrong side of Wyatt Earp on the streets of Denver. I was to find that being a part-time Big Brother wasn't going to be enough. We solved the issue by me getting a job as a bus driver at the school where he went and pretty much staying handcuffed to him until he entered Colorado State. After a blur of early-morning coffee, grubby kids' faces, and an unending march of taillights, Manuel had a law degree, married a society girl from Milwaukee, and had become director of a legal aid society in a part of Denver I wouldn't even think of going into. I couldn't be prouder with how that kid picked himself up and turned his life around.

By the time we knew we could order Manuel's cap and gown for the graduation ceremony, I determined that although I didn't have enough money scraped together to get back on the train headed east, I could barely manage a bus ticket going the longer northern route. This wanderlust had been prompted by yet another letter from Paul. Along with a picture of his new Cadillac and the house—I originally thought it was some museum—he had been provided by his congregation in Potomac, Maryland, an upscale suburb of Washington, D.C., Paul told me he still was looking for me to arrive on the train. He no longer thought I could get a pastorate in Baltimore, but he did think he had enough influence to swing an itinerant preacher position on the rural circuit on the Eastern Shore for me.

This was when he started telling me I had pissed my life away. My seminary training was pretty useless now. I hadn't taken any refresher courses in ministering and had let my credentials lapse. Having had seminary, however, should be as good, he thought, as the night classes others were taking to qualify for the rural circuit. He said that, from there, I could start relearning how to take care of people's spiritual needs and might eventually make something of myself. I could see his point and was grateful that he was still willing to look out for me.

☙ ❧

I think I could have gotten some sleep on that bus headed for Chicago if I hadn't horned in and checked out why that woman—not much more than a spindly girl—in the seat across from mine had such a frightened doe look about her. I sure did thank my lucky stars for years afterward, however, that I had been so nosy. By the time we reached Omaha, I knew that Maggy had until three days previously worked for an escort service in Denver's tenderloin district. I also knew that this happy life had been unceremoniously cut short when she was diagnosed both as having M.S. and as going blind. But it wasn't until we had cleared the billboards of Des Moines that I could make hide or hair of why she was on the bus. I think that must have been because Maggy hadn't given that one much thought herself.

After another couple of hours of riding through endless flat fields of something already harvested, Maggy confessed that she had tried to end it all with pills and liquor the day after the doctor had cheerfully delivered what she called "her lingering death sentence." But this hadn't worked—probably, she had mused, because she had already consumed enough pills and liquor over the years to build up a strong immunity. When she had come to, she had been aghast—not at what she had tried and failed to do, but that she had tried it in Denver. She wanted to go home to do it. So, here she was on the bus, headed home.

By the time we got off the bus in her Wabash, Indiana, hometown, Maggy was feeling somewhat better about her situation. In the end, the blindness won the race with the M.S., but Maggy managed to make it most of the way through Indiana State before her eyes gave out completely. We had learned Braille together because she had had trouble applying herself to that program on her own. So I was able to help her through the last of her coursework. Then Maggy took off like wildfire with an intensity that was all the more brilliant for its short duration. She found her calling as a speaker advocate for M.S. research. And we found ourselves traveling all around the upper Midwest for several seasons. She would wow her audiences and loosen their wallets real good, while I did what I could to make sure she got to her engagements on time, with enough food under her belt to keep her voice up, and wearing clothes that came close to matching. We were operating out of Indianapolis, and when we found that the various community services there were somewhat chaotic and seemed to be wasting a lot of time and money on duplicative and sometimes unfocused work, I used some of my spare time trying to figure out how to get them to start talking to each other and melding their activities somewhat better.

Maggy and I got along together real well and at some point between speaking engagements managed to fit in a ceremony. And I would have been just as happy to have stayed in Indiana, but, as had happened in Denver, several things came up at once to get me on the road headed east once more. Turns out Maggy had less time than most with M.S., and the last few months were real rough on her. But she claimed that the Indiana segment of her life had been a whole lot more pleasant than her time in Denver and that she was mighty glad she had gotten on that bus headed back to Wabash. About the time Maggy needed me nearby the most, the combined community services agency I helped put together decided it was rising to a whole new level of operation and needed someone a lot more reliable in attendance and a whole lot more photogenic than me to present to the public. And then there was another letter from Paul, who no longer had his own church but who lived in Washington, D.C., and was some sort of district superintendent. He'd always said that the ultimate goal of a shepherd was to work his way out of having any sheep in his own flock to take care of, so I guess Paul was a real success now. He certainly did look well fed and satisfied in the photo enclosed of him and his sleek wife standing by their Mercedes at the Washington Cathedral. In his letter, he said he regretted that I had now completely lost out on a ministering career, but that he still could fit me into a desk job at the district office if I stopped fooling around in Indianapolis and made it to the coast.

☙ ❧

It took a while to get Maggy's tombstone paid for. But, one day a neighbor came over to borrow the phone to call around to see if anyone was going east and could take four Siamese cats she had found on the road to a Siamese rescue center in the hills of central Virginia. That's when it occurred to me that I had been heading east for several years myself. The next day, I loaded up the old Honda, and to the chorus of four very angry caged cats, started off for Madison, Virginia, which, if my yellowed maps were halfway accurate, would put me close to Paul's place in Washington.

As it turned out, either my maps weren't too helpful or I was busy cajoling the cats when I should have been looking at the road, because, driving through the night, I overshot Madison a bit and landed in Charlottesville. After driving around there a while, I found they had bricked over their main street to make a nifty walking mall. I found out about the Downtown Mall when I got lost and ran out of road just as I was entering the downtown area.

I never asked, but Chantel must have really thought I was a sight when she came upon me as I sat there in my dusty Honda in dawn's early light, where the asphalt was divided from red brick by a couple of metal barriers. I was looking bewilderedly at the flickering fairy lights in the trees and was mewing softly to lull the cats when Chantel hefted her ample bosoms on the passenger windowsill and scrunched her ebony face down to where she could look me in the eye. Her hair radiated in gray and black wisps from an expressive face that managed to display humor and slight concern simultaneously.

She never once asked me why I had been mewing, but, upon hearing that I was headed for somewhere in the countryside between Madison and Orange to deliver four Siamese orphans, she whipped out a cellular phone and took charge of my life. As luck would have it, the woman who ran the rescue center had come into Charlottesville for a breakfast meeting at The Nook Restaurant not far up the Mall from where I had landed. So we arranged a delivery on the spot, and I never saw Madison.

All of the excitement seemed a bit much for Chantel, and she was huffing and wheezing pretty seriously by the time we'd heard the last from the cats. Gracious as well as commanding, she offered me a slice of sidewalk for that night under a colonnade at a big church near the Downtown Mall and across a small park with a bronze statue of General Lee astride his horse. It was still pretty cool at night even here in the South, though, and Chantel was looking pretty delicate despite her massive bulk. So I told her I'd love to, but I already had two rooms reserved down at the Days Inn, and I couldn't see why either of them should go to waste, so why didn't she take one of those rooms for the night and, if she would, perhaps she could lead me to a couple of the former presidents' homes I'd heard were about these parts.

Over the rest of the morning and into the afternoon, I saw Jefferson's, Madison's, and Monroe's houses. As far as I could determine, though, none of them were at home. Chantel never questioned why I had two rooms reserved at a motel, and she never left me alone long enough to make a call. Luckily, the Days Inn had two rooms available when we putted up to the big carport they'd been kind enough to slap on the front of their building. I got the impression while we ate that evening at the Red Lobster attached to the motel that it had been some time since Chantel had gotten a good meal. She was a great conversationalist and told me all about how her family had been important merchants in Charlottesville going almost as far back as the days of the three presidents—Jefferson, Madison, and Monroe—whose shadows enveloped the area. Seems her family's shop had been on the main street just about where I had rolled up to the Downtown Mall—although, of course, her daddy's business and those of several other black families had disappeared in the urban renewal frenzy that had predated the walking mall craze. Chantel herself had proven to be unmovable, however, and still held court on the Mall in front of what had once been the family shoe store. For all her worldly ways, Chantel confided to me between chews and coughs that she had never seen the sea and surely would like to do that before she died.

I didn't like the look she gave when the subject of death came up, so I quickly said that I had never seen the Atlantic myself and had, in fact, left the Pacific shore some time ago with the intention of seeing the eastern shore and was just then on my way to Washington, D.C., to get that done.

"Honey," Chantel giggled at me, "Washington, D.C., ain't on no ocean. If you want to see the ocean," she said, "you have to go east, not north." I guessed then that I hadn't done a very good job following that old map that had brought me into Charlottesville. But I couldn't say I wasn't glad to see that town.

‍‍‍

ಙ ೞ

Toward late afternoon of the next day, Chantel and I pulled up next to the sand at the poorer end of Virginia Beach. Chantel was a lot weaker by then than she had been the previous day, and I now understood why I had thrown Maggy's wheelchair into the trunk of the Honda back in Indianapolis rather than leaving it behind as the neighbors had suggested. As I wheeled Chantel out onto the sand as far as the wheelchair could go, she was giving off little clucking sounds and an occasional "Oh, my." It eventually got dark enough that we could barely see the water, but still Chantel sat there and stared out to sea. After a long stretch of silence, she gave a larger sigh than normal, trailing off into a disturbing cough, and allowed as how it was a very nice ocean but not quite as big as she had thought it would be.

The deep smile lines on her face, however, belied any disappointment she might have expressed.

I was able to find a small rundown cottage just off the beach that, along with a few others, rented by the day. Chantel died three days later, but we had managed to get out on the sand every one of those days.

I called Paul to tell him I was still on my way to Washington but would be a couple of days getting it done. He lit into me something fierce—the usual declarations of how I was just floating around and wasting my life on minutia and had wasted all that training to be a minister and how it was impossible to understand how identical twins with the identical training could turn out so different. He said he was tired of trying to hold me up and that, if I couldn't make it to Washington in the next three days, not to bother to come at all. All I could do was say that I was sorry and that I was sure I would be there in three days. I certainly couldn't argue with his point.

☙ ❧

It took two days to make final arrangements for Chantel. While I was packing to leave, I heard one real corker of a domestic fight going on in the cottage next to ours. I can't say I was surprised. The young couple and their two toddlers had been in the cottage when we arrived, and they obviously had not been having a pleasant vacation. The man was a drinker, and the woman had skittered around like a frightened rabbit for days trying to keep the kids quiet and out of his way. But even when she had taken them out on the sand and settled them into making sandcastles, he would weave his way out there, scream at her about something that hadn't been done right, and set both kids off before returning to the cottage, jumping into his Camaro, and roaring off until late in the night.

When I carried my bag out to the Honda to leave for Washington, his Camaro was kicking up dust once more, and it was loaded down so heavy I could tell the man didn't intend to come back. I was just closing the trunk when the woman staggered out of her cottage and collapsed into a weeping heap on the steps. She looked beat up pretty bad. As I walked over toward her, all I could think of was that I wasn't going to be making it to Washington in time. In spite of all the good intentions in the world, I had once again proven to be a big disappointment to Paul.

Well, I guess I just wasn't cut out to be a minister. At least I had seen the other ocean, which is what we both had set out to do.

The Edge

It was a special time for Lisa, the hour before she had to be in school, her first of two daily workouts at the rink. The fairy lights in the trees of the Downtown Mall were still working their magic when she and her coach entered the walkway around the corner of the Regal Cinemas and bustled the one block west to the ice park across from the Omni Hotel. The lights up in the rafters were bringing sparkles to the virgin ice of the rink. A small group of morning watchers, coffee cups in hand and all set for a shot of early-morning pleasure before heading off to their offices on the Mall, were gathering in the mezzanine lounge at the east end of the rink.

Good, Lisa thought. Looks like she had the rink to herself today and an audience as well. An audience was important. She was going to the regional juniors this year, and she didn't plan on staying at that level very long. As soon as she made it to the national level, her ability to perform before a crowd and to get that crowd behind her would be all important.

Wasting little time getting her skates laced, Lisa soon was flying onto the ice. Just two warm-up laps around the rink and she glided down to the east end of the oval and did a double flip jump right in front of the gathering gallery. A smattering of applause gave her fuel to take off for the other end, circle before she got there, and fire off a double toe loop jump in the very center of the rink. This time the applause was fuller, although she knew the jump hadn't been perfect. She had double footed slightly as she had come down. She hated it when she did that. And she also hated it when the audience wasn't discerning enough to separate the great jumps from the simply pretty good ones. She was known for her jumps. They all had to be perfect. It was her strength.

Her coach was yelling something at her from the boards. "The routine, Lisa. Stick with the routine."

Dutifully, she circled the oval twice more, getting a feel for the firmness of the ice and limbering up. She went into a scratch spin and followed that with a back spin. The applause was pretty sparse with those, though, and she knew she hadn't done them all that well. Suddenly, she exploded out of the spin, raced down to the west end of the oval, circled and flew back, executing a double double Salchow jump under a spotlight near the east end. The show of audience appreciation at this point was gratifying.

"Spins. The spins first, Lisa," she heard from the boards. "That's what you need work on."

Irritation gripped Lisa, and she spun around and headed for the west end, almost colliding with another skater.

Where'd *that* guy come from? Lisa's irritation skyrocketed. *This hour is only for the training skaters. How'd that old geezer get onto the ice? I hate it when I have to watch out for someone else when I'm practicing.*

The "old geezer" thought was a bit unkind, but Lisa's perspective could be forgiven. She was barely fourteen, while the new skater on the ice was clearly pushing forty and had gotten a little thick around the middle.

To clear her irritation, Lisa glided down to the west end and did another double Salchow. She could hear the applause from the other end and felt a bit better. So she came up the rink, past the old dude, who was still just skating around flexing his muscles, and then she performed a rather nice triple flip jump for the gallery. Louder applause, and well-deserved applause she thought, even though she had had to touch down slightly with her fingers at the end.

She skated out toward the center and was just about to try a double Axel jump when she was thrown off by a premature round of applause. She ended up only doing a single and coming much too close to the boards right in front of her coach.

"Spins," her coach hissed at her. "Work on the spins."

She didn't even hear him, though. Why the premature applause? She looked out onto the ice and saw that the other skater had started a routine. A strong, finely edged forward spiral down the ice from the west end had gotten the gallery's attention, and the applause had come when he had exploded into a double toe loop at the end. He had now skated back to the center, where he went into a camel spin and then smoothly down into a sit spin. This time Lisa's coach joined in the applause. This irritated her even more. She pushed off and went into a layback spin of her own, which caught the audience's attention.

But then their eyes had gone back to the other skater. After a couple of glides around the arena, he had come to the middle and tried a triple Axel. He almost made it around the third time. But he touched down on both feet and wound up in a tumble on the ice. Coming back up and brushing ice shavings off his pants, he smiled and gave a little "well, I tried" boyish shrug. The audience applauded his failed attempt at an especially difficult element—and his good-natured response to the fall—even louder than it had applauded the spins that had worked.

Lisa came out near him and went into a fast camel spin of her own. Her spin was much faster than his had been, and her leg was much more parallel to the ice. But the spin was fundamentally flawed, because she had traveled across the ice from her centering. The audience acknowledged her accomplishment in achieving an elegant position. Something about their applause rang hollow, however, as if they knew that the traveling had marred the execution, and Lisa came out of the spin and went into another jump, a triple Salchow this time, to regain their attention.

In the meantime, the "old guy" had skated around the rink, done a triple toe loop jump at one end and a double Axel at the other end and come back out into the middle for a death drop into a sit spin and back up into a scratch spin. He obviously was into a long-practiced routine, as the audience could almost hear the rhythm of music in the background and pick up on a story being woven before its eyes. His form no longer was the most crisp and the speed was a little slow, but the edging was precise, the hand movements perfect, and the joy of skating evident in his eyes.

The crowd had gathered in strength and the applause was thunderous.

Lisa's eyes blazed. She pushed off, sped around the rink once to gain momentum and, lifting one of her legs, went down into a hydroplane maneuver from the west end, coming back up and going into a triple toe loop right in the center of the oval. Too much adrenaline was working, however. She overcompensated on her timing as she went up into the jump. Thump. Down she went on her bottom, and she slid away off to the west. The humiliation was too much for her to bear. Right there in front of everyone. But then she heard the applause and looked up in time to see the flash of the second of three splits the other skater was performing, the first to the south, the second to the east, and the third to the north. The applause was thunderous. The audience—what should be *her* audience—hadn't even noticed her fall.

Shoulders down in dejection, arms akimbo, a frustrated Lisa skated back to her coach. There were tears in her eyes.

"Who *is* that guy? He ruined my practice."

"No, Honey, you ruined your own practice. He may be just about beyond his audience time now, but he has had his time in the lights. You are pushing the gun with finding yours. We call it the edge. He may be more than twice your age, but he's still got the edge, and all you've got now is the monster jumps. That's Dick Carsters. Third in the nationals in his time. As I remember it, he made quite a splash for Charlottesville. Think this skating park may have been built to play off his fame. Hope you watched the edging on his opening forward spiral, because when we return this afternoon, you're doing nothing but spirals—no more jumps, you hear me?—until you've done at least one spiral as well as he did this morning. Then we'll start talking about whether you deserve an audience."

Where There's a Will, ...

"Bah! Quit that. I'm not listening to you." Flora reached out to turn off the alarm and only managed to knock it on the floor. She rolled over and covered her head with a pillow, but it was still buzzing at her insistently. So annoying. She scooted to the end of the bed, stretched out, and slapped the clock under her nightstand. There. The muffled sound was almost soothing now.

For forty-two years she had heeded the call, jumped out of bed, and played Donna Reed all day. And where had it gotten her? She was alone now, unwanted, unneeded. Thirty-five years as a foster parent, substitute mother to twenty-one children, followed by two years as a caregiver for a husband who was dead long before his heart gave out. Three months alone in a silent house where too many memories screamed at her.

Depression is what the lady psychologist had called it. She just needed to get back into the workforce for a while. Yeah right, she had wanted to retort. Little Miss Psychologist wasn't going on sixty-three years with no skills beyond helping people get from here to there—children from a bad situation to a permanent home or independence; a husband from a good-hearted, hard-working helpmate to an address in the Monticello Memorial Gardens.

They'd done all of those aptitude and job skill tests, and for the last three weeks she'd been ripping plants out of her garden and trying to sell them to the morning people down on the Downtown Mall. She could already see where *that* was leading. Her yard was beginning to look like someone was frantically searching for hidden treasure without any prospect of finding

Photo by Stacey Evans.

any. And she could already tell that, come June, her plants would begin to wilt on the Downtown Mall before the sun started coming up. The psychologist had said to just go out and do the least little thing to occupy her time until the depression passed. Flora had taken her literally and had gone straight to the least little thing she could think of doing.

After trying that for only two days, she had skipped a day and marched right down to Family Services as soon as they opened and told them she was ready to take another foster child. Three strikes and you're out, they had told her: too old, no husband in the house, and, they had heard, she was being treated for clinical depression. They'd loved her previous work as a foster mother, but there were quite clear state and city regulations standing squarely in the way. Flora had given some thought to having her hair dyed, trolling the bars for some man drunk enough to agree to a marriage of convenience, and going over to Parties-R-Us for a happy-face mask.

But instead, here she was, in the darkness before dawn, trying to think of a reason to get up and haul her philodendron over to the Mall. She was in luck, however. The alarm clock had buzzed its last, and now she could just roll over and pretend that it had failed to wake her up.

She couldn't do it. She was awake now, and she was the most conscientious person she knew. It was a curse. She'd fight it, though. Pulling the covers over her head, she buried herself into the sheeting and mumbled aloud to the Almighty.

"A sign. Show me a sign that my impatiens are needed over on the Mall, or I'm taking the day off. I'm sure there's an *I Love Lucy* rerun I've never seen. And the Springer guy is beginning to grow on me."

Silence. Just as she thought, she was meant to sleep today. But then a gust of wind at the window caused her curtains to billow inward and the first rays of the morning sun hit her bedspread. Flora groaned, rolled over and sat up on the side of the bed. She'd lost again. She'd hurry on over to the Mall with the last of her budding lily of the valley. But right after she'd given up on selling anything, she would head straight off to Bed Bath

& Beyond for a much thicker bedspread, one that sunlight couldn't penetrate.

She felt quite a bit better once she had reached the Downtown Mall and had begun setting up her table. She had staked out a choice spot near the York Place complex of shops not far from the ice park at the west end of the walking mall. She had to admit that she had started making some friends down here; she would miss them when she'd moved on to something else to do. But moving on was something she very much intended to do. She had been a foster mother as long as she could remember. That's what she was good at and that's what was good for her. She'd just have to put some more time into figuring out how to get back into that.

It was already light when she reached the Mall, but it was still early for life on the street. She waved at Officer Shifflett as he passed and noted that that poor bedraggled street woman Sondra was still asleep on the bench over by where they were knocking down that block of buildings. She was usually up by now. In fact, by now that other woman, Chantel, was usually here too, and doing her screaming thing at the construction crane. Flora hoped Sondra was all right, and, although she knew the woman was touchy about anybody fussing with her if she wasn't up by the time the construction noise started, Flora determined that she'd go over to make sure everything was OK. Maybe she'd use the excuse that she didn't plan on staying around long this morning and wanted to give Sondra something for lunch just in case none of her other sources panned out.

That reminded Flora that she had also brought one of those little glass snow-bubble thingies for that young woman who tooled down the Mall in her motorized wheelchair contraption most Tuesday and Thursday mornings. She looked up the Mall to the east and saw that, indeed, the young woman was working her way down to the west again this morning. Moving along at a pretty good pace too.

Flora was watching the woman roll closer when she heard the moan and the whispered, but very distinct, "Hush, now." She looked around at the stores running along the south side of the Mall but didn't see anything peculiar. She heard the moan again and thought that it was coming from 2d Street, just around the corner from the Regal multiplex. She quietly, but quickly, stole around the corner, and there they were just on the other side of a dumpster.

"What's wrong, son?" Flora asked. "I heard you cry out. Are you hurt?"

The boy, somewhere around ten years old and a little scruffy, looked up and answered, "No, ma'am. I'm fine. I've just got a little tummy ache. I'll be all right." He said he was all right, but his eyes looked real sad. But right away, they didn't look sad anymore. Rather, the boy took on a real scared look and jumped up and looked around.

"Where's Jimmy?" he cried. "He was just here."

Flora had no idea where—or even who—Jimmy was. But she was now able to see that the boy may not have lied to her about being all right, but that little girl he'd been shielding under him didn't look at all well. Now Flora knew where the moaning was coming from—although that gash on the boy's arm didn't look at all good either.

"Oh, you poor dear," Flora cried and knelt down on the sidewalk.

The boy got even more wild-eyed and was beside himself with panic. He tried to shield the little girl from Flora at the same time he was trying to spy where this Jimmy person had gotten to.

Flora took command. "You go look for Jimmy, son, I'll help your little sister—she is your little sister, isn't she?—over to my stand. When you've found Jimmy, then we'll begin to fix everything up."

Something in the reassuring manner Flora had shown helped the boy make up his mind. He went off into the Mall, and by the time Flora had carried the little girl over to the chair by her plant table, she could see that the boy had found Jimmy, quite evidently another younger sibling, over by the park bench where Sondra had been sleeping. Sondra was sitting up now and checking through her rag bag.

The little girl was obviously sick and completely exhausted. She felt feverish and was only semiconscious. Flora didn't waste any time. She had mustered help to track down Officer Shifflett in no time flat, and the whole entourage had set off for the hospital in a jiffy. Flora never bothered to find out what happened to her table, chair, and wilting plants.

⊗ ⊗

"It's pneumonia, son," the doctor was saying. "She's been outside for some time, hasn't she? And she hasn't had much of anything to eat, either, has she?" Something about the doctor's manner and the white coat conveyed the charge that someone had most assuredly been mistreating this little girl.

Everyone—the doctor, Flora, Officer Shifflett, and the Family Services worker—was looking at the older boy, whose name turned out to be Michael. At least everyone was looking at him except for little Jimmy, who had taken an instant liking to Flora and was playing a game of going through her purse and giving loud voice to delight at everything he found. A big reason why Jimmy had taken so readily to Flora probably was because she had let him do this without hesitation and was taking an equal share in delight at whatever he'd discovered.

Silence. Michael didn't seem to be in the mood to talk.

"Where have you children been?" the Family Services worker looked down at Michael and asked. "And where did you come from?" She seemed to be looking for someone to blame, as well.

Flora ruffled little Jimmy's hair, discovered a wallet in her purse for him to concentrate on for a while, and turned in her chair to face Michael. "They just need to know about Brenda so they can help her, Michael. The faster they know what her problem is, the less pain she'll be in. Can you help the doctor, please, Michael? You've taken good care of her up to now, but now the doctor has to help her with this illness. And here, show the doctor your arm. You need some help too."

The story came out in a rush then. The previous Saturday Michael had gotten supper ready for the children and his grandfather out at their farm near North Garden, south of town. It had gotten quite late and the grandfather hadn't appeared. Michael put the other children to bed early, and when he saw they were asleep, he went out into the night. He found his grandfather under the tractor in a ditch. He'd gashed his own arm when he unsuccessfully tried to lift the tractor.

The only other relative he knew they had was his mother's mother, who he had been told lived somewhere in downtown Charlottesville. She and his grandfather had never gotten along and she hadn't come out to see the kids in more than two years. But all Michael had known was that he needed to get into town to get her to come out and help his grandfather. He couldn't leave the two younger children alone, though, so they had all set out in the middle of Saturday night. It had taken them until early this morning to get down to the edge of the Downtown Mall. Michael had managed to carry Jimmy most of the way, but Brenda had finally dropped where Flora had found her, and Michael had spent the rest of the predawn hours wrapped around the other two to keep them warm.

After getting the particulars as quickly as he could, Officer Shifflett went over into the corner and started making phone calls for someone to get out to the North Garden farm. Soon thereafter, he himself took off.

"We'll have to get these children into temporary homes right away until we can find the grandmother," Mrs. Otis, the Family Service's worker, said.

"Homes?" Flora asked. "Don't you mean one home? After what they've been through, they'll need to be kept together."

"I doubt that's possible. In fact, I'm sure it's not," Mrs. Otis answered. "We have a real shortage of placements just now."

Michael went into panic again and jerked his arm away from the doctor, who had been assessing the damage. "Apart? No, no way, lady. I'm the only one who's taken care of Brenda and Jimmy since Mom ran off. They won't go with anyone else."

"Ran away?" Mrs. Otis said with dismay. "You mean your mother is still alive and could come back at any time? Oh my goodness, this makes it all the more difficult. It will be very hard to place you under those circumstances."

"No it won't," Flora declared. "I'll take them. You know I'm certified. I'll take them and take care of all of them together for as long as needed, no matter what is going to happen on a permanent basis."

Michael gave her a look of great relief, and tears formed in the corners of his eyes. Jimmy snuggled closer on her lap and started to recount the dollar bills he'd liberated from her wallet.

"Now, Mrs. Howard, you know that won't do. You *were* certified, but you're no longer certified. You were in yesterday, and Mrs. Van Dyke went over all of that with you. Our hands are tied. There are both state and local certification rules, and they couldn't be breached short of a court order. We'll just have to think of something else."

Michael looked crushed, and the tears started to flow. *Good for that, at least,* Flora thought. *That child needs to have a good cry.* She'd go to him, but she was fighting a bigger battle just now.

"Well, at least we can hold off on what needs to be done for just now, can't we, Mrs. Otis? The little girl is in the hospital, and Michael needs to be there for at least a while too. Isn't that right, Doctor?"

"Well, this doesn't look too—" Flora's piercing look stopped him in midsentence. He looked at Michael and then at Jimmy and then back at Flora. "Yes, that's right. We'll need to clean and dress this wound and then he'd better stay here for a bit under observation."

"In the same room as his sister, don't you think, Doctor?" Flora's question wasn't really a question.

"Yes," the doctor sighed. "I guess that would be best all around."

"And I'll take care of Jimmy for the afternoon. That would be all right with you, Michael, wouldn't it? You need to look after Brenda, and that will be no place for Jimmy to be. So I'll just take him back to the Mall. We'll ride on the carousel and maybe have an ice cream cone from Chaps."

Wise beyond his years, Michael caught on fast and agreed readily. Jimmy had heard the words "carousel" and "ice cream," and that was all he needed to know as a reason to part with his older sister and brother for the afternoon.

Mrs. Otis stood there, trying her best to reason out why this wasn't all just fine. But she took too long in figuring it out, because when she had organized her quite logical objections, she looked up to find that she was alone. She'd return to Family Services to report what was happening and then she knew where to find Mrs. Howard and Jimmy—near the carousel or at Chaps on the Downtown Mall.

CB ED

Flora and Jimmy were sitting on a bench not far from Chaps on the Downtown Mall when the first blow fell. Jimmy was having the time of his life. First he'd tried to make up to an elderly couple sitting on one of the other benches. But the man had been too grumpy and the woman had been too grabby. Then he'd started exchanging funny faces with a bearded man having his lunch at the Hardware Store Garden Café, but that man's wife hadn't liked that and had made the man stop playing. None of this got Jimmy down, though. He'd then started trotting east on the Mall, fascinated at the sight of a woman wearing two different-colored shoes, but when Flora had gone after him, he had scampered right back to her. He was of that carefree age and had been taken care of real well. Flora could see that. It was all a game to him.

That's where Officer Shifflett found them.

"I'm afraid the old man was gone when we got out to the farm. He probably died even before the kids noticed he was late for supper on Saturday. You know it was pretty primitive out there. They didn't have a phone or a car that I could see. They must have kept pretty much to themselves, living off the land. It's hard to believe that is going on in central Virginia. There's so much money floating around here, you'd think we wouldn't be that close to poverty and misery."

Flora didn't say a word; she had assumed that what they'd find at the farm was what they did find. She wasn't sure she agreed with the misery part, though. If they asked the children, she was pretty sure they'd say they had a pretty good life with their grandfather out there. She took Jimmy up on the bench beside her and patted his arm. He hadn't understood anything Officer Shifflett had said, thank goodness. His eyelids were getting heavy, and the policeman let him drift off, his head in Flora's lap, before he gave her the rest of the bad news.

"Worse, we couldn't find any trace where the mother might have gone off to. And even worse than that, we *did* find the grandmother. She's over in the Alzheimer's unit up on Cedars Court. It's likely she hasn't recognized anyone for some time. That's probably why she stopped going out to the farm to visit the kids."

"Such a shame," Flora said quietly enough not to disturb Jimmy. "They're such nice children, and such trouble they've seen. I'd hate to have had to decide what to do out at that farm. I'm not sure I'd have managed as well as Michael did. You know, I'd like to have these children, Bob. It wouldn't even matter if the mother showed up in a month or two and took them back. They have some illness and grief to get through, and I have something I need to get over too. They need someone to keep them together just now. And I need them to put myself back together. I wasn't going to get up and come in today, and I made a deal with God and lost. But, you know, I'm not sure at all that I lost."

"Well, I'd sure like to see you and these kids together too, Mrs. H. But I'm afraid I haven't given you all of the bad news there is to give. Family Services found three separate placements for the kids and are drawing up the papers now. It shouldn't be long until Mrs. Otis is over here to pick Jimmy up."

Flora's shoulders sagged and she looked down at the angelic face of the fully content Jimmy, as he burrowed his head further into her lap and brought a little thumb up to his mouth. He popped it in and began a gentle sucking, and Flora heard—and felt—him sigh deeply. She had to lift her head up then, though, because she didn't want her tears to fall on his face and wake him up.

As she looked up, the sun broke from behind a cloud and a brilliant ray found its way through the leaves of the trees and hit her full in the face. A breeze came up and set the leaves aflutter, and the sunbeam was broken down into a mottled array of soft warmth. Flora didn't think long before she had made up her mind.

"Bob, I need you to do me a favor. A big favor."

"Sure thing, Mrs. Howard. As long as it's legal, of course."

Where There's a Will, ...

"Jimmy and I are going to go over there behind the fountain on Central Place. There's a bench over there that has more privacy than this from those walking around on the Mall. Could you watch out for Mrs. Otis, and when she comes, keep her at bay for about forty-five minutes? Tell her you think you saw us at the east end of the Mall riding the carousel."

"Now, I said it had to be legal, Mrs. Howard. You aren't thinking of running off with this little guy, are you? Remember his brother and sister at the hospital. That would put them in a real panic. We'd just have to find you and bring you back, and we'd be right back where we started."

"No, Officer, nothing illegal, I promise," Flora laughed for the first time in hours. "Just the opposite. You know they have a saying for times like this."

Officer Shifflett gave her a questioning look.

"They say 'where there's a will, there's a way.' I've always believed that, you know. I used to be a very optimistic person. I've just let worries push it into a back drawer for the last six months or so. Now, please go and look out for that Mrs. Otis."

As Officer Shifflett moved up the Mall, Flora took a cell phone out of her purse and started to punch the buttons.

ଓ ଓ

"There you are, Mrs. Howard. For some reason, the police officer thought he'd seen you up at the other end of the Mall. At the carousel." It had taken the woman from Family Services just a bit over a half hour to find her from the time Officer Shifflett had gone off.

"Yes, we saw him up there too," Flora answered sweetly. But she felt anything but sweet underneath. Mrs. Otis had found them much more quickly than she'd hoped. Flora took a quick look beyond the Mall, up toward Lee Park. "As you can see, though, Jimmy got sleepy. We mustn't disturb him. This all tired him out so much, you know." She obviously was playing for time, and Mrs. Otis wasn't fooled.

"We've finished our paper work on the children, Mrs. Howard. I'm afraid I'm going to have to take Jimmy now."

"But you mustn't wake him. He's much too—" But then Chauncey Willard showed up by the bench, a bit out of breath, but present and accounted for. And Flora didn't have to try to put Mrs. Otis off any longer.

"Well, hello, Chauncey," Mrs. Otis said. "What brings you out of Juvenile Hall this morning?"

"I just came over to tell Mrs. Howard that her foster parent assignment for this child and his brother and sister is all set up."

"But that's impossible," Mrs. Otis declared in dismay. "That just isn't possible. We've already spent some time with Mrs. Howard pointing out that state and city regulations just won't allow that. What has she told you?"

"She hasn't told me anything," Mr. Willard said. "It's all right here in Judge Hawley's order. Mrs. Howard has custody of all three children until and unless a close relative steps forward to claim them. And she's eligible for foster parent support from the city."

"But that just won't do," Mrs. Otis retorted, a glimmer of triumph in her voice. She wasn't really dead set against Mrs. Howard getting the children. Mrs. Howard had a sterling reputation all the years she worked with foster children. But rules were rules, and they couldn't start bending them just to please circumstances. That would just lead to chaos. "Hawley is a city judge. There are state regulations too. He can't override those."

"No, that's true," Mr. Willard responded. "But there's this other paper too. With this, all the state regulations are satisfied."

"Here, let me just look at that. What? Now why would he do such a thing? According to this, Judge Hawley and his wife have also signed on as co-foster parents. Why Hawley is one of the strictest, no-nonsense judges on the circuit. What could possibly have led him, on such short notice, to—?"

Mrs. Otis had run out of gas and words, giving Flora her first chance in some time to wedge in a comment.

"Oh, that's not so hard to figure out, Mrs. Otis. You see, Judge Hawley was my foster child number three."

Good Customer

"Here comes your good customer, Trixie. Right on the dot. Just remember that I've got him the first week in May. We'll see if he's as good a tipper for me as he is for you."

"I don' know, Becky. Maybe I'll just have to come back into town every morning just to serve Mr. Turner his breakfast."

At 8:15 sharp, just like for the last seven years, Mr. Turner appeared from around the corner, walking briskly toward The Nook Restaurant.

"Oh, Gawd. There's that girl again in her motor contraption. She's going to do some serious harm if she don't slow down." Trixie didn't want Mr. Turner to wind up on the disabled list rather than sitting at his favorite table for his usual. But it looked like he was safe for another day. He had seen the girl coming down the bricked walking street and had turned to greet her. But she was staring off through the trees and across the Mall at one of those young business-suit types and had barely missed Mr. Turner in passing. Good, Trixie thought. She had enough on her mind not to have her schedule thrown off.

Trixie couldn't imagine why Mr. Turner had become one of her breakfast regulars here at The Nook, as he owned his own restaurant up away on the Downtown Mall. They didn't serve breakfast there, but that didn't mean they wouldn't serve it to their owner.

He shuffled in the door and pressed those big hands, with those long fingers, on the tabletop and eased his considerable bulk down into a little round-bottomed chair that hardly looked strong enough to hold him. Just the imposing—she once would have thought, intimidating—appearance of him reminded Trixie of just how amazing it was that she now looked forward to his appearance every weekday morning. Where she had been raised up in the hollows between Crozet and the Shenandoah National Parkway running across the crest of the Blue Ridge Mountains, she had been taught to run for the barn to get her pa and her brothers whenever a black man dared put a foot on their property. And Mr. Turner was one mountain of a black man—and as old as the hills in whose shadows she had grown up and whose embrace she had fought so hard to escape by coming down to Charlottesville for a job.

"Morning, Mr. Turner. Strong coffee with cream and sugar as always?"

"Thanks, Trixie. Yes, as strong as always. Nobody can make strong coffee like The Nook."

He said the same thing a good four days out of five. It meant he was in a good mood. A good tip this morning. But, it had been years now since Trixie had salivated after those great tips Mr. Turner dropped on her table. There was much more to Mr. Turner than his tips. They had become the best of friends, comfortable with each other without going to any special pains. She had to admit that to herself, although she certainly wasn't going to go up in the hollow and scream it at her pa's barn. Didn't even think she'd be able to admit it to Evan over at the sawmill on 250 west near the Crozet turnoff.

"Two eggs over easy with sugar ham and toast, as usual?"

"That's right. I've got to gather up the energy to limber up and do some practicing for this afternoon."

"You don' need no practicing, Mr. Turner. You're the greatest there is already."

"Thanks, Trixie. That's why I come in here every morning. You're the best picker-upper for an old man that could be."

"Oh, go on. You come in here for The Nook's strong coffee, and you know it."

"That's why I came in here for the first four years," Mr. Turner admitted, "but for the last three it's been because I don't think I could have made it by Veta's passing without good, steady friends like you to meet up with every morning."

Trixie turned to the counter in embarrassment. Mr. Turner wasn't usually this forthcoming with his feelings. She felt flattered that he'd think she had helped him adjust to his wife's death, but she felt plenty tongue-tied whenever conversations got more than an inch below the surface. She took Mr. Turner's OJ off the counter and returned to the table, determined to lighten the conversation as best she could.

"Well, I've heard rumors that you have some new living arrangements now, and maybe you won't be coming around of mornings much anymore."

Mr. Turner put on a big smile. "I'll be gone for a couple of weeks or so come next month, that's for sure. Gonna have a little vacation—and not alone for a change. But I don't plan on any new living arrangements gettin between me and my breakfast at The Nook."

"Aw, gee, Mr. Turner," Becky said as she swung by his table. "Trixie's going to be off the first part of May too, and she promised her best customer to me while she was gone. Now I won't have nothin to look forward to in the mornings. Bad enough that Trixie's goin off to get married."

"Married?" Mr. Turner exclaimed. "Why you didn't tell me about this yesterday, Trixie?"

"Well, I doubt Evan thought about it much before yesterday, either, Mr. T. He doesn't do a whole lot of thinking beforehand. But there's a tractor show down in Nelson County starting May 1st, and Evan decided that the best thing that could happen on this earth was to get married and spend his honeymoon watching tractors pull things around the fairgrounds. I've been trying to pull Evan in for more than a year now myself, so I guess this is my best shot."

"Congratulations to you—to you both. You can tell your Evan for me that he's getting the cream of the crop. The best of luck to you both."

"Thanks, Mr. T." But all of a sudden, Trixie didn't look all that thankful. She abruptly sat down on, more like collapsed into a chair at Mr. Turner's table and hid her face briefly with her hands. Mr. Turner let her be for a few seconds, and in time she reappeared from behind her hands, reached into her pocket, and lit up a Virginia Slims. Mr. Turner didn't much like people smoking around him, but this always was a signal that Trixie was pretty wound up about something. She didn't do much smoking herself and usually didn't get near a cigarette while she was working.

"Whatsa matter, Trixie?" Mr. Turner finally asked. "Second thoughts about your young man?" The sad-eyed look she gave him made his heart wrench.

"Naw, thanks. Evan's the one for me. I don't have no complaints in that department."

"Then what is it? I hate to see you sad, especially at a time that should be bringing you the most enjoyment."

"Yeah, right. Weddings are supposed to be the highlight of a girl's life, ain't they? I guess I just always got tied up with the fantasies that every girl carries around about their weddings. Just because I was raised up in the hollows don't mean I didn't have the life of a fairy princess mapped out. Evan's the right Prince Charming—at least in looks and in having a good heart in the right place, and he's a hard worker—but I was no different from those girls in Farmington and Keswick. I wanted it to be storybook perfect. You know, frilly white dress, three-tiered cake, that wonderful little stone chapel on the Keswick road, a small orchestra, and three nights at the Greenbriar. So here it comes: my only good church dress, a justice of the peace in Crozet, five days at the Nelson County tractor pull, a rented bungalow on the side of the highway, and back to work for both of us."

"Your dream doesn't sound all that pushy to me," Mr. Turner said softly. "You know, Veta once admitted that she had had a fantasy about her wedding too. But we didn't even have a tractor pull to go to. I was down in New Orleans trying to make a go of it with stiff competition. Seems before we thought of having a honeymoon again, Veta no longer felt up to it. It seems pretty bad planning on the Almighty's part that when we're young enough to enjoy life, we don't have two nickels to rub together, and when we've reached a level of comfort, we're too busy to enjoy life and we just sit on useless bank accounts. Until one day life comes and strikes us down. It all seems so senseless, or maybe God's just a big joker."

"Now, don' let me get you down, Mr. Turner. Evan's a real hunk. I'm going to have a ball in that rented bungalow with my man. And you've got yourself a nice vacation for two planned as well. That's great. That's just what you need. You've pined away on your missus too long. I met her a couple of times, there toward the end, and she told me she wanted you to get more out of life than you had to that point."

"A couple of times?" Mr. Turner snorted. "You was over at that hospital more than I was. And you know what, I'm just as good as that orchestra you've been fantasizing. So, you got that part covered."

"No, you're better than I ever imagined, Mr. T." I'll check out whether there's anything you can play on at or near the Crozet Baptist church's social hall, and you're on. But hold up. You can't play at my wedding. You're goin on vacation that week."

"The hell I am until we've gotten you married. You don't think I'd leave town and miss your wedding, do you? I'll just start my vacation after the festivities have wound down."

Trixie didn't know why this gave her such a lift, but it did. She briefly thought about her pa and her brothers, seeing Mr. T. show up at her wedding. But it was past time for them to join the real world, anyhow. She'd just give them a good talking to beforehand, and then they could just decide for themselves whether they would be there.

She bounced up and went for Mr. Turner's eggs. The morning got pretty busy along about then, and every time she thought of checking on her good customer, he looked pretty deep in thought. He also was doing some figuring with a pen on his napkin, as he often did when he was working on his business plans. Trixie hoped that he wasn't having second thoughts about his new living arrangements and his coming vacation—or about telling yet another woman that he was putting their plans off to take care of other business. She hadn't lied about Veta wanting him to get on with his life. They'd been such a nice couple. She decided she'd hate not having him at her wedding—a strange thought, it occurred to her, because up to fifteen minutes ago she had had no intention of inviting him to her wedding—but she couldn't see him putting off his vacation plans for her. She'd sit down and talk it over with him again before he finished his breakfast and left.

Next thing she knew, Mr. Turner had finished and was gone, and Becky was standing over his leavings with a very strange look on her face.

"Whatsa matter?" Trixie asked, as she ambled over. "Mr. Turner forget to leave a tip for the first time in his life?"

"Not exactly," Becky said with in a small, distant voice.

Trixie moved Mr. Turner's plate and saw that he had left a check this morning rather than his usual cash. It was made out to her, it was in the amount of eight thousand, seven hundred, and fifty-seven dollars and twenty-nine cents, and it was marked "one breakfast and one storybook wedding." On the napkin he had left at the table, Mr. Turner had tallied out the estimated cost for a white lace wedding dress, rental of Grace Episcopal Church in Keswick, rental for the Crozet fire house hall and a baby grand piano, a three-tiered cake from Chandlers, catered refreshments and champagne for eighty guests, four nights for two at a B&B in Nelson County, and three nights at the Greenbriar. The seven dollars and twenty-nine cents was tallied out as the cost of his breakfast.

Invisible

Marybeth rolled slowly around in circles in front of city hall for several minutes, building up a good pout. The eager-beaver civil-servant types were showing up for work early, but if they paid her any mind, she certainly didn't notice. She was sure she was invisible to them. Just why would anyone notice a young woman dressed in orange and purple, with a red baseball cap, turning tight circles right in front of the steps to city hall, anyway? Scenes like that must exist out here every day. Of course, she herself had only been coming out here on Tuesday and Thursday mornings for the past three weeks, but there must have been many more bizarre things happening out here for the city workers to notice on the other three mornings of the workweek. It couldn't be that they were embarrassed to take any notice of her, a misshapen, scarred cripple in an oversized wheelchair. Oh, no, that couldn't be the case, if her analyst was right. There had been a time when she had been noticed for her beauty, but not now. Now everyone made a point of looking away without seeming to be doing so on purpose.

She gave up on her little experiment with the city workers and revved up her motor and rolled over to the eastern edge of the Downtown Mall. The sun was starting to come up behind her—rising behind Thomas Jefferson's little mountain—and was now bouncing off the side of the Blue Ridge Mountains in the distance to the west. As the sun's rays started to pick out the twinkling lights woven through the branches of the trees marching down the bricked shopping street, the lights flickered off to give way to a new day. Another balmy, beautiful day in the lush, rolling hills of central Virginia. But Marybeth wasn't having any of that. Beautiful days were for other people now. Her days were now filled with pain, despondency, and rejection.

As Marybeth maneuvered her motorized wheelchair into position for what she was determined would be her last prescribed and useless promenade down the Downtown Mall, her cart clanged up against one of those historical markers. As she well knew from previous visits to the Mall, this told her that this bricked-over stretch of shop-lined avenue, most recently the downtown segment of Charlottesville's Main Street, marked the journey of Three Notch'd Road. This had been a road with an interesting past. It was surveyed by Thomas Jefferson's father and opened up the mountains and what was then the Wild West to the Virginia pioneers.

One recent day, having tried everything else she could think of, Marybeth's analyst had brought her down here to the eastern end of the Mall and had pointed out that sign. Just as this street had opened the world of the American West to Virginia settlers of old, her analyst had said, this road could reopen Marybeth's world.

How insensitive. The analyst, of all people, should know that Marybeth couldn't stand any of those "road" metaphors. How could there be life for Marybeth after that terrible automobile accident, especially since she herself had been the drunken driver involved? The analyst had said that Marybeth only needed to let her life rebuild, not to fight it every inch of the way, but what did she know about anything?

The analyst was so sure that all Marybeth had to do was roll down this Mall six times on six different days, and that she would see from the way people opened up to her and befriended her that life *was* worth living, that she wasn't just a cripple tied to a chair who was invisible to everyone.

Well, Marybeth knew that that was a bunch of poppycock. But the analyst had told her not to come back until she had taken those six trips down the Mall, and Marybeth's insurance support was only good as long as she continued seeing this analyst. She couldn't win for losing.

But she *could* show the analyst just how wrong she was. This was her sixth and last trip down the Mall. After this, she could go back to the analyst's office in triumph and tell her how dumb the whole idea had been. Why, Marybeth had even worn the loudest of colors, but no one had been nice to her or had made any effort to befriend her in her previous five trips down the Mall—just as she had known would be the case. She didn't see any reason why she should point out to the analyst that she herself hadn't gone far out of her way to talk to, let alone be civil to, anyone else during these trips; that she had scheduled them all for early in the morning when the only people on the Mall were in a hurry to be somewhere else; and that she could manage a pretty fast clip in this motorized chair of hers.

In fact, the only one who had talked to her at all was the police officer, Shifflett, who had told her more than once that this wasn't any Daytona 500. Well, she knew that. At the Daytona 500, the cars and their drivers were the heroes, the center of attention, and she'd certainly proved that wrong here. Besides, she'd already been in a speed race with a car, and that was what had put her where she was today. She just wished she hadn't survived that wreck. Everyone else had died. Why not her? And everyone had said it was all her fault.

Taking a look down the Mall and not seeing much of anything stirring, she revved her motor and roared out of the rising sun. One third of the way down the Mall, and so far so good. Just two of the night people jawing at each other near the carousel, not noticing her a bit, as she knew would be the case.

She caught sight of a group of preppy-looking college boys from up at the University. They were sitting in The Nook Restaurant's outdoor café area, laughing and punching each other, and egging one of their own to go on down the Mall. He had a bundle under his arm and had a scared look about him that Marybeth found attracting in spite of her determination to prove that no one would bother to make contact with her in this experiment. Although he was laughing along with his cohorts, he was only doing so with his mouth. Marybeth could tell by his frightened eyes and stiff facial muscles that he was being sent off to do something he didn't want to do. Forced into a game, just as she had been forced into this game. She longed for the young man to notice her, but, of course, he didn't. There was a time when he would have noticed her and would have been delighted if she noticed him. But the car wreck had changed all of that.

The young man steadied his bundle and started west down the Mall, just as Marybeth's cart came abreast of him. She cut the motor some. His back was to her now, but she thought just maybe she'd get a little ahead of him and then look back and make eye contact. Maybe there really was someone on the Mall this morning she could connect with.

But just as Marybeth got into position, she nearly sideswiped that big old black man going into The Nook Restaurant's indoor dining room. She had seen him going into that restaurant the previous Thursday and had thought he was going to say something to her then. He looked mean. She thought that he probably had been the one who got Officer Shifflett to get after her about driving too fast on the Mall. She really wasn't supposed to be on the Mall at all with anything motorized, but her analyst hadn't thought much of this excuse for not trying this out. Nasty old man; she was almost sorry she had missed hitting him. She was even more sorry—and disgruntled at the old man and the world in general—when she got control of her cart only to find that the college guy was now too far down the Mall for her to catch up to without making a spectacle of herself.

She had to slow down a bit through here, anyway, as she was getting to an area where she'd almost been proved wrong the last time she came to the Mall. Yes, there was that woman with the bookstore that was closing. They'd made eye contact the previous week; maybe the woman would notice Marybeth today. But no, the woman had come to the door of the shop, seen Marybeth coming down the Mall, and gone back in. And there, that woman who slept over on that bench at night. She was always up at this time and usually with another woman who was jabbering up a storm at the top of her voice. There she was today, pretending she was asleep. Obviously not wanting to notice Marybeth. Probably thought she was too good to talk with a cripple, even though she was just a homeless bag lady herself.

Oops. She hadn't seen that little boy. Almost ran him down. What was *he* doing out here in the early morning? But she wasn't worried about him. All his limbs worked. Somebody would pick him up and play with him. He wasn't invisible like she was.

There was that plant lady. Always looking friendly and talking earnestly with everyone around her. But not with Marybeth any of the previous mornings she'd come down here. Today the woman saw her, made eye contact, and looked like she might be ready to say something. But then she turned abruptly and disappeared around the corner near the movie theater building. Now if that didn't tell Marybeth all she needed to know about what people in this world thought about her, nothing did.

Then, seeing a pert little blonde with ice skates strung over her shoulder and a man walking with her and showing her all sorts of attention only depressed Marybeth all the more when she got to the western end of the Mall with its hotel on one side and ice rink on the other. Those ice skates said it all. Marybeth had once been pretty good on skates herself. But now there was no feeling in her legs at all. The image of those ice skates hurt real bad.

Completely absorbed in her own misery and in how badly people were treating her, Marybeth failed to stop at the end of the walking mall but continued right out into the turning circle in front of the hotel's front door. There, a large SUV was just pulling away from the hotel door and moving toward her, building up speed to enter the street in a lull in the traffic there.

The young man at the wheel was concentrating on the street traffic. Marybeth, however, was now determined to get someone to notice her, someone to concentrate on her, just her. She kept on moving, eyes locked on the young man at the wheel. At last, he turned to look in front of him, and then she had what she wanted. He was looking at her, completely focused on her. She was now quite visible, connected to another human being. They opened their mouths together, screamed together, their destinies now forever entwined.

Photo by Stacey Evans.

Just Two More Years

Alberta Adams went over to the door and looked out on the Downtown Mall. No long line waiting to get into the Commonwealth Bookstore. She unlocked and opened the door and looked first west, down toward the Omni Hotel, and then east, up toward city hall and the amphitheater. Except for that poor young girl in the oversized motorized wheelchair, the area looked pretty deserted for such a lovely morning. She was glad she'd remembered to pick a few books out to send over to the medical apartments for the girl to read. Only a few more minutes to opening, and not a soul in sight who looked like they were waiting for last call. She sighed deeply, relocked the door, and retreated to the back of the store, where she would count the minutes until she could open for her last day.

The last day. All these years she had told herself that she'd do this for fifty years and then sell out to some young couple for enough money to be able to keep the upstairs apartment. But now both dreams had been shattered. A book chain had come to town and weakened her position enough that she had to close. She hadn't been able to find a buyer for the turnkey business offering. A bank had bought the building, and she was not only being evicted from the storefront as of tomorrow but also from her apartment upstairs as well. And two years short. She had always kept her eye on that fifty-year goal, which had sustained her through some bad times as well as some good, and she had only managed to eke out forty-eight. Just two more years. That was all she had counted on.

But it was only two years. Why should she feel so sad? Maybe because she hadn't really set any other goals for herself in life. She'd been content with spending nearly every day of the last forty-eight right here in the bookstore, living life vicariously through her patrons. Most of them had become friends, family almost. She had never thought of having a family of her own. For years, the elderly patrons who had come in to browse and visit were her parents and all of the little ones were her children. Thus, this had become a serious goal for her. She was going into the solitude and isolation of a retirement home without having achieved her only real goal in life. She knew nothing about the activities of the elderly: crocheting, bingo, and so forth. But then she thought back to one of her all-time-favorite books on the new lifestyle of seniors, gave a little chuckle, and added motorcycling, fencing, and spelunking to her list.

But all she knew about were books. She had no idea how she would fit in at Rosehaven. She felt defeated, a failure. Served her right. She'd been such a "know everything" all her life—and had wasted all of it without really venturing beyond the Downtown Mall. She had started here before there was a Mall; everything she had needed had been close at hand forty-eight years ago, and all of it was still close at hand on the Mall.

She went to the desk and looked at the inventory list of what she had left. Too much. It would drain even more of her savings to get it all moved out overnight. And the storage space she had rented didn't come cheaply either. Why had she insisted on sticking with her old-world arrangement with the book distributors and bought her books outright rather than take them on returnable consignment as the big chain that was putting her out of business did? Volume. That was it. She only was able to continue to get the hot new releases before the other bookstores in town by keeping to her old arrangement. Well, it was coming back to bite her in the bustle now.

She really did need to turn some profit out of the last of these books, or she couldn't swing the suite of rooms she had picked out at Rosehaven. She had thought that at least some of this stock would go today, especially since she had marked it for "pay what you can." She had been looking forward to at least getting good books into the hands of some folks who could not otherwise afford to indulge.

Oh, well, she thought. It won't be so bad. I did some figuring last night, and I'll still be able to afford that small room on the first floor, the one with the air-conditioning system under the window and where I'll share a bath with Clara. I do hope Clara is tidy.

The time had come. Alberta marched purposely to the front of the store, unlocked the door again, and switched the sign to Open.

"Stand back, don't anyone get trampled," she announced to the empty space out on the Mall in front of the door. But the space hadn't really been empty. Just as Alberta turned around, a middle-aged man in a white shirt with an American flag logo on it passed by. Alberta recognized him as a waiter at the Hardware Store Restaurant up the street. He obviously had intended to just scurry by on his way to the restaurant, but Alberta's strange statement to the sparsely occupied Mall at this time of the morning had brought him up short.

As Alberta retreated into the store with an embarrassed giggle, the man entered and started to browse the shelves. Within minutes, he had made two selections and brought them to the desk.

Ah, the first sale of the day, Alberta thought. Somehow she had always been a little tense until she had made that first sale. And she had always kept a mental chart, like the thermometer design they use to keep track of church building fund-raising programs, that marked the level of what she could afford to eat and buy that day from the day's accumulated profits. Half way up the thermometer and she could have a slice of that peasant white bread from Our Daily Bread; if she hit the top of the thermometer, she could have a slice of Black Forest cake from Hot Cakes. For no reason she could figure out, as the man approached the desk, she was thinking: *An extra tube of toothpaste for when Clara mistakenly takes mine.*

"Ah, a book on the writings of Thomas Jefferson and the new edition of *Gray's Anatomy*. An intelligent, if eclectic choice."

"Yes, ma'am. I've needed to get my own copy of *Gray's* for some time. I'm glad I thought of it right after the new edition came out. Here's my Visa card."

"How much should I put on the card for the books?"

"Excuse me? Don't they have price tags on them?"

"Yes, but didn't you read the sign when you came in? I'm closing the shop and this is the last day, so we've got a 'pay what you can' sale going."

"But won't you take a loss if I pay less than the price marked on the book?"

"Well, yes, some—depending on how much less you pay—but the retail price does, of course, have some profit margin built in for expenses."

"Looks to me like you still have expenses. So, I'll pay the retail price. I didn't come to America to do less than my part."

"Thank you, that's nice of you. Where did you come from?"

"From Guatemala."

"Oh, I've always wanted to visit Central America—in person, that is—I've often visited there in my books."

"Yes, well, I'm very glad to be living here now, though. Thanks for the books. Goodbye."

All she had missed by living her life within the four brick walls of this building. But they had been good years, and there were all of those people she had watched grow in their horizons and helped discover the wonderful world of books. Charlottesville was a highly literary town, and Alberta had done more than her share of promoting literature here. She had kept a stock of really good books that the big chains, with their emphasis on high-volume sales from transitory best-seller thrillers, wouldn't bother with.

Over the years she had given prominent display to the books of any local author, no matter how new or inconspicuous. And she had helped many authors make the leap into the publishing world by sponsoring readings and writers' classes in the mezzanine space she kept for gatherings and for the readers who came in to explore rather than to buy. More than a handful of current internationally renowned authors had gotten their start on her mezzanine. And many children and young people grew up loving books because she had let them read deeply in whatever subjects took their interest in the comfortable armchairs she had scattered about the store rather than hassling them to "buy or git." She even had a back room, where she and some of her friends entertained as storybook characters at children's parties. She had thought she made quite a charming Little Bo Peep, until some little tyke who was much too smart for his britches asked if she wasn't really playing one of the sheep because she had grown so wrinkled.

Alberta had returned to the front of the store, where she saw Renata from the Raven Art Gallery down the Mall appearing for work. Renata had acquired her interest in art right in this bookstore as a girl whose ambitions far outstripped her family's ability to indulge in such luxuries as books. Similarly, Glenda, the manager of the swanky Hamilton's Restaurant, who had just appeared in the door of that establishment across the bricked Mall, had been guided by Alberta to the management books that had led to her landing that job.

At that moment, Glenda caught Alberta's eye and started across the Mall. She examined the half-full display cases at the front and Alberta's sale sign with some consternation before she entered.

"What is this that is happening, Alberta? I've only been away on vacation for two weeks and have come back to find you selling out. Have I lost track of time? Didn't you always say you'd be here for exactly fifty years? It's only been about thirty hasn't it?"

"Oh, land, no child. It's been forty-eight. You can feel free to take those years off my age, but not off my time here on the Mall."

"But forty-eight isn't fifty. Why are you leaving? You aren't sick, are you?"

"No, of course not. Just a little tired. Tired of fighting progress. A bank wants to open here, and we all know the power of banks. What's that expression? 'Follow the money?' Well, I've always wound up at a bank when I've followed the money."

"But what will you do now? And is the bank letting you stay in your apartment upstairs?"

Alberta shook her head. "No, I'm moving over to Rosehaven."

"But you're too young to retire and leave us and go to a rest home. I grew up with you being here. God, this makes me feel old."

"That's fine with me, I can use the company."

"But, seriously, Alberta. Are you sure you're ready to give it up, and why Rosehaven? There are better homes here in town."

Alberta looked away so Glenda wouldn't see her eyes mist up. "There's really not all that much choice. I haven't saved enough to start over again. And if I don't sell this stock by closing time today, I'll be lucky to get into a home as good as Rosehaven."

Glenda looked around the store with sad eyes. "Our cook told me that folks think you were doing this because you were tired of working. And we all thought you were well fixed for retirement. Well, at least come on over to the restaurant for supper. I'll treat you to a closing party, even if it's just the two of us. And I promise, we'll only talk about the authors you like."

After Glenda left, Alberta was actually grateful to be alone for a while. She had had no idea closing down would be this hard. She hoped that the rest of her customers for the day wouldn't want to reminisce about what once was and try to talk her out of what had to be.

But Alberta wasn't alone for long. Shortly after Glenda departed, Mrs. Elizabeth Potter-Hanson from out at Keswick Hill sailed into the shop. She gave a tight little smile to Alberta in passing and then started walking up and down the aisles of half-full bookshelves. Alberta could guess what section she was in by the tapping of her cane. It wasn't long before she had returned to the desk with an armful of children's books. Alberta started to say something to her, but Mrs. P-H had already turned and tapped back down an aisle. Soon she was back with another armload of teen novels.

"Regressing in our reading habits are we, Lizzie?" Alberta observed when it was evident that her longtime friend's hunt in the stacks had concluded.

"Nope. I soon expect to have some new life in my house, and I want to be prepared." While she was answering the question, Mrs. P-H had been writing out a check, which she ripped out of the checkbook with a flourish and tossed on the desk. "I trust you don't need to see several forms of ID."

"Not this time, Dear. You haven't walked out of here without paying for your books since 1963—and that was because of the riot going on up the street a bit. But, but—"

Alberta had taken a look at the check and was having trouble forming her words. ". . . but I think you need to be more careful with your banking habits, Lizzie. This check is made out for eight hundred dollars. You got the decimal point in the wrong place."

"Sign on the door says 'pay what you can,' doesn't it?"

"Yes, but—"

"You've been pretty honest up to now, Bertie. This is no time to renege on advertising promises to the customers. The sign says 'pay what you can,' and, as you well know, I'm richer than Midas. These books are worth eight hundred dollars to me. So bag 'em, and button your lip. Glenda tells me she's throwing a dinner party for you tonight at Hamilton's, and I've invited myself. So I'll see you later."

And before Alberta could say a word, that ship had sailed. She was quickly replaced by Mrs. Henrietta Stowe-Byrd, who looked in the front window momentarily, entered the store, walked back to the desk, reverently placed a violin case in the corner by the cash register and out of harm's way, and strolled the aisles of shelving. To Alberta's estimation, she was looking at the empty shelves along the top of the bookcases rather than at the books.

When she returned to the desk, she said, "I see you have some of my books in the window, Bertie. Do you have any more copies here?"

"Why, yes. They go very well, but I had ordered enough to get me through the summer."

"Well, I can't stand to see them here in a closeout sale. I'll take all you've got. Total up the bill."

"I can't charge you for these, Henri. Why don't you just go ahead and take what's left for free? I've made a pile of money off your books over the years."

Mrs. S-B snorted in derision. "I've been insisting forever that none of my books have to go for less than retail. I don't plan to mess up that record now." Alberta gathered up all copies on hand of her friend's books, and, as she was totaling up the transaction with shaking hands, Mrs. S-B's attention had returned to the top of the half-empty bookcases once more.

"These are ten footers, aren't they, and solid oak?"

"Yes, they are. And they've aged wonderfully. I'm surprised they didn't sell. These are hard to come by. They'll be even harder to store until I can get rid of them."

"Don't I know that. I'll give you thirty thousand dollars for the lot."

Alberta's jaw dropped. "I don't think they're *that* precious. And what would you do with all of these bookshelves?"

"We are redoing the library out at Rivanna's Rest, and I haven't been able to find the bookcases I need. These will do nicely."

"But *this* many?"

"You've seen the library at Rivanna's Rest. I'm surprised you even asked about how many I need. Besides, I'd like to have some spares. As you said, bookcases like these are hard to come by. Oh," she said, as she picked up her violin case, "it's a pity you can't come over to the noon concert at Christ Episcopal. I have a feeling that will be a performance to remember. I'll tell you about it at Hamilton's this evening."

Alberta didn't mean to be impolite and not respond to Henrietta's comment on the concert, but she was in a daze until several minutes after Mrs. Stowe-Byrd had left. Not only was she getting top dollar for the bookcases, but she didn't need as much storage space now and wouldn't have the aggravation of getting rid of them. She already was reassessing her position at Rosehaven. She was no longer thinking in terms of that small first-floor room and shared bath. A nice-sized room with its own bath in the back on the second floor was also available.

"Alberta. Alberta. Are you all right?"

It was Renata from the Raven Gallery.

"Certainly," Alberta answered, her attention back on the business at hand. "Just thinking about how long Henri and I've known each other. We've had a lot of good times. Some knock-down-drag-out fights too, I must allow."

"I just came in to gather up all of your art books. We've decided that, since you are closing, we will start our own little section at the gallery on art books. Wholesale prices plus 10 percent OK?"

The door opened and another friendly face appeared.

"Hi, Renata."

"Hi, Laura Grace. What brings a competitor to the doors of the Commonwealth Bookstore?"

"Mr. Eads sent me over. Even though Read It Again Sam specializes in used classics, we hate to see the type of books Alberta carries become unavailable in town. We'd like to take over whatever inventory she hasn't sold. Is that OK with you, Alberta? Good. Oh, and Renata, did Glenda tell you about the dinner for Alberta at Hamilton's tonight? Hope you can make it."

Alberta hadn't been open an hour yet, and she had unloaded it all. The second-floor back room at Rosehaven hadn't lasted long at all on her thermometer chart. Now she could take her original reservation for the two rooms and bath on the second-floor front.

"Ms. A, Ms. A, glad I caught you here. Mr. Turner and I both have favors to ask of you. Glenda just told me you were still open over here for another day." Louise, the waitress from the Moondance Café on the Central Place who had an insatiable taste for the Mahfouz novels, appeared in Alberta's vision. But she had to take a few minutes to catch her breath. Good thing for Alberta, because she was a little out of breath herself, and she hadn't stepped beyond her sales desk for some time.

"Mr. Turner is stuck with that small storefront building over by the plaza for another two years before the corporate tenants he landed want to take it over. I'd like to take the upstairs apartment to be near my work, but it's too big just for me. I hear you've lost your apartment lease here. Any chance you could come over and room with me? We've always had a great time talking about Egyptian literature, and I'd like to have the company, not to mention the help with rent. Oh, and before I forget, Mr. Turner wonders if you could relocate your bookstore over in that storefront. He'd be willing to renovate to suit, seeing as how he could promise a lease for just two more years."

"Oh, my," Alberta whispered. "I'm not sure how I will be able to tell her."

"Tell who what?" Louise, Renata, and Laura Grace asked almost in unison.

"Henri," Alberta answered. "She's going to have to make do with fewer of those bookcases now—but for just two more years. Oh, and I hope you don't mind if I don't move in for a month or so. I've decided I want to take a trip when I clean all of these books out. Central America. Maybe Guatemala."

War Souvenirs

Jack propped the bulky package against the side of the bench and sat down. He'd have to catch his breath before he went into Snooky's. It had been a long walk from the parking lot south of the Downtown Mall, the package had been hard to handle, and he was out of marching trim. The fact that he was pushing eighty didn't occur to him as an explanation for why the trip had been so tiring. He plopped down on the bench beside the package and reached into his shirt pocket for his smokes. There weren't any there. Of course there weren't, he laughed at himself. That's why he was down here in front of Snooky's with this package in the first place. No smokes, no booze, no more money from his government check, and he needed to do something to stop his hands from trembling.

Just one more look, he thought, *just so I'll remember it.* He reached over for the package and maneuvered it onto his lap. He began working on the brown paper, down at the corner, but then he stopped himself. He couldn't bear to look at it again, and he didn't need to see it now to remember it.

CB ƎO

He had been just a kid, and he was happy that most kids nowadays had no idea that the world could be so cruel. But he knew it could, and he'd gotten a lesson in that he'd never forget those months it took the 157th to cross from Africa, come up the length of Italy, and take on the Germans on their home territory. All that fighting and the mud and cold and seeing all that dying and the devastation—the senseless, needless devastation—and the effect that it had on all those people, and not least

Photo by Rick Britton.

the effect it had on him.

But suddenly his war was over and there he was, in Munich, Germany, waiting around with all the other soldiers for the decision on what to do with the vanquished and when he could go home. As it was, they'd left him there nearly a year after the end of the war, in an out-of-the way war camp just outside Munich. Not much had bothered him during those last months of inactivity. It was really quite a new experience for him. Only twenty-one and already a lieutenant, which put him in charge of something for the first time in his life, even if it only was a line of mess halls.

What did bother him, however, was to see how the church-going sanity he had known back in the States as an innocent kid didn't just snap back into focus after a big ruckus like World War II. This was no more evident to him than when he had been placed between Captain Thorpe and that old man at the mess hall door. He had seen Thorpe—it was retired Major General Thorpe now—at a reunion just a few years ago. But what would really give him comfort was to have some idea that the old man at the mess hall door had made out OK. He, of course, realized the old guy would be dead by now—he was practically dead himself and he'd only been a kid then—but it would mean a lot to know that the man had seen some better times before he went.

The first time Jack had gotten a fleeting glimpse of the man was in the gloom of a cold, rainy Munich twilight as a shuffling blur at the trash cans behind one of the mess hall back doors. Jack had remembered thinking that, if the rats had grown that large now, he was certainly glad he'd gotten his orders for home already. Jack hadn't been looking for trouble, but he was responsible for these kitchens, so when he entered the wash room, he asked the Cookie on duty—all mess sergeants were called Cookie—whether they'd had any trouble with civilians hanging around the door.

"Not much," Cookie answered. "Why, Wadya see?"

"I'm not sure," Jack had responded. "Just thought I'd seen someone over by the trash cans."

"I'm sure it was no one." Jack could tell from Cookie's manner that the mess sergeant really didn't want to talk about it anymore. Their captain, Cliff Thorpe, was a real stickler for discipline and for keeping the German civilians on their side of the fence. He could be right mean about any contact with the defeated enemy. And that meant any contact that was short of stripping them of war booty.

Most of those in the unit, all except the mess hall cooks who had one more unit coming in to serve before they could go home, had just gotten their orders to return to the States. While most everyone else was spending the meanwhile time writing their sweethearts and parents letters and making plans for their futures, Captain Thorpe was stepping up his collection activities. He was doing everything he could to acquire all the valuable artwork in Munich that hadn't had a hole punched in it by a rifle bullet or hadn't already been liberated, and he was doing a pretty good job of it. In fact, he'd been in a real good mood for days because he had heard that a famous German landscape painter was living somewhere around here. He also knew that there was an art wheeler-dealer around by the name of Helmut Bergen. It was said that Bergen could locate some of this artist's works, and he would be showing up at the camp, under a summons from the captain, in another week or so. The captain thought this Bergen could put together some of the famous artist's paintings for the captain to add to his war souvenirs.

Meanwhile, everyone within miles, American soldiers and German civilians alike, were just as happy that Captain Thorpe had something to occupy himself with other than mean-spirited discipline. And maybe that's why the old man had gotten bold enough to start raiding the company trash cans at night. Or maybe it was just the depths of hunger that had brought him there.

In any case, Jack clearly caught the old man in the act not more than three days later when he had returned to inspect the mess hall again. The man, gray and withered but with an air of dignity and intelligence about him, was wrapped in torn and dirty rags. He had lingered a moment too long in trying to find something edible in a trash barrel, and a ragged sleeve had caught on the crimped lip of the metal can when he had tried to make his escape. He didn't give Jack much of a fight when Jack laid a hand on him; Jack could tell the old man was probably too weak from hunger to put up a fight, and just as likely too far into despair to care much anymore.

The real tragedy of the encounter was that, in the ridiculously short scuffle, the man's glasses had come off his face and Jack had inadvertently stepped on them. They had very thick lenses and they also looked very expensive. Jack's first instinct had been right; this man was no professional panhandler. He was just another one of those unnumbered casualties of the wars that men chose to inflict on each other from time to time.

The man peered myopically into Jack's face and then looked down and saw that his eyeglasses had been shattered. If Jack had thought that all the stuffing had been knocked out of the old man before, he had been mistaken. The broken eyeglasses had obviously been the last straw. The man just sank down in the muck around the trash barrels and began to softly cry.

"Cookie!" Jack called.

The same mess sergeant Jack had talked to about someone nosing around the mess hall a couple of days earlier appeared in the doorway. "Yes, Sir, Lieutenant."

"Look what we have here, Cookie. Have you seen this old gentleman before?"

"Naw, can't say as I have, Sir," was the answer. But Jack could tell that the sergeant was lying. Something gave him a pretty strong indication that the soldier not only had known the old man was coming around and raiding the trash cans at night, but that he also was allowing this to happen. That knowledge had a strange effect on Jack, however. It made him feel good. And he marked from that moment the completion of his long journey away from a wartime soldier mentality, something that had been necessary to form during his trudge from North Africa just to stay alive, back to being able to be just another normal person. And that knowledge also helped Jack see the mess sergeant as an individual and not just another Cookie.

"Well, Sergeant Grisham. Don't you think we need to get this gentleman out of the rain? And do you think there's any grub left over from the evening mess?"

"Yes, Sir, Lieutenant Bradley, Sir. Just lead him over to that table over there." The smile on the mess sergeant's face was just as wide as it could be. "Would you like something too, Sir? We have some canned peaches left over from the last meal."

"No thanks, Sergeant. I think I'd best go see about getting these eyeglasses replaced. I stepped on them, so I think I should be the one to replace them. Oh, and Sergeant. Most of the soldiers have gotten their orders now and aren't thinking much about their stomachs anymore. I think we should be having more food left over now, don't you? I'd hate to see it go to waste. Maybe you could invite this gentleman in for dinner every night from now on after the soldiers have eaten."

"Yes, Sir. I think that's a very good idea, Sir."

Jack managed to find another pair of eyeglasses that night that were at least good enough so that the old man could see where he was walking, but it was nearly two weeks before he encountered the man again, and that came in almost disastrous circumstances.

The captain had managed to locate the art broker, Bergen, who was being brought to see him one evening after dinner. As fate would have it, the broker and the old man arrived at the gate near the mess halls at the same time and were in deep conversation when Captain Thorpe strode up.

The captain was in high dungeon. Not only was the art broker showing up for his audience late, but he was talking to another German civilian—inside the gate, where there should be no other German civilian present. Giving everyone around a tongue-lashing and kicking the old man out of the camp with the command that he never wanted to see the old man's face here again, the captain ordered his escort to bring Bergen back to his tent.

Both Jack and Sergeant Grisham had seen it all from the mess hall doorway. The old man was standing just outside the gate, in complete confusion and despondency. He looked up at

Jack and the sergeant with sad, defeated eyes and turned to leave.

"Just a minute, Mr. Richter," Jack called out.

"Bill," Jack said to the sergeant. "Why don't you go back and wrap up some food in a tin, and I'll go talk with Mr. Richter until you can get back."

"But the captain. He'll have our hides if we let Mr. Richter back in the camp."

"Well, I heard Captain Thorpe say he didn't want to see Mr. Richter's face in the camp anymore. I didn't hear him say we couldn't take food to Mr. Richter out of the camp. I've talked to the lieutenant replacing me here, and he's agreed to continue feeding Mr. Richter. I can find out where Mr. Richter lives. This can work if you and some of the other soldiers will agree to take his dinner to him after cleaning up the mess at nights. How does that sound?"

"That sounds just great, Jack. Ain't it just great to be able to start feelin human again? I thought I'd never get to feelin civilized enough to go home. I know this is just one old man out of so many who are suffering, but ya gotta start somewhere, don't cha?—that is, if you open your eyes and realize that it's got to be done."

Three days later, most of the unit shipped out. Everyone was happy about the move, but no one was happier than Captain Thorpe. He had gotten nearly a dozen of those paintings he had wanted through the broker, Bergen, and had gotten them for a song—at least for him; the sum probably was the difference between life and death for some German family.

As it turned out, Jack wasn't going home empty-handed either. When he returned to his room the night before they shipped out, there was a large oil painting propped up on his desk. He wasn't much for artwork, but there was something about this one that made him sit and stare at it for an hour. It was a painting of a mountainside with one of the alps in the background. Right there in the center of the painting, growing out of the mountainside in the foreground was a tall, thin, isolated pine tree, one without hardly any branches at all. There were some live pine needles on the branches—not many, but enough so that you could tell the tree was still alive. The tree stood out against the mountain opposite it, and the valley between was filled with a thick mist. The colors were luminescent and quiet at the same time, and there was both a profound serenity and a tight tension quality about the work. The tree was so scraggly, it should have been laughable, but it wasn't. And it took Jack nearly the whole hour to figure out why it wasn't. That lone pine was rising right out of large boulder and was in the bed of a dry stream that probably was awash with a tumbling torrent of water all spring as the snow melted on the mountain and then was dry as dust all summer. But still the lone pine survived; it was thin and twisted and struggling for life, but it was a survivor. Jack got the message.

He went out to ask the barracks sergeant where the painting had come from.

"Oh, it was dropped off for you by some old German guy. Sergeant Grisham brought him over. He said something about being sorry, but that it was the last one he had. Said he'd run out of paints before the war ended and just after he'd finished that painting. Sergeant Grisham said he was glad the old man told him he was out of paints, because Grisham knew where he could find some more. That seemed to please the old man mighty fine."

Jack went back into his room and searched the lower reaches of the painting. There it was, cleverly hidden in the shadow of a rock outcropping—the signature "R. Richter."

ଓ ୨୦

Jack awoke as if from a dream and was a little confused where he was until he saw the storefront of Snooky's Pawn Shop just a few steps away from where he was sitting on the Downtown Mall. Then he heard it again. Someone was calling his name.

"There you are, Jack. I was afraid I wouldn't find you."

"Hello yourself," Bill. "Nice day. A good day to be out on the Downtown Mall."

"Yep, agreed. I see you have a package there. And I noticed when I stopped by the home to visit you that your painting wasn't on the wall."

"I'd offer you a smoke or a drink, old buddy, but I'm fresh out. Out of smokes, out of drink, and out of pension for the rest of the month. Gotta do something about that."

"Aw, Jack." The two were silent for a while, and then Bill said, "I thought you were giving up smokin and drinkin."

"I have given them up. About a hundred times. Always near the end of the month when the pension check runs out." He put his hand out. "Look at that hand, Bill. Ever seen anything tremble that bad?"

"You're nearly eighty, Jack. You should be happy that hand is still moving."

They were silent for a couple more minutes.

"That's Snooky's Pawn Shop right over there, isn't it, Jack?"

"Yep."

"I think it's time I told you something, Jack. If you've gotta do it, I think you'd do better going into the Raven Art Gallery over there. I think they'd welcome you with open arms, and you'd be able to stock in enough smokes and booze to kill you twice as fast as any deal Snooky's would offer. They don't know much about art in Snooky's."

"What are you saying, Bill?"

"Let me put it this way, Jack. Remember that reunion of the 157th we went to a couple of years back and how General Thorpe was yapping on so long and hard about the great art collection he had from Europe?"

"Yep."

"And remember how I kept saying he really should get appraisals for all those German paintings he'd gotten just before your unit shipped out of Munich?"

"Yeah. That irritated me a bit, Bill. I didn't see any reason for you to suck up to that ass, Thorpe, after all these years."

"Well, that's not exactly what was happening, Jack. You know all those German landscape paintings he crowed about?"

"Yeah."

"Worthless. Not a one of them worth a pile of shinola. And I thought it was time that Thorpe knew that. I'd like to have seen the expression on his face when he got them appraised."

"Whatya mean worthless? How do you know that?"

"Remember that I stayed around for a couple of months after you and Thorpe shipped out?"

"Yeah, so?"

"I ran across that Bergen fella at Mr. Richter's one day. By the way, it's a good thing we started taking food to Mr. Richter's house. I found that there was an invalid Mrs. Richter. I had wondered why he was only eating half the food I was laying out for him and asking to take the rest home for breakfast. We upped his rations mighty fast, you can bet."

"I shoulda guessed he wasn't fighting so hard to stay alive just for himself. Thanks for telling me that. But what about Bergen?"

"Oh, yes. As I was gonna say, seems the captain ticked Bergen off real bad when he was so mean to Mr. Richter and threw him out of the camp. Bergen was awful respectful of Mr. Richter. Seems Bergen got the captain back by selling him some real bad paintings some local school children had done. Thorpe thinks they're abstracts. Shows what he knows. The famous painter he wanted to collect didn't paint no abstracts. All Thorpe knew was that there was some famous artist around Munich; he had no idea what he was famous for paintin."

"I think I get the drift, Bill. You're saying that Mr. Richter was that famous artist?"

"Not exactly, Jack. Mr. Richter was the master who *taught* that famous artist. I've kept track, you havin that painting and all. Richter is the more famous of the two now. His paintings go for a lot of money. And I mean a lot of money. I'd a told you about the painting sooner, but I thought its value to you was something other than the money it would fetch."

Jack just sat there, staring at Bill for nearly a minute. And then his face got red and sort of puffed up, like he was going to explode.

"Oh, that's good! Schoolkid doodles, you say?" was all Jack could manage to get out, because he was choking up. Then he started laughing loud and hard, and he continued laughing until tears rolled down his cheeks.

"Bill?"

"Yes, Jack?"

"Suppose you can help me get this heavy old package back down to the car?"

"What about your smokes and your bottles?"

"I just remembered how I got this painting and I also just remembered how you and I got to be such close friends. If it hadn't been for Mr. Richter and those eyeglasses I broke, I don't think I'd had ever been able to laugh again after what we went through marching up Italy and into Germany. That story you told about Thorpe and his collection of schoolkid doodles is going to make me laugh every time I think about it, and I'm going to think of that story every time I look at this painting now. I think I need a good laugh now and than a whole lot more than I need a cigarette or a shot of bourbon."

What's Mine Is Mine

Sondra knew something was peculiar for some time before she rejoined the world. The morning light was shining full in her face, and her muscles felt more cramped than they usually did when she had spent the night on that park bench in front of the block-long construction site. *How rude,* she thought. *What's the sun doin being up at this time?* She opened one eye to get her second rude awakening for the day. Plastered almost up against her face was that of a sad-eyed little boy. Just standing there and staring into her face for who knows how long.

She gave the child a funny face, which he good-naturedly returned in kind, giggled, and then romped off across the bricked Charlottesville Downtown Mall.

"T'aint no way for a woman to be awakened," Sondra mumbled belligerently. "What's the sun doin up already? I don't like being caught in my 'boodwar' asleep. T'aint civilized. A girl could get mugged and who knows what else being caught sleepin out here on her bench too late in the morning."

Sondra stood up and stretched and then leaned down and picked through her bag of treasures, making for damn sure that no one had made off with any of her stuff in the middle of the night. She looked around. The Mall was already coming to life. A perky looking girl with an older man at her side and ice skates laced together and hanging over her shoulder was scurrying off away from the morning sun. No secret there; they were headed for the skate park on the west end of the Mall across from the hotel. No use asking for a handout from them either; they would be in too much of a hurry to pay her the least bit of attention.

Across the Mall, that nice lady was setting up her plant stand. She'd be good for lunch money if Sondra wasn't able to score big off the tourists today. It was always good to have a little something in reserve for a rainy day.

She could see Ms. Alberta entering her shop up a ways too. It was too bad about her shop closing. Ms. Alberta had always passed her a book now and again. She'd learned to read that way. She was mighty proud of that; she'd gone to school, of course, but she hadn't seen the need to know how to read much at that time. Ms. Alberta had volunteered to help her get cleaned up a bit and maybe find a job too, but Sondra wasn't having any of that. She was free now, free of all constraints, and no one but one of her own kind could know the glory of that. She'd stop in when the store was open, though, because this was its last day, and Ms. Alberta was giving books away. It would be good to get a free book when that wasn't a special favor, just something that anybody could get that day.

Nothing all that special happening on the Mall this morning, but why had she awakened so late? She hadn't done anything special the previous night to make her all that sleepy. Getting up this late always put her off her schedule; she'd probably be playing catch-up all day long. She hated that—going through the day always just a couple of minutes late for everything. She had half a notion of going and finding Chantel's hidey hole and sleeping right through the day so she could get a proper start the next morning.

Chantel. This was all Chantel's fault. "Chantel. Chantel Walker. Where you at, girl?" she called toward the north, in the direction in which her friend had a covered spot picked out up near the Methodist Church just off the Mall and across General Lee's park. Sondra took a quick but careful look in all four directions. She wasn't the only one who was off schedule this morning. Chantel wasn't here. That's why she hadn't been wakened before the day people started arriving on the Mall. This was all Chantel's fault.

Ever since they had started knocking down those buildings on this block of the Mall, all but the facades of them, Chantel had been out here every day at the crack of dawn ranting and raving at the top of her range at what they were doing to "her" building. Chantel had always claimed that one of those buildings over there was rightfully hers. The little one, the one with the plain face, sitting between what had been a photo studio and the old Miller and Rhoads Department Store, the highest building on the Mall. Now some big company had come in and was building a new building all across the block. The city had made them keep the faces of the old buildings, however, on account of the rules they had about the Downtown Mall look.

Every morning Chantel would be standing out in front of that construction and screaming at them to stop knocking down her building. Today was the first day she'd missed since they'd started working. She'd been better than an alarm clock. And it was her fault that Sondra's day had been ruined even before it had got a chance to start off.

Don't know why Chantel was puttin on such airs, though. My daddy had his own business down somewhere around where the hotel now stands too. We had the best candy store there was in the city. Even the white folks would bring their kids in for my daddy's hard candy. That part of town was once called Vinegar Hill, but we usually called it Our Harlem, because it was just as grand a community for our folks hereabouts as Harlem was up there in New York City. We had night spots and entertainers that would have given those folks up in the big city a run for their money. Nearly 150 buildings on the hill, including two churches and twenty-nine businesses, all black owned and all prosperous. Yes, indeedy, we was doin fine until those white folks from up in Washington, D.C., decided that what this country needed was urban renewal. Well, by 1962, they started to urban renewal us over in Vinegar Hill, no matter that we kept our side of the city up a mighty sight better than those folks over in Belmont on the east side of town were doin.

First thing they did was to condemn our places, divide us up into smaller groups, and take us way out into the countryside and dump us onto land that no one else wanted for anything. It was that or those cheap same-same apartment complexes called the projects—or a group of shacks over by the railroad tracks. My own family decided to stay in town over by the railroad tracks, but nobody wanted to come into where daddy tried to restart his candy store, and we went downhill from there. Still, I'd probably still be in that shack they gave us if it didn't burn down one Christmas morning.

Well, once they'd moved us out of Vinegar Hill, it took them three more years to decide how to urban renewal it and to start knocking down all of those nice buildings we had built for ourselves. Twenty-nine prosperous black businesses, all knocked down. Don't know of any that came up and made a go of it anywhere else. But I'm sure them urban renewal people thought they was doin us a big favor.

Guess they decided they didn't really like the plans they had drawn up, because that end of the Mall stayed as scrubby ground for more than the next twenty years. Then when they did put something on it, the biggest piece they gave over to a fancy hotel that failed within two years and had to be bought and helped along from then by the city. I don't remember the city having to—or ever offering to—help along the businesses we had goin there before.

But Chantel always was above that. Whenever we mentioned those twenty-nine prosperous black-owned businesses that had been renewed to dust, Chantel would break in and say there really were thirty. Her daddy had been some braver, for all the good it had done him, than the rest of our community. He had actually bought a building further east on Main Street and put in a shoe store. It didn't do so bad, but not as good as our businesses over in Vinegar Hill. Most white folks were too good to go for the discounts Chantel's daddy was offering, and most black folks were too scared in those days to go that far into Main Street proper.

Chantel's daddy had his business on the Mall, but her family lived in Vinegar Hill, just like the rest of us. And a fine house they had too. But it wasn't fine enough to escape bein urban renewed, and it fell down when the wrecking ball hit it just as fast as my house did. This urban renewal business was what drove Chantel's daddy crazy. And somehow in all of the hullabaloo, some white man moved in and said Chantel's daddy had sold him the shoe store building on Main Street. Chantel's daddy was too far out of it by then to offer up any help on why he'd sold the store or where the money had gone, and Chantel got it into her mind from that time forward that that building right over there by the photo studio was her inheritance.

She wasn't too pushy about it until just of late, when they started knocking it down. For some reason, that stuck in her craw real bad, and she started standing out here and screamin at the wrecking ball every morning, rantin "Stop knocking that down. What's mine is mine," until Officer Bob comes along and gets her to move off and stop scaring the tourists.

Think she might be just about as crazy now as her daddy was in the end. For all that, she's the best friend a girl could have.

But I was relying on her to get me up this morning with all her racket.

"Chantel! Chantel! Where are you?" Suddenly, Sondra had a really bad thought. Chantel's cough hadn't sounded at all good the last couple of days. Suppose Chantel was still up under cover at the Methodist Church, dead or dying. Sondra just knew this was going to be a bad day, having been awakened off schedule like that and having that little boy give her the sad eye.

She picked up her treasure bundle and started up toward 1st Street, which led up past the park to the church. Just before leaving the Mall, she turned and yelled out "Chantel!" one more time. This time she got back an echo, but in a voice of a much lower register than hers. Down the Mall from the east end was running Chauncey Willard, their old friend from the Vinegar Hill days who had made good over at Juvenile Hall. And he was calling out for Chantel too.

Catching up with Sondra, he breathlessly asked, "Where's Chantel gotten to, Sondra? I know she's here every morning. Did Officer Shifflett move her off already?"

"Don't think so," Sondra answered. "Chantel's had a real big mouth here of late. I been right here all night. I woulda heard her if she was here. She's tryin to get them to stop knocking down them buildings over there, you know. What a fool woman."

"Well that fool woman's got her wish," Chauncey said. "That's what I've come to tell her about. I just heard up at the courthouse. The lawyers for that construction company over there just came in today to talk to a judge, and he's set them down real hard. He called in Joe Tucker, that lawyer who came up from the projects, his daddy was a friend of Chantel's daddy, it turns out."

"Cut to the chase, Man. I don't got all day. I think Chantel might be up at the church right now coughin her life away."

"Well, OK. I'll come up with you. We've got to find Chantel. Upshot is that she's right. She does own that building over there. Turns out some white man got it from her daddy without getting the deed. Chantel doesn't even know she's got a lawyer, but Joe Tucker is with the judge and those construction company lawyers now. Chantel's building is right in the center of all that construction. They're going to have to pay her a bundle whether they go ahead with construction or not. Chantel's rich, Sondra."

This didn't take all that long to sink in with Sondra. Hiking her bundle up under her arm, she started trotting as fast as she could up 1st Street toward the Methodist Church. "Hang on Chantel! Sondra's coming to help you with that cough." Maybe it wasn't such a bad morning after all. Maybe she didn't have to worry about where supper was coming from today, let alone lunch.

Readers' Choice: Gordon's Ride

Jan found Gordon right where he said he would be, although she had thought he was joking on the telephone. Always the joker. As she approached her father-in-law at Miller's patio table area on the Downtown Mall, however, it certainly didn't look like Gordon was in the joking mood. He looked very serious, his eyes closed, his chin down, and his arms folded across his chest. He was very much in his own world. A sudden jolt of fearful anticipation shot down her spine. The news must have been even worse than they'd thought. But then her irritation rose when she saw the glass of beer sitting in front of him.

"Dad, what are you doing here?"

"Am where I told you I'd be. Right here at Miller's." A little belligerent. At the same time dreamy, as if he had been dozing. Was there a sign of sadness in his voice?

"Yes, you said you'd be waiting for me at Miller's, but I thought you were joking. The first thing the doctor told you the other day when he set up this appointment was that you needed to stop drinking right away. Please tell me at least that you've had something to eat with it. How many of these beers have you had?"

"Just the one. Well, no, just about two-thirds of one, to be precise."

"Very funny, Dad. About two-thirds too much, wouldn't you say? You know what the doctor said."

"It hardly matters at this point."

"Oh." There it was. Everything she'd feared in that one simple sentence. Doctor Graves had called him back to the office for a consultation right after his tests came back. She'd had to cancel a house showing to bring him down here this morning and then had to cut another one short when he called her to come pick him up afterward. Originally, when she'd let him off at the Mall, he had said he'd just walk back home to the house on Evergreen after the appointment. He loved to walk, and he still seemed robust at seventy-four. Doctor Graves's news must have really been a blow. What was she supposed to do now? Gordon was Sam's and her last remaining parent. She wasn't ready for him to go. It wasn't just that she genuinely enjoyed him and having him live with them. She'd always had the fear that when the last of her parents' generation was gone, she'd have to start making plans for her own passing. Gordon had been her protection from all that.

She sat down across from her father-in-law, grasping in her mind for what to say and do next. But in the end it was Gordon who broke the silence.

"I called Sam too, over at his bookstore across the Mall. He should be along any minute."

"Maybe you should tell me what the doctor had to say before Sam gets here, Dad. Maybe it would be best if I knew first."

"Ah, there he is now."

"Dad, Jan." It obviously had been tough for Sam Eads to pull away from selling his used classics, but he had known that his father had been called back to the doctor's under very unusual circumstances, and the possibilities this brought up had been eating at him all morning. "Can't stay long; we're taking on most of Alberta's books from the Commonwealth closing, and I have to figure out how to get them over today and where to put them. What did the doctor have to say, Dad?"

"Well, we'll get to that, but first I have a favor to ask of you both."

"Sure, Dad, what is it?" Now that Gordon was putting him off on what he found out at the doctor's, Sam's mind was only about half on this conversation. In his head, he was already trying to remember which rental truck company's rates were cheapest.

"I want to go for a ride up on the Blue Ridge."

"Fine, Dad, we'll try to fit that in this Sunday. Oh, no, we're expecting Phoebe and Harley over for a cookout, aren't we, Jan? Well, we'll just have to look at the next—"

"Now. I'd like to go right now, son. With both of you."

"But—" Jan put a restraining hand on Sam's arm before he could go any further and gave him a very pointed look.

"That sounds good, Dad. My car is probably closer than Sam's and is gassed up. We'll take that one."

That had been easy to say. Entirely too easy. Jan's mind raced over all that she had to do that day. She was in a stiff competition to make the Golden Realtor's level this year, and she should be showing that million-five house over on Rugby Road this afternoon. But this might be Gordon's last ride. He certainly thought he had to do it right away. If they left now and didn't dawdle, she should be able to make it back in time. She just had to reach the gold this year. She'd been at silver both of the last two years, and you only had so much time to reach gold before you got to be known as an also-ran in this business.

Gordon's voice had a dreamy quality to it as he reveled in the drive out toward the mountains. "Look at those mountains showcasing that vineyard over there. Most beautiful sight. Haven't been out this way in years, and it's just across town from the house. It's true, the mountains really are blue."

Once in the car, Gordon had insisted that they take the back roads through the rolling horse country that stretched for twenty miles from the west end of Charlottesville to the Blue Ridge Mountains and the Shenandoah National Park. If they'd taken I-64, they'd have been up to Afton in about twenty minutes. This was where the Skyline Drive ended, coming down the crest of the mountains from the north, and where the Blue Ridge Parkway took up the road heading south all the way to Georgia. Even Route 250 would have gotten them there in less than a half hour. Taking Barracks and Garth Roads out to White Hall and then over through Crozet was taking considerably longer.

"I think U-Haul might be a bit more, but it's more likely to have a truck on short notice. Maybe I'll just use the cell phone—"

"Let's not do that, son. Road's pretty windy and narrow. We'd hate to go before our time. Uh—"

Jan whipped her head around in consternation. "Dad?" Gordon had winced and was rubbing his chest with a hand.

"It's nothing, Jan. Just a muscle twinge. My, look at all that white fencing and those beautiful pastures. And isn't that the Foxcroft race track coming up? Looks like they're getting ready for one of their do's."

When they reached the crest of the pass at Afton Mountain, they let Gordon choose whether they went north or south. Sam had given it considerable thought on the way up and didn't think the distance to an exit back off the parkway was any further in one direction than the other. He was already trying to gauge just how long they had to be up here. He chose south on the Blue Ridge Parkway rather than north on the Skyline Drive simply because there was a charge for the Drive and there wasn't one for the Parkway.

"Isn't this gorgeous, kids? Here, pull over at the overlook. I want to see down into the Shenandoah Valley. It's so clear today. I may never be able to get a good view like that again."

Of course they had to stop. While Gordon and Jan sat on the stone wall and looked out over the Waynesboro area below and toward the next set of mountains, Sam used the cell phone to call back down to the bookstore on the Downtown Mall and to tell Laura Grace she'd just have to hire in someone with a truck to get the books moved over. Luckily, the turnoff at Wintergreen wasn't too far off. They'd be back in Charlottesville by 3:00.

"Can't think of any better time to see Hump Back Rock. It's just down the road here a bit."

"Dad!" Jan thought this was really too much. "The climb up to Hump Back Rock is just for teenagers. We don't have the shoes and clothes for it, and don't you think you shouldn't—?"

"Oh, no. I didn't mean to suggest that we stop at the parking area for the climbing. Just beyond that there's a real nice peaceful picnic area well off of the road. I think I'd like to go there and just sit a bit. Get my thoughts in order. That is, if you don't mind."

"Sure, Dad." Sam was now resigned to having lost all of the afternoon. He knew Laura Grace would manage without him. Besides, he'd had some quiet time while driving along the parkway to think back over his life. His dad had always been there for him and had never asked much in return. Sure, he lived with them now, but it was his money that had bought the house on Evergreen and they'd been so busy with their jobs over the past several years that he'd been more of the glue that had kept everything together than a burden. He obviously had taking this ride on his mind—and if it helped him take whatever bitter pill the doctor had given him easier, then that was OK with Sam. He had to admit the drive up here and down the parkway was relaxing, even with whatever trouble his dad had weighing on his mind. Maybe his dad knew this trip would help them all face his news.

Jan's mental condition at that moment was another kettle of fish altogether. Her mind was racing, calculating and recalculating times and distances. When they had pulled into the picnic area and Sam had helped Gordon over to a picnic bench, Jan heaved a big sigh, took the cell phone, and walked higher onto the ridge to get a clear channel down to her office in Charlottesville.

When she returned, she announced that she had turned the Rugby Road showing over to a colleague. "There's a place out in Ivy that the couple wants to see this evening, though," she continued. "It's a little less, but I could keep the—"

"Look, Jan. Over there. Isn't that the mountain laurel you've been trying to get to grow in the backyard? Isn't it beautiful up here in the wild? And isn't that trillium?"

"Very nice. In fact, the Ivy house has one more bedroom. I think they said they—"

"Shh, Jan. Listen a minute. What do you hear?"

Jan listened. "Nothing. Just a lot of silence."

"Precisely, dear." A little smile formed on Gordon's lips, and he closed his eyes and drank in the silence.

Jan got the point. She didn't even object when Gordon requested that they stop in Nellysford on the way back to town for an early supper.

"Your mother and I always wanted to stop at that restaurant in Nellysford. I'd really like to do that once before I die."

The sun was sinking behind the ridge of blue mountains behind them, as they drove back toward Route 250 that evening. From the sighs coming from the back seat, it was obvious to Jan and Sam that Gordon had enjoyed his outing. Some time after the sounds from the back seat had stopped, however, Jan, having given up on the possibility of making a sale to that rich couple, began to think about Gordon's problem again. His daughter, Gloria, and her husband were off in the Caribbean on another cruise. Jan had no idea how you got in touch with people in this situation. Maybe Sam would be able to handle that. What were the final arrangements Gordon had made? She knew he had a plot next to his wife up at Monticello Memorial Gardens, but had he made any funeral home prearrangements? She knew she shouldn't be thinking about all this, but her mind was just too organized. Finally, she decided she couldn't take it anymore.

She turned in her seat and said: "What was it that Doctor Graves said today about your tests, Dad? Whatever it is, we can face it— Dad? Dad! Gordon! Sam pull over. Pull over right now. Something's wrong with your dad!"

When they'd gotten the back door open, they could see that Gordon was slumped over toward the center of the car. Only his seatbelt held him in place. But he looked so peaceful, his eyes closed and a sweet smile on his lips. He obviously had enjoyed his ride.

Either ...

At the services at Hill and Wood, Doctor Graves came through the line to offer his condolences.

"We had had no idea he was that sick," Jan told the doctor. "He looked in such robust health right up to the end."

"Surprised me too," Doctor Graves responded. "He had a great heart for a man his age. You just can't always tell when something's going to go wrong."

"But surely you knew something serious was wrong, Doctor. You called him back in to meet on his tests just that morning."

"Oh, that. That's sort of embarrassing. Just before Gordon came in, I found that his tests had been mixed up with someone else's. According to *his* tests, he was quite healthy for a man his age. All I told him that morning was that he needed to get out and about in the garden more. Needed to stop now and then and smell the roses. I told him that you two would do well to slow down a bit and enjoy life too. He responded that he'd just see about that and mentioned something about a ride in the mountains."

Or ...

When they'd gotten the back door open, they could see that Gordon was slumped over toward the center of the car. Only his seatbelt held him in place. But he looked so peaceful, his eyes closed and a sweet smile on his lips. He obviously had enjoyed his ride.

Jan started to tremble and Sam wrapped his arms around her—right out there on the side of the road. There wasn't much traffic going by, but the cars that did pass them weren't even slowing down.

Sam reached over into the window of the driver's seat for his cell phone, but his action was arrested by a dry voice from the interior of the car.

"What'd we stop for? Surely you *both* don't have to take a whiz. What's that? Can't hear you. Oh, my hearing aide fell out."

"Dad, you're OK!" Jan leaned into the back seat and gave her father-in-law a big hug.

"Of course, I'm OK. Why wouldn't I be OK?"

"What in blazes did Doctor Graves tell you about the tests, Dad?" Sam had had enough.

"Oh that. Just before I got there this morning, he found out that my tests had been mixed up with someone else's. According to *my* tests, I'm healthy as a horse, albeit an old horse. He did say I should get out and about more often. Stop and smell the roses, and such as that. He's also your doctor, Sam, and he told me that you should slow down and enjoy life more too. You're probably wound tighter than I am. And goodness knows, Jan should take time to breathe every once in a while.

Always thought she looked a whole lot better in silver than in gold. You just never can tell when your time is going to come, so it's not such a good idea to save all the good times for later. So, I decided we'd take a ride today. Worked real good. Think we'll go to Richmond next week. I hear there's a great new botanical garden on the north side. The Lewis Ginter Center, or some such. So, I don't care what you have planned for next Tuesday, we're all—"

The Game: One

"Just a glass of Lemonade for now, thank you," said Shelley.

"And one for me too," requested Tiffany. "Oh, and maybe a bowl of chips. We're expecting a couple of others before we order lunch."

Dennis, Max, and Megan, knowing just how late Jeff and Luis often were in showing up, went ahead and ordered full lunches.

As the waiter headed into the Hardware Store Restaurant building with their order, Shelley stood and said, "I guess I'll go in and freshen up. Want to come along, Tiff? They've got that Pachinko machine near the women's room I'd like to try out. I just adore games." The two left the Hardware Store's roped-off open-air Garden Café area and followed the waiter off the Charlottesville Downtown Mall and into the main restaurant. Megan gave a little snicker and Dennis looked at her sharply.

"Say, that waiter looks familiar," Max said.

"He should," Megan answered. "That's Rafael. He's the star of our microbiology class at UVA."

"I wouldn't laugh at that," Dennis said. "A lot of people have to work jobs like this as they go through school. I've had to do a lot of things to keep my Harley in gas, and I haven't even gotten around to trying out college yet. I'm hoping my next wife is richer than the last one was. It's probably even harder for this dude to manage school because he's old enough to have a wife and his own kids to support and he's Hispanic."

"Oh, I wasn't laughing at Rafael," Megan responded. "He's a really good guy, and he's really smart too. I think he's already got a lot of degrees from where he came from in Central America. I think the degrees just don't do him much good here in the States. I was laughing at Shelley and Tiffany. If they only knew they were both off sprucing up for the appearance of Jeff, each thinking she is his one and only."

"Both still carrying the flame?" asked Max.

"Yep, and neither seems to be able to catch onto the other's hopes and dreams. But, shh, they'll be back any minute. Tiffany forgot her purse. Of course, she's so ditsy, she probably won't even notice."

"Speaking of hopes and dreams," said Max, his voice full of hope. "Remember that I asked you to go—"

"Here, quick, Dennis, pass me Tiffany's silverware and napkin," Megan cut in. "Let's see how long she goes without noticing."

"Well, I'm sure glad we went ahead and ordered our lunch," said Dennis after Megan had concealed the napkin and silverware. "If Jeff has any inkling of what's waiting for him here, he'll never show up. It looks like we might have a pretty boring afternoon ahead of us."

"Oh, I wouldn't worry about that," said Megan with a smile of welcome for the returning young women. "Tiffany isn't good at waiting. She'll have us doing something before we can get bored. We'll probably wish we had been left alone to be bored."

True to Megan's statement, Tiffany wasn't able to sit still for very long. She became more agitated as the tables of the Garden Café began to fill up and the waiter took away the empty chair that had been next to her to accommodate a party at the adjacent table.

"I do hope Jeff gets here soon," she said with a bit of irritation in her voice. "They're running out of chairs here."

"Not any faster than they're running out of silverware and napkins," quipped Megan. Tiffany knit her brow and started counting the napkins and silverware at the table.

"No problem," Shelley purred. "We still have one empty space here by me. Luis will just have to go find his own when they get here."

Tiffany looked up, a little confused, and then, having lost count of the silverware and napkins, started counting them out again, this time pointing with her fingers and forming the numbers with her lips. Megan stifled a giggle, and Tiffany looked up again suspiciously. Max swept in before Tiffany could form a question.

"I know, let's play that game Jeff thought up the last time we met down here at the Mall."

Shelley's eyes brightened. "I remember. That's what we did when Jeff brought me here on our first date."

Tiffany looked up again, not sure that she had heard correctly—not even sure what she had heard Shelley say.

"I think that was before I met you guys," Dennis said. "About the time I was hiding from my wife."

"Yeah, right, you're always talking about having run away from your wife," Shelley said. "You're not old enough to even be married."

"Well, what we do is that whoever won the last round picks out someone within sight of this table at the Mall," Max pressed on with the game, "and then two of us have to make up a story about who they are and what they're up to. When that's done, the rest of us vote on which is the best story. Shelley, you can start by picking somebody out. And Tiffany and I will be the first to make up stories."

Shelley laughed. "So you do remember that game. Of course you'd pick Tiffany to compete with."

Max ignored the jibe. "Is that OK with you, Tiffany?"

"Wait a minute. I think we're short a napkin and—"

"How about you, Megan?" Max plowed on, as he tried to catch Megan's eye. He didn't like the way she had moved away from him when he had asked her again about Saturday night.

"Yeah, yeah, whatever." Megan had answered, but her attention was not on Max. Her voice trailed off as she caught sight of a young man turning the corner into the Mall and heading slowly in their direction.

Well, hello, gorgeous, she was thinking. *Please, please be coming to the café. Yes!*

Max caught this new focus of Megan's interest and scowled.

The Game: One

"OK, OK," said Shelley. "Let's see. Oh, I know. Look over there at that Oriental furniture store. There's a soldier. It looks like an army officer, and he's standing outside the store and bowing and scraping with that old Chinese guy in the Oriental dress. OK, Max, quickly, what's the story of these two?"

"Yep, yep, that's a good one. Hmm. OK, OK. The army guy is from that army spy place that used to be here just off the Mall and that's now out 29 North. He's a spy for the Chinese and is selling secrets to the old man to ship to China in furniture."

"Not bad there for a minute," Dennis said with a snort. "Right up to the part about shipping Oriental furniture from the States to China. They've brought the furniture *here* to sell, Genius."

"OK, Tiffany, your turn. What do you see?" Shelley asked.

"It's more what I don't see," Tiffany whined. "Everyone has a napkin and silverware but—"

"The solider and the Chinese guy, Tiffany. Focus." Shelley was really getting into the game.

"Oh, I think the army guy is buying some Chinese furniture for his house."

"That's it? That's your guess?" Max said. He couldn't believe it. He'd overshot on his answer and thought he lost this round. But Tiffany's understatement had certainly trumped his overstatement in stupidity.

"OK, I vote for Max's story," announced Shelley. "How about you, Dennis?"

"Tiffany."

"Tiffany?" Max roared.

"And you, Megan?" Shelley asked.

"Huh?" Here. Here. There's an empty table right here beside me. Yes!

"Who's story was the best? Tiffany's or Max's?"

"What? Oh, Tiffany's, I suppose."

"That's no fair," Max thundered. "You weren't even listening."

79

"That's OK, Max," Shelley said soothingly. "It's early in the game yet. We'll let you play the next round. You can play against Megan. Is that OK, Megan?"

"Yeah, sure, fine."

"OK, Tiffany, your turn to pick someone out."

"Okie doke. There, how about that high school kid over there looking in that jewelry store window? OK, Max?"

Max took a look and screwed up his eyes in thought. He wasn't going to blow this one. Then he looked over at Megan—to see that she seemed to be mooning over a guy who had just entered the café and was seated at the table right next to her. Max's heart did a flip-flop.

"The boy is going into the jewelry store to buy a present for his first girlfriend," Max said.

"OK, your turn, Megan," Shelley said.

"No, wait, I'm not finished," Max said. And then in a voice with a bitter edge to it, he said, "He'll spend everything he has. She'll accept it but dump him immediately for a football player. Now, it's your turn, Megan. Megan? It's your turn. What's your story for the boy at the jewelry store window over there?"

"Yeah right. I see him," Megan said, trying—but not all that hard—to refocus her attention from the dreamboat at the next table to the game. "A kid standing in front of that jewelry store, moving his weight from one foot to the other. My guess is that he just has to go to the bathroom and is looking for some store that will let him use their john." After delivering this assessment, Megan's attention snapped back to the young man at the neighboring table, and Max's spirits fell another twenty points.

Dennis gave a hearty laugh. "Right on, Megan. My vote goes to Megan."

"I vote for Max," Shelley countered. She would have voted for him whatever his story, as she thought he'd gotten a raw deal on the first vote. "Tiffany?"

"I don't think Megan's story was very nice," Tiffany answered in a very prim voice. "Max's story is sad, but I'll vote for him, because I don't think Megan should use bathroom words at the lunch table."

The Game: One

"OK, Max wins. You pick the subject now Max," Shelley said. "Dennis and I'll make up the stories."

"Does anyone have an extra napkin and silverware?" Tiffany asked hopefully.

Max looked around the nearby area of the Mall. That's when he saw a toddler go up to an old woman and an old man sitting on a bench and the old man shooing the boy away. He pointed this tableau out to Dennis and Shelley.

"The man hasn't really brushed the little boy off to be mean," said Shelley. "The old man has a terrible, communicable disease and he doesn't want the little boy to be exposed."

"Oh, I agree the man is concerned for the little boy," Dennis counters, "but he's shooed the boy away in anger. My story is that the woman has spent much of her life behind bars for stealing a baby from a hospital. The man has given up everything to care for her and to try to keep her from the temptation of repeating her crime. He has realized too late that bringing her to the Mall and into this crowd was a mistake, and he's pushed the little boy away to protect him and out of anger at himself for bringing the woman here."

Tiffany began to cry softly. "I don't think I like this game. That story's too sad. And . . . and I don't have a napkin."

"Oh, here!" Shelley said, taking the napkin and silverware from the empty place beside her and plopping it down in front of Tiffany. Tiffany's little sobs subsided with a crowning hiccup.

"I'll take that as a vote for my story," Shelly concluded. "Max, who are you voting for?"

"You, of course. How about you, Megan?"

But Megan obviously wasn't paying a bit of attention to the game anymore. She was deep in conversation with the young man at the adjoining table. Max started to pull at her arm, but Shelley interceded.

"I got two votes, anyway. It really doesn't matter. I win. It's my turn to pick someone out. Dennis and Megan can do the guessing." This time, Shelley took a long time choosing a subject. Eventually a woman walking slowly along the side of the Mall caught her attention. She seemed to be in a daze. "Her. What's her story? Megan can start."

Max turned in his chair. "OK, Megan, what's your guess on that woman over there with the strange shoes? Megan? Shelley, Megan's gone. Did you see where she went?"

Just Call Me Rose

Ted could see as he approached the Ming Court that the intricately carved teak and rosewood tables and chairs were tumbling out onto the bricks of the Charlottesville Downtown Mall again. This was a never-ending struggle between the stubborn Ke Mushui and the Charlottesville authorities, who bent over backward to be tolerant, but whose sense of propriety had its limits.

Not that Ke Mushui and his wife, the indomitable Leng Taohua, were a tumble-down sort of couple. They were anything but that, and Ted was sure that Madam Leng knew the exact whereabouts of every *yi fen qian*, or one-cent piece, that had ever passed through her claws. But they had not been gone long enough from the narrow shopping streets of Tianjin, China, to have grown out of the Oriental merchant game of starting the sales day by staking as big a claim on the potential sales territory in the front of the shop as they possibly could. This invariably would be followed by spending much of the rest of the day making further inroads into the sidewalk displays of the surrounding merchants.

Ted knew he really should try to explain this one more time to the owners of the Oriental furniture store, but he just liked and respected the irascible old couple too much. Besides, he didn't want to be involved in the relentless stripping away of their tenuous hold on their customs and traditions. They had already lost so much of themselves in their flight from China.

As he approached the shop door, the smells of camphor and of fine old wood, aging gently in the filtered sunlight streaming into the Downtown Mall, wafted forth, bringing back sweet sensations of the hillside looking down into the harbor of

Photo by Rick Britton.

Aberdeen on Hong Kong's Victoria Peak and, inevitably, of his Rose.

A somewhat stooped, but still lithe and noticeably fluid old Chinese gentleman in the men's version of a white cheongsam, the traditional skirted Chinese dress with a Mandarin collar, separated from the shadows of the shop door and flowed out to greet his guest. Master Ke usually wore an impeccable Western three-piece suit, and his attire this afternoon reminded Ted of the rigid demands of the ceremonial occasion.

The old man stopped in front of Ted and bowed deeply. "*Ni hao* (Hello), Major Ted."

Ted attempted to bow his head even lower than that of the older man. "*Ni hao, chang ren* (Hello, Father-in-Law)."

"*Ni chi fan ma* (Have you eaten yet)?" The man's head dipped a bit lower.

"*Wo chi le, xie xie* (I have eaten, thank you)." Ted failed in his attempt to get his head below that of his father-in-law, not least because he had started off a good foot taller than the older gentleman.

"*Hau le, hau le* (Good, good). Come inside out of the sun."

Ted followed the merchant into the dimly lighted shop, which was literally stuffed with the wealth of Asia. He was led through a maze of carved teak armoires to a very private little nook that had been preserved at the side of the showroom, far from the main aisles that traversed the Oriental treasure trove. There Ted found, as he expected, three ornately carved traditional rosewood throne chairs and a round wooden table. The table was topped with an intricately cut scene of ancient Chinese sailors on a wave-tossed sea engaged in a fight to the death with a huge sea serpent. This piece of furniture had long been both a mystery and a comfort to Ted. Despite the elaborate carving, you could put the smallest cup anywhere on the table and it would not tip over. Also, the table stood sturdily on impossibly thin, curved legs. The most striking thing about this table for Ted, however, was the little piece that had been sliced out of the rim closest to his host, leaving a ragged edge that marred the overall impression of the fabulous artwork the table had previously represented. In a store like this, Ted knew that his father-in-law normally would just destroy such a damaged piece of furniture. But Ted also knew that this was the family's most prized possession. A tea service with two cups and a flask of rice wine and three delicate crystal goblets rested on the table in front of the old man.

Ke Mushui leaned over and lovingly traced the edges of the marred area, now smoothened with time and attention, although no effort had been made to repair the damage.

"*Xiao Bennu* (Clumsy little girl)." The old man affectionately whispered the family name of his daughter as he almost absent-mindedly traced where she had fallen against the table and rendered it useless as a sales object many years previously. "She will join us presently, but in the meantime, can I interest you in a cup of *cha* (tea), and we will talk of our shared past. I am honored by your visit to my inferior shop."

೧೩ ೮೦

Ted initially had regretted having come to the concert at the Bhirasri Institute that evening. He didn't even know what had drawn him there after the ceremony at the JUSMAG, the Joint United States Military Assistance Group, building just around the corner from the Bhirasri on Bangkok's busy Sathorn Road. Years later he told himself that he had come for the classical music, but he had always known that it was because he'd been told it was a good place to pick up girls. He had only walked about three city blocks from JUSMAG, and it was mid-November already, but the afternoon's military ceremony had required him to wear his full summer dress blues. Thus he was sweltering by the time he reached the art institute's outer courtyard.

He had taken off his dress jacket, bought a cooling drink, and was standing under a giant orchard plant at the edge of the flagstones, waiting for the doors to the air-conditioned concert hall to open, when he heard a plaintive "Oops." He felt a cold liquid pour over the jacket he had draped over his arm and down the side of his leg.

"Oh, I'm so sorry. I'm just so clumsy." The voice had a mesmerizing soft sing-song quality about it, and when he looked up, he was struck with the conflicting thoughts that she was at the same time the most comical and the most beautiful woman he had ever seen. As long as he lived, he couldn't forget the way she half cocked her head and set her mouth into a mock pout. She was thin and more than a foot shorter than he was and was dressed in a pure white floor-length cheongsam, with mid-thigh slits on either side. Over this, she wore a crimson brocade loose jacket with elaborate frog fastenings, and there were red sparkles in her jet-black hair that twinkled in the courtyard's torchlight. She was enveloped with the slight, compelling scent of orange blossoms.

"That's quite all right," he managed to stammer. "I had been contemplating something much more drastic than that to cool myself down." They just stood there, gazing into each other's eyes for the longest moment, and then he finally broke the tension. "But here, you're in the need of a drink now. Let me get you another."

When he returned, they engaged in a short round of nonsensical and nervous chitchat until she broke the tension when she stepped back and directly on the insole of a prissy young man with a slicked-up pompadour and an apparent serious aversion to having his foot stepped on.

"Oh, dear," she cried. "There, I've done it again. 'Little Clumsy,' that was my childhood name. And I certainly seem to be living up to it tonight."

"Xiao Bennu?" he asked.

"You speak Mandarin?" She was surprised.

"*Buhui shuo, buhui shuo* (cannot speak). I'm sorry, I'm just starting to learn."

"Well, my name is Meigui. But you can just call me Rose."

"Rose, what a beautiful name." And it *was* a beautiful name. He would come to think of her by another name altogether, but he would never deny her the right to her own choice of name.

"There, I hear the bell. We must go take our seats now."

"Are you with someone? I hate sitting alone. Would you join me?"

"I can't," she answered with the charming tilt of her head and a melodious little laugh. "I'm afraid I have an assigned seat."

And she swirled around and floated off in that half-step gait that was dictated by the tight cheongsams of Oriental women.

Ted entered the concert hall with a perplexity that was not dissipated when he found a seat. As far as he could determine, there were no assigned seats at the concert. The house lights went down. And when the audience had quieted down, Ted began to hear, rising up from only a slightly perceptible hint of a sound, the most haunting melody he had ever heard. It was the sound of a single flute, and as the lights on the small orchestra came up, he saw and understood. Rose was playing the flute, and he knew in that instant that Rose would be his wife. He was almost irritated when the rest of the orchestra pieces, one by one, joined with the strains of Rose's flute until she was just a single, harmonious aspect of that haunting melody.

At the end of the concert, the orchestra lights went out, and when the house lights came back up, Rose was gone. Ted was unable to find her in the dressing area, but he had faith that he would not lose her. He went out the very next morning and had a pendant designed just for her: a fully opened rose in diamonds. The tips of the petals were set in rubies. He hung the pendant on a gold Thai baht chain and carried it with him, close to his heart, waiting for the time when he would again encounter his Chinese rose.

The next time he saw her was under surprising circumstances. His duties with JUSMAG required that he help keep track of a band of arms smugglers in Bangkok's Chinatown that was bringing in arms from China's southern Yunnan Province through Laos for use in Cambodia. He was doing a visual checkout of the gang's warehouse off of Bangkok's Charoen Krung, or New Road, at dusk one evening, when he saw Rose exit the warehouse in the company of the head of the smuggling clan. The shock of seeing her under these circumstances was so profound that Ted hesitated too long before calling to her. By the time he had crossed the road, she had gotten into a three-wheeled samlor taxi and had left. As it was, Ted almost came face to face with the Chinese smuggler, which, if that had happened, would have completely fouled up his mission.

His next sighting of Rose was under similar, just as shocking circumstances. He had gone up to the former U.S. air base near Udon Thani in Thailand's far northeast to receive some communications equipment the Thai air force was turning back to the American military, when he saw a small convoy of surplus troop transport trucks go past the gate of the base from the direction of the Lao border. Rose was sitting in the passenger seat of the first truck. She was dressed in camouflage gear, but he was sure, at least at the time, that it had been Rose. Later, when he returned to Bangkok, he convinced himself that he was just so head over heels in love with Rose that he must be seeing her in every attractive Oriental woman who passed by. And to help counter his nervous concern about her, he gave Rose a new name. Henceforth he would think of her as his butterfly, flitting along the surface, appearing here and there, only to disappear as quickly. Somehow this image of Rose kept him from thinking other, more sinister thoughts.

His fourth encounter with Rose was the charm. He reluctantly had agreed to attend a Songkran water festival celebration for the American community on the lawn of the American ambassador's home on Wireless Road. When he arrived at the party, it was already in full swing, and a line of Thai dancers was trying to teach the ambassador and several other guests how to do the intricate hand and foot movements for the dance. They were all in a line, weaving here and there, arms undulating away from and above their bodies, fingers bent in unlikely positions, telling a story of a flood and the drowning of a beloved queen on the Chao Phya River. Without notice, the center of the line collapsed into a laughing pile, as one of the dancers stopped dead in her tracks.

Ted knew in an instant that the fall had been caused by his butterfly. Rose had seen him. As usual, she herself had managed to avoid the fall she had caused, and she danced across the lawn, her white and scarlet striped sarong flapping in the breeze, and fell into his arms. She never ceased to amaze and enchant Ted—not before, not at that moment, and not later. Rose hugged him as if she also knew they were intended for each other and as if they saw each other on a daily basis. Ted reached into his breast pocket, took out the rose pendant and necklace, and fastened the necklace around Rose's neck. Rose gave him a brilliant smile, followed by the most delicious kiss he had ever enjoyed, and then tripped back to where the dance line had reassembled.

Ted watched her weave in and out, now sharing a laugh with the American ambassador, now showing the accomplished Thai dancers that her fingers were just as flexible as theirs. Ted had no idea how long he watched the dancing before he realized that Rose was gone. But as soon as it occurred to him that she no longer was there, he knew that it would be futile to try to follow and capture her. Such was the nature of the butterfly.

%%

More than a year was to go by before Ted saw Rose again. But not a night followed day in the interim in which he did not think of his precious butterfly. Through it all he maintained the certainty that she would be his one day.

The next sighting of Rose was just as unlikely as any of the previous ones, although by now Ted had lost both the shock of seeing her in unexpected places and the confusion that perhaps he was only seeing what he wanted to see—and that it was all a mirage. Ted had been transferred from Bangkok in the spring of 1994 to be assistant U.S. military attaché in Hong Kong. Shortly after his arrival, a friend took him to Happy Valley for the horse races. There, after the third race, in what inexplicably did not surprise him in the least, Ted saw the familiar color combination in the winner's circle. Rose was wearing a smart white suit, accented with a red wide-brimmed hat, red gloves, and red shoes. Ted didn't mind the way she was stroking the nose of the winning horse, but he wasn't at all pleased to see the possessive manner in which the horse's owner was holding her elbow. Ted had only been in Hong Kong for a couple of months, but he had been there long enough to have seen the file the embassy's security unit had on Chang Zhoulu, the ancient *toumu*, headman, of the colony's oldest and most notorious smuggling *tuanti*, or association. As he knew would be the case, Ted managed to work his way through the crowds only in time to breathe in the exhaust of the *toumu*'s departing Bentley and to receive a particularly pointed staredown from one of his henchmen.

Not less than a week later, Ted thought he caught a glimpse of Rose disappearing into the shadows of the herbalist market in one of the worst parts of Wan Chai, and he was definitely sure that he saw her three weeks after that when he was crossing back to Wan Chai from Kowloon on the Starr Ferry. He was sure this time, because when the young woman in peasant dress who was floating by on a large dilapidated junk and who had caught his attention looked up, she waved at him, tilted her head to the side, and flashed him one of her brilliant, pouty smiles.

Ted was now beside himself with frustration and anticipation. And less than two weeks later, when Rose, resplendent in a low-cut, billowy crimson gown with a white-lace shawl swirled by him at the Governor's Ball on the arm of the colony's deputy governor, he could take her just flittering in and out of his life no more. He searched the governor's mansion high and low and eventually ended up out on the balcony, high on Victoria Peak and overlooking the night lights of one of the world's busiest harbors below. But he couldn't see what was one of the most spectacular night vistas available to man. He felt close to defeat and was thoroughly dejected.

As he was fully engaged in cursing his luck and all of those in the city below who were obliviously going about their business, the sound of a familiar, haunting tune began to imprint itself on his consciousness. He looked around frantically and soon determined that the sound was coming from a garden that started off to the side of the balcony. As he moved more quickly toward the sound of the flute, the music increased in volume. By the time he saw the secluded gazebo, he could smell the hint of orange blossoms. And by the time he could see the flash of light off the flute and the diamond and ruby rose pendant, Ted could see that the pendant was all that his elusive butterfly was wearing.

Ted and Rose were married in the late fall of 1996, at an absolutely outlandish celebration at the gaudy Tiger Balm Gardens in Hong Kong, famous for its tasteless garishly painted concrete abominations cascading willy-nilly down the side of a steep hill. Ted didn't care in the slightest. He only had eyes for his butterfly—and this in spite of the large clan that Rose had accumulated in Hong Kong and that Ted somehow had to get out of Hong Kong before the Communist Chinese takeover of the colony the next year.

Rose had told Ted that she had been eluding him, even though she had known they were fated to be together, because she had taken as her all-consuming priority the delivery of her extended family in Tianjin, which had been persecuted by the Communist authorities for decades, out of China and to safety. Although she had succumbed to Ted's pursuit at the governor's mansion, she had told him she couldn't marry him because she had this daunting task to fulfill and could not think of her own needs until the task was completed. If she didn't get her family somewhere safe through Hong Kong before control of the colony reverted to China in 1997, she was sure the task would be impossible. If they had lived in the south, she might be able to manage another route, but Tianjin was just too far north for a whole family to traverse across the country to safety.

Even after Ted had pledged that he would take responsibility to get her family out of Hong Kong and to the States in time, Rose had hesitated, saying that she would still have to be away for prolonged times and that she couldn't tell Ted anything about what she was doing when she was away.

Ted didn't care. He had never cared. He had seen who she had been dealing with, and he didn't even want to know what sorts of business she was embroiled in. He knew she was a butterfly and that the only way he could keep her as she was and could have any hold on her was to let her roam free, unfettered and unquestioned.

So, shortly before they had married, Rose's extended family, at least forty of them—Ted had quickly lost count—had mysteriously appeared in Hong Kong. Ted had been prepared to move heaven and earth to relocate all of them to the States before the reversion of Hong Kong, but this had all gone far more smoothly than he had anticipated. Then for a few short years, Ted and Rose maintained their unusual marriage. He continued with his work at the American consulate in Hong Kong, while

Rose reveled part of the time as a diplomatic wife in the exotic city and simply disappeared part of the time, only to reappear without explanation and without seeming to have missed a beat in her busy activities. No one at the consulate seemed to mind or even to notice her absences, and Ted was never, to his surprise, ever questioned about her lifestyle.

But there did come a day when this lifestyle came to an abrupt end. Ted found himself flying to Beijing to bring his wife, no longer his butterfly, home. This was followed by the flight to the States and his assignment at the army's foreign technology research center near to where Rose's parents had been relocated in Charlottesville, Virginia.

ఇళ ಏಲ

Ted's father-in-law sighed and carefully placed his empty tea cup on the marred family heirloom table. He seemed to be very tired, but also very satisfied with his reminisces of his recent life and his family's escape to the Charlottesville Downtown Mall. "*Haule* (It is good)" was all he said, and then he cocked his head to the side and smiled a little smile that made Ted's heart skip a beat, and sat perfectly still, as if in anticipation of the last act of a play.

On cue, a lilting sound of miniature bells could be heard and the scent of orange blossoms wafted into the dim nook.

"She is coming," Ted's *chang ren* said simply, as he put the empty tea pot and cups to one side and moved the flask of rice wine closer to the center of the table.

Madam Leng entered the room, her half-step gait caused by her tight white cheongsam setting the small bells in her hair combs to tinkling. She crossed to the remaining chair and eased herself down, sitting ramrod straight on the chair's edge.

"Major Ted," she rasped in acknowledgment of his presence, as she bowed her head a fraction of an inch and placed two items she had brought with her on her lap. The items caused Ted's heart to constrict painfully—the presence of just one of the items would have been enough to have caused him excruciating pain. One object was a picture, framed and under glass—one of the wedding pictures of Rose and Ted. It was a candid pose taken of Rose, who could be seen in the foreground, clowning on a concrete camel at Tiger Balm Gardens, while Ted, barely discernible in the background, tried to maintain some semblance of dignity. The other object was a long-stemmed rose, a perfect rose that was white at the foundation and rose to scarlet on the tips. The stem bore a single thorn.

"It was good of you to come, Major," Madame Leng said stiffly. "You gave me to understand last year that you would not come again. But anniversaries are necessary. At least they are for we Chinese. This is the fourth, but we will continue them into the afterlife."

"Yes, I understand, Mother-in-Law," Ted responded. "Of course I'll be here for the anniversaries whenever I can."

With that, Madame Leng leaned over and poured wine into the three crystal goblets and then handed one to Ted and another to her husband.

Madame Leng took the last goblet and put it to her lips. But she did not drink. Lifting the glass high, she said in a strangled voice, "To my dear Meigui." Then in a louder, more strident voice she screamed, "*Hao jiu* (good wine)," and dashed the crystal goblet to the ground at the foot of an ancient rosewood armoire.

Master Ke sat, withdrawn into himself for several moments. Then he raised his wine goblet to his lips and drained the glass in one long swallow. Raising the empty goblet, he said in a more even, and gentler voice than his wife had used, "To my brave *Xiao Bennu*." Ted noticed that his father-in-law was lovingly stroking the mar in the table top with his free hand. Then in a small voice, Master Ke gave the toast, "*Hao jiu*," let the crystal goblet simply drop from his hand to shatter at his feet, and dropped his chin on his chest.

Ted's turn had inevitably arrived. As he lifted his goblet up, his last unexpected encounter with his wife rushed through his mind in a blur. The call in the middle of the night when she had been gone on one of her absences for longer than usual. The explanation at the consulate that she had been working clandestinely for the U.S. government for nearly five years and had brought more than a hundred important Chinese artists, scientists, and political activists to freedom in the West through both Hong Kong and Yunnan via Thailand. The regretful disclosure that she had been captured in Beijing and had just been publicly executed. And the long trip to Beijing to bring her body back to Hong Kong to rest in her mother's family crypt near the crest of Victoria Peak.

Ted worked his free hand between the buttons of his shirt and grasped the diamond and ruby rose pendant that hung around his neck on a gold Thai baht chain. "To my beautiful butterfly," he whispered. But then he faltered. It only now occurred to him that, despite all of his intentions, he had tried to control his wife after all. He now, suddenly, understood just how greatly his wife had valued her independence. And understanding that, he realized he had to give up the illusion that she had ever been his butterfly. He cleared his throat and once again whispered a toast. "To Rose." He followed this with an almost unheard *"Hao jiu."*

He could not bring himself to break the lovely crystal goblet any more than he had been able to bring himself to try to fetter the free flight of his wife, Rose. He simply put it down on the top of the carved table. But, ironies of ironies, the edge of the glass found the one flawed measurement between the ridges of the design in the tabletop, and the goblet fell over and shattered.

All of Ted's energy had drained from his body. The ordeal was not completely over, however. The three figures hunched over the table, as Madame Leng placed the picture of her beloved daughter face up on the table top. She then pierced her finger with the single thorn on the white and red rose and forced a drop of blood onto the glass of the picture. As the three closest members of Rose's family leaned over the photography and each in their own way relived the memory of her precious life, their tears mingled with each other's tears and with the single drop of blood, until the visage of the playful Rose in her red wedding dress with the white trim was just a blur.

The Present

I thought that what had caught my attention was how the teenaged boy moved a few paces away from our front window and then stopped dead in his tracks and then, after a short pause, squared his shoulders and marched back to our window, where he stopped again only briefly before entering the store. But it wasn't his movement that made me notice him. It was his eyes, those sad eyes.

"Hey, look at that kid out front, Tina," I had said to the other sales girl in the Geldhaus when the boy had first stopped in front of our window. "We'd better keep an eye on that one. He's been looking at the stuff in the window for some time but not really looking at it, if you know what I mean. I keep telling Mr. G. he shouldn't put the good jewelry in the window. Some day one of those kids is going to put a brick through the window, grab some of that stuff, and be down the Mall and in the crowd before we can do anything about it. But look at him, so sad looking. Such sad eyes. Maybe he just needs to get something for his girl and realizes he can't afford anything in that window."

Tina put down the silver tray she had been polishing and started to come around the counter.

"No. It's OK, he's going away," I told her. "Pay attention, kid. You're going to knock over that old couple. Must be getting warmer; haven't seen that pair out on the Mall since last summer. Her always yapping away and him looking so sour. Boy, I hope I don't live to be that old and doubled up. Oh, but look. The kid stopped and turned around and is coming back. I guess he likes his girl too much to let his shyness win out."

The Present

The boy seemed to have found a new determination, because he came straight to the door, which set off that annoying bell when he opened it, and walked right up to the counter in front of me.

"Yes, sir, welcome to Geldhaus, fine jewelers. Can I help you with anything? We have some nice school pins—both UVA and the area high schools."

"Um, no, I'm not looking for anything to buy. I was just wondering—"

He suddenly seemed at a loss for words and only half as brave and determined as he had been when he walked in. I didn't help. So far I didn't have a clue what he had come in to get, and Mr. G. always said not to assume too fast that the customer is looking for something cheaper than you might otherwise convince them they can't live without.

"Is this Mr. Gelton's shop? Mr. Gerhard Gelton?"

"Yes, it is. Did you want to talk with him? I think he might be in back, but he's working on a setting right now, and we don't like to disturb him when he's doing that."

All of a sudden the boy looked about ten years younger and ready to cry.

"But if it's important," I rushed on, "I can go get him." I don't think I could have stood it to see the boy cry. His sad eyes alone melted my heart. He was going to be a real killer with the girls in a year or two if he could keep that look.

"No, it's OK. Maybe you can help me. My mother said my father used to shop here—even before you moved to the Downtown Mall. And I think he knew Mr. Gelton pretty well." There was a pause, as the boy absentmindedly played in a tray of cheap stickpins on top of the counter. "Do you—?" He cleared his throat and looked up at one of the dim corners of the ceiling. "Do you perhaps keep any records of things ordered but never picked up?"

"I'm sorry, I don't follow. What to you mean?"

And then it all came out in a rush. "Well, I think my father may have bought something in here sometime before the second week in January and then not picked it up. I'm just checking on whether that could have happened. And, and, of course, I'd take it now and pay for it."

"Well, I don't know. That's possible, of course. What did he order?"

"I don't know."

"You don't know? This is getting a little complicated. I think I'd better go get Mr. Gelton. Tina," I said with a meaningful look. "Could you watch after the shop while I'm gone?"

Mr. Gelton was none too happy to be interrupted, the old grouch. Such a grump and miser. Never a kind word for anyone and wouldn't walk across the room to do a favor. I'd have found other work a long time ago if I didn't like his long-suffering wife, Milly, so much.

"Whadcha want? Can't you see I'm finishing up Milly's anniversary present?"

I couldn't help myself when I saw the exquisite diamond pavé heart pin. "It's gorgeous, Mr. G. She'll love it." I wasn't too sure about the last comment. Just the other day Milly had told me that she bet Mr. G. would give her another of those heaps of stones he makes for their anniversary, when she'd really settle on a kind word for someone from the old coot. Well, to each their own, I guess. I wished for the umpteenth time that I had married a jeweler—although I could certainly see her point about wishing that Mr. G. could be a lot nicer.

"This other one's very nice too," I said, picking up a diamond and ruby cross pin, with inferior but still very good stones. "Who are you making this for, Mr. G.?" I asked. "I don't remember an order for one of these. Such an interesting design."

"Don't know myself," he grumped back at me. "I just had this urge to make that one. Something just kept nagging at me that I could find a use for that. The arrangement of the stones just kept cropping up in my head. So I went ahead and made it. Now skeddadle so I can finish the heart before I forget which stones I was going to use."

"I came to tell you there's a boy out front to see you, Mr. G. He says something about his father having had something made here and that it's on layaway, but he doesn't know what it is. I thought you might know what he's talking about."

"In a minute, in a minute."

I went back to the shop, and the boy, Tina, and I sort of wandered around nervously for several minutes, waiting for Mr. G. to finish the broach and put in an appearance.

Eventually the curtains to the back swept aside and Mr. G. came in, muttering to himself something nasty about having been disturbed. Then he looked at the boy and said, "Don't I know you? Aren't you Pete Jones's kid?"

"Yes sir," the kid answered softly. "I'm Pete too, Pete Jr."

"Good man, Pete. We served together for many years in the Lion's Club. Sorry to hear about his passing. Met your mother too. Mary Elizabeth isn't it? Cancer wasn't it that got him? And it had a grip on him for quite some time, didn't it?"

"Yes, sir. Thank you, sir. Yes. The chemo seemed to have worked and then he had that heart attack and went so fast. Mary Catherine, sir. My mother's name is Mary Catherine."

"Ah yes, Now I remember. Well, what can we do for you, son? Carol says you think your dad may have ordered something here and not picked it up."

"Yes, sir. Maybe he did and maybe he didn't. And maybe he ordered it somewhere else. The thing is, sir, it's my mother. She's so sure that he ordered a birthday present for her and never got to pick it up. It's not the present itself that's worried her—it's just the thought that his business isn't finished. That keeps eating at her, sir. Dad died just two days before her birthday in January. He had been going to chemo right up to New Year's and he still had managed to get her a Christmas gift. Both Mom and I had offered to take him out in early January so he could get her a birthday gift, but he'd just told us he didn't need to go out. I know he must have planned something. Mom gave me a list of the stores where she thought he did most of his shopping. I've already been to every one listed on the Downtown Mall. If he didn't order anything in here, there's just one left to check out at Barracks Road and then I'll have to go back and tell Mom I couldn't solve the mystery."

"And you've been in other shops on the Mall and asked them this question?" Mr. G. asked.

"Yes, I'm sorry. It's sort of embarrassing—going in and asking to check with so little information to go on. But it's my mom, sir. They thought everything was getting better, and then he died right before her birthday. She's just been so depressed, and this has been eating away at her. I think it will help if I can just tell her that I checked and there's no present coming. It's been several months, and she still runs to the mailbox as if something might be there that was on back order or something."

"Well, the order book is over here on the counter. We'll just check to see if—"

"I checked through the book while you were talking, Mr. G.," Tina said quietly. "I couldn't find—"

"We'll just take another good look," Mr. G. overrode her. "Hmm. I'm not sure. Maybe yes, maybe no. You say you had no idea what he might of been thinking of getting her?"

"No, sir. I think I did ask him once or twice, and he just smiled and said Mom was worth something really special this year. But I don't know. With all those medical bills and expenses, maybe he just ordered her some flowers on the phone and the order got messed up. Mom loves flowers." The boy was acting like he was at the end of a distressing school assignment and was just so happy that it was over that he didn't care what grade he got anymore. He was even inching toward the front door. I felt so bad for him that he had had to go into several stores on the Mall and give that little story. But at the same time, I wished my son were more like him.

"Just a minute. You stay right there. There's an order form here that suggests there might be something in the back room."

"Ah, yes, I found it," Mr. G. said after having been gone what seemed like an eternity. "Your mother was right. Your dad did order her gift from here. If I'd been the one who took the order, I'm sure I would have remembered it. He always came here for his special gifts. We had been friends for a long time. He was a good man. Uh, I guess I said that before."

The Present

The boy hadn't said anything when Mr. G. returned, but his eyes had gotten really big. Then, with as much dismay as admiration, he said, "Oh, sir, it's so beautiful, and it looks so expensive. I'm sorry, but I'm afraid we don't have enough—"

"Yes, a really good man and always a great customer, your dad," Mr. G. broke in. "Most customers don't put more than 10 percent down when they order something special like this. But this order form says he paid the full amount when he ordered it. Don't find as good a customer as that anymore. I think your mother will like that. He ordered the design especially for her, you know. See that little engraving there on the back? Aren't those your mother's initials? M. C. J.?"

I had remained completely speechless from the moment Mr. G. had reappeared with the pin. When the delighted boy had left with the gift in one of our best boxes and with the fanciest wrapping we could find, Tina brushed back a tear and said, "Such a nice boy, wasn't he?"

"Mr. G—" I finally managed to stammer.

But Mr. G. cut me off. "Well, I said I knew I'd find a use for that other broach, didn't I? Don't fuss. Get back to work, both of you. There are customers to serve."

My eyes rotated around the room and then I stared out onto the Mall. There wasn't a customer in sight. "Mr. G.," I said a bit more loudly than necessary. "You said you were making the diamond and ruby cross for an unknown occasion. That I understand, and you did a wonderful thing here today—and to be honest I don't understand that too well. But you didn't give the boy the cross pin. You gave him the diamond heart you made for Milly. And it was engraved with Mrs. Jones's initials."

"I know, I don't understand that myself. Not the engraving part. I pride myself in my quick engraving work, although it's a good thing I had already checked with the kid about his mother's name. But I don't know why I gave him *that* pin, either. It's just that I got back there and saw those two pins together and thought of what I would want to do for a wife who had taken care of me through a fight with cancer, and then I just couldn't give him the second-best broach. What I said was the truth. Pete Jones had always been a good friend to me. Came to the hospital to see me that time I had the broken leg, and I didn't visit him while he was sick—not once. And that's one fine kid he's got. It's a good thing I made that other broach. I just don't know what I'm going to tell Milly. You won't tell her she's getting second best, will you?"

"No, *you* will, Mr. G.," I answered. "Tina and I will close up tonight. You go on home. Stop at the florists and get Milly some flowers you think Mrs. Jones would have enjoyed receiving, take Milly out to a nice dinner, give her that cross pin, and tell her what happened here today with the Jones boy. And I mean tell her everything. Trust me, it will be the anniversary present she always wanted from you."

Sad Eyes

I thought that what had caught my attention was how the boy moved a few paces away from the jewelry store window and then stopped not more than ten feet from where Madge and I were walking and then, after a short pause, squared his shoulders and marched back to the store window, where he stopped again only briefly before entering the store. But it wasn't his movement that made me notice him. It was his eyes. Those sad eyes. I staggered back a bit and almost knocked Madge down as I plopped on a miraculously available bench on the bricked Downtown Mall.

"Hey, Dutch, why can't you tell a person when you've decided to sit? No consideration; no consideration at all. But, then, I guess we have walked a good bit from over at the home. My, isn't it nice out here on the Mall? We should do this more often. But, lands, what a crowd already. We're lucky you found this bench. You know, I was saying to Helen just the other—"

ঙ ৪০

Those eyes. From all those weeks we were plodding up the Italian peninsula from the landing at Anzio on the boats from Africa, all I can seem to remember is those eyes. I guess I should count that as a blessing. When I get together with the guys—fewer every year—and hear them talking about all the trouble of taking and holding Monte Cassino, I should be so lucky only to remember those eyes. Everywhere we went, it seems, there they were. Small kids standing by the road as we passed, dirty hands and feet. How could they stand it with bare feet in the snow? But it wasn't the feet. It was the eyes. They stood there, no expression, no complaints, no smiles—with the saddest eyes I ever seen.

☙ ❧

"—and she, Miss High and Mighty. Do you know what *she* said? 'Just don't let it bother you, Madge. She'll just have to answer for that when her day comes.' Well, it never bothered me, of course, I says, that's not the point. Land, Dutch, that's an ugly face. You could scare off children with that look. Oh, but I guess not. Look at that nice little boy over there. Look, he's staring at you. Maybe it's your beard. Oh, what a beautiful boy. But such sad eyes. Just like the boy I always told you I wanted."

I could see her face was puffing up again, and I wanted to stop her from going into it. And I might of stopped her with a backhand, but here we were out in the open on this hotsy totsy Mall, with everyone passing by and all.

"I never could figure out why you changed, Dutch. When you left for the war, you was all in favor of having a family. And I would have had the start of one to show you when you got back if it hadn't been for that fall."

She stopped, and I grabbed for her hand—if for no reason other than to keep my own hand from swinging out—but she built up steam again. Back to that old script.

"A boy. We should have had a nice little boy. And then you came back all sullen and distant and negative about a family. My mother told me I should of left you right then. And I wish I had listened to her. Jumping down my throat every time I brought it up. And now look at us. Old and dried up and of use to nobody. Oh, hi there, Honey. Decided to come over to give us a closer look? What a pretty ball. Green and blue. Can you say green? Green? Oh, do you want me to have the ball? No? Oh, you want *him* to have the ball? Look, Dutch, he's trying to hand the ball to you. Go ahead, Honey, give the ball to gramps. Oh, Dutch, whatcha do that for? Now you've scared him. Don't cry, Honey, he didn't mean it. It's a pretty ball. Let *me* see your pretty—"

☙ ❧

Sad Eyes

Cold and snowy again. But now it was years later, and we were in another war. Korea was so much different from Italy. But I guess snow is snow wherever. It was those sad eyes that caught my attention. We weren't supposed to fraternize with the locals who lived near the camp—never could trust them, we were told. But whenever I took my unit out on patrol, there he was, standing at the side of the road with his little sisters in tow as we left and then still waiting at the gate when we returned. Never knew his name. All he would say—maybe the only words he knew in English—was "Shine, mister?" And then he would look at my boots and then back up into my face with those sad eyes.

By the end of the third patrol, I couldn't take it no more. Sure, I said, and I let them come over to my digs, where I sat and watched as he cleaned my boots up real nice. I would offer his sisters and him a little candy, which the girls would take with a little smile that didn't seem to change the sadness in their eyes none and which he would always politely refuse. After a while, when the boots was all spiffy and some color had come back into the kids' faces in my warm tent, the boy would hold the boots up for my inspection, and he would accept a few small coins. Once I tried to give him more, but he carefully separated out the coins that were above his normal fee and handed them back to me. Don't even know why I let him shine my shoes. Korea was the muddiest hole I ever saw. Couldn't keep those boots looking clean for more than five seconds after I left the tent.

Then came the day when not just the boy and his sisters were waiting for me at the gate, but there was his mother as well. The same sad eyes. She had brought an empty pot and a spoon with her, and somehow they got across to me that I was being invited to dinner. I didn't want to go, but the boy and his sisters obviously wanted me to come, and I didn't feel I could insult them.

"Better watch out for all your gear when you go," my Korean sergeant said. "You can't trust these people." We had had several break-ins at the camp at night, and even had some of our weapons stole. The only way I could see to put a stop to it was to tell all the Korean guards that if they caught anyone doing that, they should make sure that person couldn't do any more stealing—and that if it didn't stop, I was going to start holding the guards themselves responsible for what was being taken.

I don't know if the dinner was a success or not, but the mother and her kids seemed happy. I felt so guilty at eating from what little they had that I had brought some rice and a little meat from our own chow hall—probably not more than I would have eaten myself that evening, though. After dinner, the boy started pulling on my boots. He wanted to shine them. But it was later than I should be out of camp, so I said no, not tonight. I could see that he was real anxious to shine them shoes, but I tried to get across to him that I couldn't stay longer. When I left, I could see that the sisters and mother had gotten happier than I'd ever seen before, but that the boy was still looking at me with those sad eyes. I tried to give him the money that would have covered a shoe shine, but he just sadly handed that back to me.

Later that night, long after I'd gone to sleep, there was a commotion, shots and all, like I hadn't heard for several weeks—not since we fought off that assault on our position by the North Koreans—or maybe Chinese—who knows for sure? As I turned up the lantern, the Korean sergeant threw open the flap to my tent and entered all smiles. No more problem with thieves in the night, he said. They had caught a local stealing from the camp and had taken care of it. Any other thieves would hear about it and would stay away now.

"What do you mean, taken care of it," I asked.

"Like you told us," was the reply. "We caught him with these, and we shot him. Now all the others will know the price of theft from this camp."

He stood there holding out my boots. My shined boots. I didn't have to ask who they had shot.

☙ ❧

"You grouch. You mean, dried up old grouch. Now look what you've done. The boy is crying and running off, and his grandmother is looking at us. How could you be so mean?"

Sad Eyes

Tears started to well up in Madge's sad eyes, and she looked away. And in looking away, she wasn't able to see that I had started to cry as well.

The Wedding Plans

Megan zeroed in on him as soon as he turned the corner near the bank and strolled on toward where she was sitting with her group in the Hardware Store Restaurant's Garden Café.
Well, hello gorgeous. Please, please be coming to the café.
It did look at first like he was making a direct line for the café under the trees at the center of the Charlottesville Downtown Mall. But then he hesitated near the door of the Mole Hole Gift Shop. He stooped down, picked something off the ground and handed it to a woman who had been standing in the doorway to the shop. She accepted what seemed to be a white glove without even acknowledging his presence, and, with a nod, the young man started off in Megan's direction again.
Yes! Oh, what a gentleman. Old World. A rarity.
Megan looked over at Max, who was sitting next to her at the table and bantering back and forth with Shelley and Dennis about a man in uniform talking to an old dude in a Chinese dress in front of a furniture store on the other side of the Mall. It was no contest. She returned her attention to the young man, who had reached the entrance to the Garden Café and was checking his watch and looking up the Mall. At length, Rafael, the waiter, stopped to talk to him and then led him into the café area.
Here. Here. There's an empty table right here beside me. Yes!
The waiter seated the young man right beside Megan. They were at two different tables, but for all practical purposes they were right across from each other and were almost directly face to face. Megan was beside herself. Was her hair combed? Did she still have any lipstick on? He was a dream; could have been a

male model, but not at all plastic. Tanned, which highlighted a little scar at the corner of his mouth—not enough to distract from his looks; just enough to be intriguing. Football? No, with his clothes, it would be lacrosse or polo or a yachting accident. Something expensive and exotic. Max asked her a question, but she just waved him off. Was she drooling? That wouldn't be good. She pulled herself together and acknowledged Max's question.

"Yeah, right. I see him. A kid standing in front of that jewelry store, moving his weight from one foot to the other. My guess is that he just has to go to the bathroom and is looking for some store that will let him use their john."

Megan looked back at her Prince Charming. He wasn't paying too much attention to the extensive menu. Most of his energy was engaged in looking from his watch to the entrance to the café to his watch. He did respond to the waiter, though, when he came by for a drink order. And that was when Megan saw the cool blonde wafting in their direction. Right then Megan was sure that her prince wasn't going to be alone for long, and, as the waiter departed with the drink order, thankfully blocking the young man's view of the approaching princess, Megan knew it was now or never.

"That was quite chivalrous."

"Excuse me?"

"That was quite chivalrous. I saw you pick up that woman's glove over at the Mole Hole. She didn't bother to thank you. So, for all women everywhere, thank you."

"Don't mention it."

Oh, my g-a-w-d. I'm in love. The young man had flashed her a radiant smile, the scar near his mouth becoming a handsome dimple that Megan could barely resist.

"She was wearing mismatched shoes. What do you think of that?" Megan couldn't believe she had been given time for a second question. Ah, yes, the blonde was standing over there talking to those two executive types at the table just inside the entrance.

"What? Who?"

"The woman in the entrance to the Mole Hole. Her shoes didn't match."

"Yes, I noticed that. I'm sure that's a clue to why she didn't thank me for picking up her glove. She seemed quite distracted. Must be having a really bad day."

"Chivalrous *and* sympathetic. That's very becoming."

The marvelous smile again.

"My name's Megan. I recommend the peanut soup here. It's great."

"Well, hello, Megan. My name's—"

"Chad, honey. I just was talking to Stanley and Josh over there. They say we shouldn't worry about this morning's drop in dot.com stocks. They think FNS is rock solid. Oh, why couldn't you have gotten a table on the other side of the restaurant? Another ten minutes and I'll be in the sun here."

Another ten minutes and you'd be sitting here alone, Honey. Chad. She knew he'd be something like a Chad. "Chad, could we take the Rolls tonight? Clarence didn't have time to wash the Jag." "Chad, could you stop by Foods of All Nations on your way home from the club for some caviar? We're down to our last barrel."

"Chad, I don't have long to eat. They're in such a turmoil over at FNS today. I've just got to be there for all the big decisions. Why didn't you go ahead and order? You know I always have the tuna salad here."

"I thought we'd have some time to talk today, Cathleen. We need to start pinning down our wedding plans."

Whoa. Wait just one minute. Tragedy time. Chad, you do not want to be doing this. She's an iceberg, and unless your last name is FNS, you're not going to be getting near the attention you deserve.

The waiter approached, and Cathleen ordered the shrimp salad. Chad said he'd take a club sandwich. "Oh yes, and a bowl of the peanut soup."

Yes!

"Well, let's discuss what we can before you have to go back to FNS. I was thinking that beautiful little stone, English-style church out beyond Keswick, Grace Episcopal. You know, the one where they bless the hunt every year."

"Oh, God no. We could never stuff 300 people in there. There will be more than 100 just from FNS alone. Maybe Keswick Hall for the reception, but it's got to be something bigger for the wedding. I'm thinking Christ Episcopal here in town. They've got those Tiffany windows."

Nope, certainly can't get married without Tiffany windows, now can we?

"Well, I wasn't really thinking of a big fancy reception. Maybe just a group of our friends over at Miller's. You know I've been talking with Dave Matthews, and he said he and the band would do a special evening for us."

You know Dave Matthews? He'll do a special gig for you at Miller's? Hello, Cathleen. Are you ever in luck!

"Yuckee do. You know my parents don't like Dave Matthews's music. They want to get a small orchestra down from New York. Oh, look, there's our chief financial officer, Mr. Purdy. I'll be just a minute. I've got to tell him something. Oh, and there's our CEO, Mr. Crawford. Oh, pooh, he doesn't see me waving at him."

Cathleen was on the run again, and Megan was going for it.

"I couldn't help overhearing. I'd die to be able to get married out at Grace Episcopal. It's almost magical out there. It's just like a little chapel I saw when we were living in England."

"You've lived in England? I love it there. Where in England?"

"Henley. Henley-on-Thames. My dad was connected with BBC Monitoring Service near there at Caversham Park. Do you know the place?"

"Sure do. That's where they have the Henley Cup Regatta, the crew races." He involuntarily raised his fingers to the scar at the corner of his mouth.

Bingo. I was close. Not yachting. A rowing race accident.

"And the Dave Matthews Band. What a way to celebrate your wedding. I think that's just wonderful."

"OK, Chad. I'm back. But can't stay long. Mr. Purdy says they're just about to start a powwow over at FNS, and I can't miss that."

111

No, we certainly couldn't miss that, could we, Cathleen? You've got the world's greatest man sitting here, and you just have to go to a meeting on saving the dot.coms, don't you? Nope, no contest.

"Well, what do you think about the honeymoon, then? I thought a cruise around the Caribbean, and I know of a restored shotgun house with a small pool we can rent for a couple of weeks in Key West. A boat goes with it."

"Oh, no, I can't be away from FNS for any length of time. Three nights tops. Just time for shopping and a couple of plays in New York. And you know I burn too easily—no beaches. Whose phone is that? Oh, it's mine. Hello? Yes, yes, I just heard about the meeting. What's our strategy going to be?"

Chad looked so forlorn, sitting here playing with the remnants of his club sandwich. He obviously finished the peanut soup with relish, however.

Megan had to take advantage of the moment. She had to think of just the right thing to say: "The house in Key West wouldn't be anywhere near Decatur Street, would it? I try to get down there every couple of years. Love the water around there."

Then she took a deep breath. Giving him the sweetest smile she could muster, she went for broke. "What kind of boat goes with the house? I'm trained to cocaptain a Hobie Cat."

Cathleen's phone call came to an end. "Well, OK, see you in a couple of minutes. Ta, ta. Sorry, Chad, I've gotta go, we'll have to discuss this . . . . Chad?"

Max and friends had moved on to a new phase of their game. "OK, Megan, what's your guess on that woman over there with the strange shoes? Megan? Shelley, Megan's gone. Did you see where she went?"

The Game: Two

Shelley and Tiffany had given up on Jeff and Luis joining the eclectic group of twenty-something friends at the Hardware Store's Garden Café anytime soon and had ordered their lunch. Tiffany was busy picking the tomatoes, meat, and cheese out of her chef salad and scraping the dressing off to the side, while Shelley and Dennis watched Max return from the telephone booth in the indoor restaurant, his dejected gait telling them that his trip had been fruitless.

"Was she at home?" Shelley asked Max as he plopped down in his chair.

"Nope."

Shelly wished Megan would just stop leading Max around and drop the ax on him. These university kids were so fickle, she thought. She was glad Jeff didn't act this way. He was up at the University too, but he wasn't like the other guys up there. He was steady. He didn't seem to mind at all going out with a townie hairdresser like her.

"While you were in there, you should have tried calling Jeff to see if he'd left yet," Tiffany said, most of her attention devoted to dragging a boiled egg quarter out of her salad and dropping it, along with the other ingredients she was rejecting, on the substitute napkin Shelley had given her. It was then that she discovered she was making the napkin unavailable for its intended use and started looking around in panic.

Max had looked at her sharply when she mentioned making a telephone call to Jeff and grabbed at Tiffany's distress over her napkin situation to change the subject. "Here. You can have your own napkin back, Tiffany. And you can have Megan's too.

She took yours earlier and I don't think she'll be back to use hers."

"Oh, did Megan steal my napkin?" Tiffany asked. "She's such a meanie. She's always mean to me just because I'm not wasting my time going to college like she is. Helping my Daddy with his horses takes enough of my time. Oh, that reminds me. Are you meeting Jeff and me at Miller's tonight, Dennis?"

"Jeff and *you?*" Shelley's head had snapped up.

"Naw," Dennis answered. "I've got a date with a woman who's too old for Miller's."

"You and older women again, Dennis," said Max. "All a part of your married before to an older woman story?"

"Oh, let's start up the game again," said Shelley. "With Megan gone, though, we'll have to change the rules. The winner will choose the subject, the other three will make up stories, and the winner will pick the new winner. Dennis, you pick the first subject this time."

"OK, what about that man and boy at the table over there? They look pretty sober. Tiffany?"

"Hmm. Let's see. OK, OK, I got one. They both ordered something new off the menu they thought would be interesting. And then when their lunches came, they decided they'd prefer what the other one was having. And it made both of them sad."

"Not bad, Tiff," said Shelley with a smile. *For a ditz,* she was thinking. "But I think there's a deeper story there. The man looks like a straight-laced CEO type. So impeccably dressed and ramrod straight. The kid's just a typical sloppy high school boy, maybe a little pudgier than most. I'll say they are a particularly mismatched pair in a city 'big brother' mentoring program, and they're both being tortured by the experience."

"And your story, Max?" Dennis prompted.

"The man's an old pervert. He's picked the kid up off the street and is treating him to lunch to get more friendly."

"Oh, Max. That's awful," squealed Tiffany. "What made you think that up?"

Max gave her a hard look. "I have no idea, I'm sure."

Dennis chose Shelley as the winner. She picked out an old man pausing before he entered Timberlake's Drugstore.

The Game: Two

Dennis was the first to provide a story. "His wife is dying a lingering death, and the man has struggled out of a sickbed himself to come get a prescription for painkillers filled. The two of them are trying to collect enough pills to overdose and escape their pain."

"But Timberlake's delivers prescriptions," Tiffany said.

"Oh, Tiff," Shelley said. "You ruined the story."

"But they do. I know. They're bringing Valium out to my mother in Farmington all the time."

"OK, OK, what's your story?"

"I think he's just meeting an old friend at the soda fountain, where they've been eating lunch together for many years."

"Thank you for your contribution, don't phone us, we'll phone you," Shelley quipped. "And you, Max?"

"He's an old pervert looking for—"

"Oh!" Tiffany exclaimed.

"Dennis wins," Shelley broke in. "I suggest you hurry up and pick another subject."

"OK." Dennis looked around the Downtown Mall for a long time, and then his attention was riveted on someone stumbling along toward them, keeping near the south-end storefronts on high heels. *Geez, what in the hell?* "There, over there. That . . . person in the dress coming up the Mall. Tiffany?"

"Oh, my. A woman who made someone mad at the salon where Shelley works, and they did a real job on her?" It was more a question than a guess.

"Bingo. I think we have a winner already," Dennis announced. "But see if you can top that, Shelley."

Shelley watched the figure coming closer to them, struggling along on spike heels and keeping as close to the shadows at the fringes of the Mall as possible. Tiffany's reference to her hair salon had ticked her off just a little bit. "Oh, I don't know. I'm afraid to say what I really think. So, I'll say it's Tiffany's mother going to Timberlake's to pick up her Valium."

Dennis laughed heartily, as Tiffany pouted. "I don't think that's very funny," she whined.

"This is going to be a hard decision. Can you compete with that, Max, my man?"

"It's Jeff arriving for lunch."

"Max!" Shelley and Tiffany exclaimed in unison.

"That's not nice at all," Tiffany said in dismay. "Why have you become obsessed with those mean thoughts? Just because Megan went off with that other guy. He looked really nice. You've been dumb thinking Megan wanted to date you."

"Dumb? Me dumb? You and Shelley are the dumb ones. You both waiting here for Jeff to show up. Well, let me tell you something about you two and Jeff."

"Max," Dennis broke in. "I don't think you want to continue with that."

"You two need to wake up and smell the . . . smell the pansies." With that, Max jumped up and flounced off.

"Coffee. He got it wrong. It's coffee," Tiffany said, as she started munching the lettuce from her salad.

Decision Point

Uh, oh, I really must have screwed up the drill this time. The colonel has never taken me—just me—to lunch before. At least as far as I can remember. We usually just try to stay out of each other's way. I stay at school until suppertime and then there's no problem with going to my room to hit the books the rest of the evening. Was it the grade in biology? Or did Mom tell him I sassed her the other day? Time for the inquisition and the firing squad. Boy, does he ever look out of place here on the Downtown Mall. Starched collar, perfectly knotted tie, shiny shoes, buzz cut, commanding air. I'm surprised the waiter didn't salute after taking the menus. Greater surprise that the colonel didn't order him to drop and do fifty push-ups for not saluting. Gotta control that thought. Can't start giggling. That will only make it worse.

He can't look at me. Every time I get brave enough to look at him, he's staring off down the Mall at some different point—staring, but not seeing anything. I think he must be even more nervous than I am. Good. Must have asked for an iced tea refill three times already. New thing for the colonel to seem so nervous—especially with little insignificant disappointment me. The athlete and war hero. Both football and basketball all-state in high school and that fancy basketball scholarship to Georgetown. Tall, thin, and handsome. Must have wondered just what rock I crawled out from underneath. The hero of the Lost Battalion at Duc Loc; most decorated man in his division; the best bayonet instructor in the army.

I know, that's it. It's military school time. Military school instead of the University. Too much independence at the University. I knew it would come to that. It is that D in biology. That must be what it is. All the other A's don't matter. Kid can't do the sciences, there's nothing the kid can do in the modern world. No matter that more than half the kids in the class got D's or F's and that Mr. Kasel is being reviewed. One of those teachers who writes on the board with one hand while erasing with the other and expecting us to understand it all. Have to make a separate appointment just to ask a question. But they know what I think about military school. I want to be an actor. I don't want to learn to bayonet anybody.

"Son."

"Yes, Dad."

"Uh— Nice place, isn't this?"

"Sure is."

"The Hardware Store's got the nicest café on the Downtown Mall. Right in the center of everything."

"Right."

"And we couldn't ask for a better day. Not too hot and not too cold."

"Uh huh, right."

Silence, as the two looked off in separate directions, making a big show of appreciating where they were sitting at the outdoor café under the trees, the breeze rustling the leaves ever so slightly. The son saw a friend from school, Petey Jones, over in front of the Geldhaus jewelers. He waved. But Petey had already turned away. He stared intently into the shop window, but he went inside before the son could decide whether yelling across the walking street was worth a withering look from the colonel and ten days of KP duty. In the meantime, the colonel's attention had been arrested by the shock of realizing that the figure that was scooting by on the other side of the street was a transvestite, and a not very accomplished one either. Shorter, thicker heels would have been more appropriate if (s)he didn't want to be noticed. But maybe that was the whole point. In broad daylight on a public walking street. The colonel's nostrils flared and the corners of his mouth turned down. He turned and noticed that his son was now looking straight at him. The eyes. Such sad eyes.

Now it's coming. He can hardly stand being here with me. He's really got the mads about something. Here comes Lecture Number 32. Stop slouching. Sit up straight. Slouching only makes you look even fatter than you are. Chest out. Stomach in—at least to the point that is possible. Elbows off the table. Look respectful when I'm talking to you. We know how to fix that attitude, boy. A couple of years at the Fork Union Academy should fix that. Maybe not enough for a football scholarship, but maybe enough that we can get you into VMI. Forget it, Colonel. You've had your chance. You don't like my grades now, just wait until you see what I can do at Fork Union.

"Uh, Son, I wanted to take you out to lunch today to discuss a proposal your mother and I have been mulling over."

Drum roll. The guillotine blade rises slowly to the top. Nice move, bringing mother in on it. No use thinking I can get anyone on my side on this, right?

"Dad, I'd really rather not—"

"Your mother and I have been talking ever since that production of *My Fair Lady* last month, and we wondered whether you'd like to go to acting school and get some voice lessons before or instead of going to college.

And there it is, folks, the Fork Union— Clash of symbols. What was that he just said?

"Excuse me, Dad, what—?"

"We wondered whether you'd like to make a try at the professional stage. You were so good in the musical and we talked with the drama coach, Ms. Drapel, and the music director, Dr. Conor, and they both said—"

"You talked with Dr. Conor? He thought I was for shit in the musical. He and I fought the whole time we were putting it together. And you and Mom didn't say much at all about it. I know you were embarrassed to even be seen at the play. I'm surprised you came at all. You didn't come to *Bye Bye Birdie* last year."

"I know. I'm sorry about that. I thought my assignment in Turkey would end soon enough, but they kept me over, and I just couldn't come back in time. And we haven't reacted very much to your performance yet, because, quite frankly, your mother and I are still in shock. I know you were spending every evening this spring at school in rehearsals, but you have always found something to do at school in the afternoon rather than coming home early. Two years ago when you were in *Brigadoon*, you told us you had a speaking role, and you also spent every afternoon at school during practices. We talked the play and your part in it up to all our friends, and then when we came to the show, it turned out you played a bartender in the background and only had one line. Then last year you had that good character role of Mr. MacAfee in *Bye Bye Birdie,* and we did get a lot of compliments on your performance. But I'm afraid the whole thing didn't make much of an impression on me, as I was off setting up a communications post on the Turkish border and having a lot of problems getting that done.

"But this year, even though you spent a lot of time at rehearsals, you didn't tell us anything about what you were doing in the play, and we showed up to find you were the lead. And you were a great Henry Higgins. After the show, everyone came up to us and told us how wonderful you were. We were very proud, of course, but we were totally unprepared for the play. We've been shocked and embarrassed ever since. You took me back many a year. You looked just like me up on that stage."

"Just like you? I don't understand."

"I was in a couple of plays in high school, you know. I loved it. Almost thought of going into theater work myself."

"No, I didn't know. You never told—"

"I also sang when I was younger. I remember that I sang on the radio for a couple of years. We had a quartet back in Montana. Sang cowboy songs like 'Cool Water' and 'Tumbling, Tumbling Tumble Weed' on the radio in Billings. Had a ball. And you sounded just like I did. I was a tenor too. I think you sing a lot better than I did, as a matter of fact. And Dr. Conor said—"

"But I thought, Dr. Conor—"

"I know, you think Dr. Conor didn't like what you were doing in the musical. But you were wrong. It was Mrs. Danner who got us to go talk with Dr. Conor after the show, and he told us he thinks you have the talent to make a profession of the musical stage."

"Mrs. Danner? Mom's friend, Mrs. Danner?"

"Yes. She's a piano teacher, you know, and she's a friend of Dr. Conor's. She was busting to tell us after the show. Dr. Conor, who didn't know she knew us, told her that you were so good in *Bye Bye Birdie* last year that he thought you deserved the lead role in your senior play. He picked *My Fair Lady* just for you, so you could do Professor Higgins. And then you showed no interest in trying out for that part. You insisted on trying out for the Doolittle character role, and you seemed so resentful throughout the rehearsals because he had cast you as Higgins instead. Dr. Conor wasn't mad at you—and he praised your performance to high heaven. He was just frustrated because you didn't seem to want the Higgins role and he couldn't let you know in front of all the other kids that he had picked the play just for you."

A long pause of silence, while the waiter brought the bill and the flood of information sank in. Tears welled up in the eyes of the son. No longer sad eyes. Now eyes that sparkled. But he was determined not to let his dad see him cry.

"But, Dad. You never told me before. You never told me you had been in plays yourself and sang. I thought you thought I . . . I thought you were ashamed of—"

"We're so proud of you, son. Your mother and I think you're a great kid. I know I haven't—"

Another moment of embarrassed silence as the waiter swept by with the credit card slip to be signed.

"So, Son, interested in acting school? We talked to someone up at the Arena Stage in Washington, and he recommended—"

I can go. I can do it. Years of acting school. Competing for parts. On the road. The smell of the greasepaint; the roar of the crowd. He understands how it feels up there under the lights. I can choose. They'll let me choose.

". . . So, what do you think?"

Thank you, thank you, thank you.

"Thanks, Dad. But you know, I've been thinking these last couple of weeks of high school myself. I sure do like acting and singing, but I think I'd like to do it in my spare time rather than trying to do it as a job. I think it will be more fun that way, and I won't have to worry about having to make enough money from it to live on. I think that would take a lot of the pleasure out of it. I liked living overseas when the family got to go with you on assignments. I think I'll just go on to the University and then I'd like to work on something to do with world affairs like you do. Maybe something simple, like secretary of state."

This brought the tension-breaking laugh from the old man that the son wanted at this point. A few more seconds of silence, this time much more comfortable than before.

"Dad?"

"Yes, Son."

Thank you, Dad. I love you, Dad. I'll never forget this. Nothing else up to this point matters.

"Let's stop at Ben and Jerry's on the way home. My treat."

"Yes, let's. I'd like that. I'd like that very much."

The Feud

He hadn't been in Timberlake's in an age. The place had gone downhill quite a bit, as most any drugstore that was a hundred and ten years old would do. But he just recently heard that it had been refurbished, so he decided to go on over today and have his lunch there. He had to admit that he had, in fact, heard about the renovations. But he hadn't come over sooner because he had not wanted to be cheated of his memories of the place as it once was.

It was a little sliver of a store, only about twenty-six feet wide. But it ran back for a block. He could always remember that his mother would bring him in to shop for all of those mysterious unguents and remedies they kept up front, such as Pointer's liniment salve and Dr. Clampton's bunion pads, that he'd always assumed had long since been outlawed by the FDA. He was sure they only were available at Timberlake's because they were somehow grandfathered and never actually left the dusty shelves. And while his mother would shop, he and his little sister would go all the way in the back, where there was a soda fountain that could have come straight out of the Mayberry television show.

Egg salad sandwiches and an ammonia-infused ice cold Coke in a glass that billowed at the top, where the ice gathered and acted as a dam against the easily bent paper straw. That's what his sister had always ordered. It was what she still always tried to order at a lunch counter, always to be disappointed when it just didn't taste the same as she remembered Timberlake's serving. And the Timberlake's soda fountain, with it's red-plastic-covered chrome stools that were easier to spin than the

Timberlake's, Mole Hole, Hardware Store block. (Photo by Stacey Evans.)

law really should have allowed, was always what he thought of whenever he saw or heard of egg salad—or of his sister, Cora, for that matter.

As he walked into the front door shortly before noon, he was happy to see the "On the Downtown Mall since 1890" sign out front where it always had been. This sign had always struck him as a bald-faced lie that no one seemed to challenge and he couldn't understand why not. He didn't quibble that Timberlake's might have been on this stretch of street for more than a century, but he knew for a fact that the Charlottesville Downtown Mall itself hadn't been here for more than twenty-five years. Before that, this had been Charlottesville's Main Street, with cars and narrow sidewalks and all.

However, he took the familiar sign as a good indication of what was going on inside, and sure enough, as he entered the store, he could see that very little had changed. He almost closed his eyes as he passed the shelves of Pointer's liniment salve and Dr. Clampton's bunion pads, because he just knew they had messed up—or what they would have claimed as modernized—the soda fountain area. But there it was, just as he remembered it. He almost could see his little sister attacking that block of ice at the top of the Coke with a paper straw.

"Why if it isn't Mr. Chauncey Willard. How nice of you to drop in and visit with us in the new century."

"Hello, Joyce. I see you're still here. How's life on the other side of the tracks?"

"Oh, Belmont's becoming right upscale these days, Chauncey. The arts and crafts movement has started its moving into the neighborhood, and it won't be long until the likes of me will be forced even further out of town. Need to see a menu?"

"I reckon not. At least not if your menu hasn't changed much more than this counter and these stools have in your recent renovation. I like what you've done—or haven't done, I would say."

"Thanks. We still feel like it's home."

"What *has* changed? Did you just strip the rust off the chrome, do some dusting, and put some brakes on these stools?"

"Well, we did get new bathrooms, ones with running water in the sinks rather than across the floor."

"Go no further. I think this renovation idea was just great."

"So, if you don't want to see a menu—"

"I'll just have my regular." Let's just see if she's kept her edge and can remember my usual.

"I'd like to say that the health authorities won't really let us serve any toasted cheese sandwiches and French vanilla Metrical shakes anymore, Chauncey, but that would be a lie. I'll just try to be busy across the counter while you combine those in what must be a cast-iron stomach."

And just then Joyce Donnell's business at the other end of the counter did pick up, as an elderly gentleman came in, sat down near another elderly gentleman, and immediately started raising a ruckus.

"That's my seat, Walt. You know that."

"Don't see no names on it, Ed. You might have sat on this stool for a while in the early fifties when I was off to war and you were here servicing all the war widows, but I do believe I started sitting here in 1942."

Ed made a great display of finding another seat, just two stools over, and spreading his newspaper out far and wide on the counter.

"This ain't no reading room, Ed. Keep your classifieds out of my hominy."

"Whew. What's that you doused yourself with, Walt?"

"It's called 'Midnight Mystery.' It's $4.95 a bottle up at CVS. Don't sell it here in Timberlake's. Brand's too new."

"Well, there's no real mystery there, Walt. Would you move downwind, maybe about three store's worth?"

No response, so Ed made a big drama of moving around on the other side of Walt.

"Quite a pair," Chauncey whispered to Joyce when she brought him his sandwich and shake.

"Oh, those two? All bark and no bite. They've been feuding since not long after we saw the last of you here. Used to be best of friends. Were—still are, I think—next-door neighbors out in Fry's Springs." Joyce went off to take Ed's order.

The two old men sat, fuming to themselves for a bit, while Walt continuously stirred his empty coffee cup and Ed pretended that it took him more than five minutes to work through the Tuesday *Daily Progress*.

"Walt, you need to keep that dog of yours on a leash, or I'm going to have to call out animal control again."

"Well, if your cats didn't come over and try to do their business in my azaleas, the dog wouldn't get riled and chase them back over into your yard. Speaking of which, I've put in an order to bring that oak tree down."

"Don't even think of that, Walt. Marge and I planted that tree on our tenth anniversary. That tree stays right where it is."

"Well, your tenth anniversary was a good foot of age rings ago, and that oak is half in my yard now. It's dead, just as dead as your and Marge's marriage, and it's leaning toward my house. Not that I blame it. If I was growing in your yard, I'd lean as far away from your house as I could too."

"Don't you go talking about my Marge like that, Walt. That dispute was your Gert's fault, and you know it."

The feuding continued, as Joyce returned to Chauncey to see if he wanted anything else.

"Tell me you're satisfied now and aren't going to order your usual for dessert, Chauncey."

"Nope. Same as always. I'll have a hot fudge sundae, and don't spare the fudge, the nuts, the whipped cream, or the ice cream, for that matter. If you have to skimp on something, I'll take a smaller spoon."

"Chauncey, I don't know how your stomach takes it. Why bother with the Metrical shake at all?"

"Cuttin here and there allows me to go a little heavier on the hot fudge. But tell me something before you go get it. What were those two talking about when they said their wives were fighting?"

"Oh," Joyce lowered her voice another notch. "That's what started the feud between those two in the first place. Their wives disagreed over what to stuff their Thanksgiving turkey with sometime in the mid-eighties, and the fighting just sort of snowballed from there."

"You'd think that being neighbors and all they'd have patched that up by now. Can't the wives see how much damage this has done to these two? They obviously were a real comfort to each other at one time."

"Oh, the wives had made up by that Christmas, but Walt and Ed didn't notice. Or, my theory is that they *did* notice but that they discovered it was more fun to be yapping at each other than being civil all the time. It's not like they avoid each other. They both appear here at the same time for lunch nearly every weekday. And another thing. When it looked like they weren't ever going to make up, I *did* go and talk to their wives and learned a thing or two. I learned that when Walt went into the hospital unexpectedly for a serious operation, Ed was the first one down at the Red Cross donating blood for him. And not long after that, when the bank was ready to foreclose on Ed and Marge's mortgage, I heard that Walt marched right down and bought up the paper and had the bank tell Ed that they'd been mistaken and that his payments were lower, not higher, than they had told him. No, I think we can just let this situation lie and step back and watch the fun."

As Joyce finished her assessment of the Ed and Walt act, Walt went up a couple of decibels in volume on the other side of the counter.

"No, I don't want that. I'm not going to take that. Well, I'm not going to be a baby about it. I won't take it out of my wallet now that you've put it there. But I'm not paying for that." With that, he grabbed his wallet and shuffled at a pretty good pace for a man his age to the bathroom.

Joyce went over to the other side of the counter. "What was that all about, Ed? Is Walt OK?"

"I reckon he'll be OK."

"What did you do to him? You-all pick at each other all the time you're in here on the best of days, but this was pretty over the top for a reaction from Walt."

"It was just the photograph, I suppose."

"What photograph?"

"The photograph of his new grandchild."

The Feud

"Ed Mahoney. If you don't let loose with more information than that, you'll have a might bit more trouble with me from now on than with Walt. What did you do to the photograph of his new grandchild?"

"I didn't do nothin to it. I just gave it to him."

A couple of seconds of silence, and Ed could see that Joyce was reaching for a seltzer bottle from behind the fountain, so he decided to be a little more explicit. "Walt didn't have that picture of his grandson. I had it taken. I went over to Waynesboro and paid to have it taken. That grandson was born about four months ago, and up to last month, it was touch and go on whether it was going to live. The baby came out with something wrong with its heart, and they're only now breathing a little easier about its chances."

"I don't understand, Ed. Why did *you* have the picture taken?"

"I've seen that before. Marge used to work in the newborn nursery over at the University hospital, and she always told me about this special trauma that some of the parents of the real sick ones had. They'd refuse to have photographs taken of their sick babies. They wouldn't always know that that was what they were doin, but it was like they were afraid to have something permanent made of a baby that they didn't know was ever going to come home or not. They were torn between not getting too attached to it and smothering it with love and attention. Then, the times when a baby did die, and no one had taken a photograph, the parents were even more upset because they discovered there really was no choice on whether they were going to get attached to the baby, and now they had nothing to remember it by. I've watched Walt since the baby was born at New Year's, and I think he's been suffering that trauma."

"So you took it on yourself to—"

"Yes I did. Ever since Valentine's Day, I've asked to see pictures of Walt's grandkids and he always brings out a whole string of them—but never a picture of the new baby. So, two weeks ago I went over to his daughter's house in Waynesboro to see what was what. The baby started crying and puttin on a fit the minute I came in the door. I figure he's goin to take after his granddad in that respect. But, well, I saw that the baby wasn't all that fragile anymore, and none of us can guarantee that even our healthiest young ones are going to live from day to day. So I treated Walt's daughter to a pile of baby photographs over at Gitchell's Studio. Must say the mother seemed relieved when that was done, and she didn't have nearly as many worry lines when we reviewed the proofs than when we first went into the studio. But I really had it done for Walt. He seems to have lost his edge on account of this worry. It's hardly been worth fighting with him since New Year's."

Joyce reached over the counter and gave Ed a hug, which she figured—rightly—was just about the right punishment for his little antic. Ed turned beet red with embarrassment and secret pleasure.

"Uh, don't you think someone should check on Walt?" Chauncey broke in to ask. "He's been in there a pretty long time."

"No, I reckon we should give him another ten minutes or so," Ed answered. "It takes a while to get over puffy eyes so no one will notice, and he's been saying that the bathroom turned out to be the best part of this renovation at Timberlake's. Besides, I have a thing or two to get in with him over this loud Beethoven crap he's been playing late at night over at his house, and I haven't quite decided yet what I can say to rile him the most."

The Gauntlet

Whew, made it out of the restroom without anyone seeing me. Wouldn't that have been a gas to have been discovered there right off the bat? All the way down the Downtown Mall to city hall. That's a long way. Long enough even if I didn't have to make those stops. Stop that nervous laugh! It will only attract attention. OK, assigned stop one. Across the lobby and ask for directions at the desk.

"Welcome to the Omni Hotel. May I help you, … ah … Ma'am?"

"Yes, please. Where is the Cat House, please?"

"Just take those doors over there out onto our bricked Downtown Mall shopping street and go down to 5th Street and turn right. You can't miss it. Hello, Sir, Ma'am. Welcome to the Omni. May I help you?"

Go ahead, turn away from me as fast as you can. Just how many question marks were in that question of yours? No use getting pissy, though. First stop taken care of. The voice. Too much waver. Either have to get control of the nerves or speak as little as possible—probably both. There's the door. Just one more look back to see if I'm being followed. Yes, there's Hank. And over there, there's that blond guy. Can't remember all the names. How the hell did I get into this mess? Oh, and there's one of the people who had been behind the reception desk. Moving in this direction, but not directly. Probably making sure I leave the hotel. Not quite the clientele they prefer, I'm sure.

There, out the door and at the top of the Mall. Bright sunshine, and these panty hose are so hot—tight too. And why'd I choose to wear these heels? I'm sure I could have gotten away with something with lower and wider heels. Why didn't I think of these things yesterday? Yeah, right, if I'd

131

given this much thought, I wouldn't be out here at all, with those two guys following me. Just don't let any of the girls see me.

Oh, Gawd. Why'd I say that? There's Karen, going into the skate park. And she's with Don. Those bastards. They've set me up. She's looking over here. Just keep on walking. Not too fast. Yeah, right, as if that was even an option with these heels. Just a little further and I'll be by them. Don's moving around, getting her to look my way over his shoulder. Stop that! She's looking. She's looking straight at me. But she doesn't see me. She's looking right through me. Yes!

Into the Gaming Place.

"You know, that computer game, 'The Adventures of Mighty Joe.' It's for my nephew's birthday."

"Sorry, we haven't had that in months. But I could order it for you, if you—"

Turn your head, dammit. He's just now looked up.

"No, thanks," backpedaling to the door. "I'll check somewhere else. Thanks, thank you very much."

Watch it. Hair caught on mobile hanging from the ceiling. Quickly, pull it away. Wouldn't that be something to laugh about?

The door shuts on nervous laughter and a "Hey, Gill, come quick. Over here. Get a load of—"

Have almost made it to the jewelry store. Hey, watch out, kid! You'll knock over that old couple. The old man would probably land on my feet. I'll guarantee you that these heels won't take another 220 pounds. Oh, good, that's caused everyone to look at them; I can slide off and look into the window of the needlework store until the walkers thin out. Just another sweet young thing looking for something to embroider or needlepoint, or whatever. Am I still being followed? Yep, but the old couple have moved up to those benches and are playing with that little kid, and nobody else seems to be gawking. So, three quick breaths and on past Central Place. That'll be the real test. OK, girl, back straight, tummy in, chest out—and push off.

Youch! How is one supposed to walk on brick with heels? My ankles are taking such a beating. I'll be in no shape for the dance tonight. OK, stop giggling again.

No, I certainly do not *want any of your Indian bracelets. Just get out of my way, crumb bum! Why do they allow these street vendors out here anyway?*

"Yes, very pretty. No, no thank you. No, not today!" *Geez, am I ever going to get to the end of this street?*

Past the Central Place but coming up on the Hardware Store and most of the outdoor cafés. But I was supposed to make another stop somewhere around here. Oh, that's right. I have to price sheet sets at the Palais Royale. Silk sheet sets. Who thought that one up? I'm not even sure I know what a sheet set is. Maybe they have a back door, though. I could get off the Mall, and take the less-traveled Market Street down to where I can come back to city hall. I could shake those guys then. Give them something to think about for a change. But no, I'd have to go by the police station then. Bad idea. Very bad idea. Good, they don't have the bright lights on in here. I might just about do this.

"Yes, they do feel so silky. Yes, yes, lovely. And how much would these be in azure? My Reggie says nothing is too good for our guests. His parents are coming—they haven't been here since we moved in near the club out at Farmington, and we'd like to have everything just right for them. How much would the queen set be?"

"These run about $500 for the set, but we do have some better-quality sets over here. Have you ever seen such a lovely shade of lavender? Here, take your sunglasses off, dear, and bring that pillowcase over to the window. Ohh—"

"Oh, no, no thank you. Yes, it's a lovely shade of lavender. I have to meet someone at the Downtown Grill for lunch, but then I'll be right back. She'll help me decide between the azure and the lavender. Both are just as lovely as can be. Bye for now."

And at the tinkling of the doorbell upon retreat: "Ann, did I hear you with a customer just now? Ann? Ann. What's wrong?"

Back out on the street. Was that Professor Gwathney's wife at the back of the store? Can't think of that now. Just a couple of more blocks and one more stop. Geez, would ya look at that group sitting right out in the center of the Mall at the Hardware Store's café? Got to be the night regulars at Miller's. It's going to be tricky getting past them. Shelley's there with them; and Dennis is there too, and that babe from microbiology class is walking over there with that professor. Head down; pretend you're looking in that antique store window. Oh, good, they're looking over at the Mole

On the Downtown Mall

Hole Gift Shop. Who's that dame over there? She really looks whacked out. Her shoes don't match and she moves like she's a zombie. Good style overall, though. Bet she isn't getting pinched by her pantyhose. Would'cha listen to me. I must be going over the edge. Gotta get past these cafés and then the crowd will thin out, and I'm just about home free.

There, this is 4th Street. The Cat House is on 5th. Hey, who are you looking at, Lady? Oh, cripes. You aren't a lady. What's going on here? Where's Hank and that blond guy?

A quick look around to see if Hank and the blond guy are still in tow, which they are. Both have gotten ahead, and are looking back. Hank has a grin a mile wide, and the blond guy is about bent all the way over with laughter.

The "woman" stands there at first, dead still, like a deer in headlights. The resemblance is remarkable. They could be twins, except the "woman" obviously has learned to carry "herself" better—and her makeup is much more expertly applied. Their suits are a near match, however, and they could have gotten their wigs from the same lot. The "woman" recovers first, acquires a very tentative, shy smile, and takes a step forward, taking on a look of happy recognition and instant acceptance. "Her" near twin stumbles back, turning onto an ankle yet again, and almost falling to the ground. The "woman" is there in an instant, saving the fall with strong arms. But there's a strangled gurgling sound, and the near twin breaks away and hobbles across to the other side of the Mall and up toward 5th Street. The "woman" follows at a slower pace, drawn like a gnat to the light bulb.

OK, that's it. Those guys aren't going to get away with this. That wasn't the least bit funny. No one else who's been through this told me about that part. Here's 5th, there's the Cat House off on the side street, and this is the very last stop.

A pert little saleslady with friendly eyes comes out from behind the counter. As she focuses on her customer, her eyes narrow a bit, and slight frown lines appear around her mouth.

"Yes, were you looking for anything in particular? Excuse me, I didn't hear what you said."

"Yes, please. I am looking for a toy for my cat." Someone out on the sidewalk clears their throat, and Hank and the blond guy appear just outside the doorway, straining to listen to every word. Checking up.

"I mean, I am looking . . . I am looking for a furry stuffed toy for my pussy."

"Ah, yes, I understand," the saleslady says, as she relaxes, returns behind the counter, perches on a stool, and resumes pricing a pile of cloisonné cat broaches.

"Don't you Phi Sig boys have any imagination?" She is speaking loud enough for Hank and the blond guy to hear her from their reporter position just beyond the entryway. "This is the third year in a row you've used this for hazing week—and the University says you aren't even supposed to do any hazing any more. It seemed sort of cruel and degrading to me the first time you used this for your fraternity initiations, and I don't think it's improved all that much with age. I hope your new crop of brothers have more constructive ideas for using up your energy."

"Yes, Ma'am. Sorry, Ma'am." And Steve is out of the Cat House in a flash, nearly pushing the giggling Hank and the blond guy over, as he dashes around the corner and into the arms of his new fraternity brothers who have gathered in front of city hall before all go back to Miller's for a celebration.

"You did good, Steve."

"Way to go, champ."

"Nice legs, sweetie."

"You guys. That dude you had decked out like me and headed back up the Mall was just too much. I had no idea *that* would happen.

"What dude? I don't know anything about another dressed-out guy."

"I thought you'd fold back at the sheet shop," blurts out Hank, as he and his compatriot join the celebration.

Steve basks in the limelight of a rite of passage survived for a good half minute. But something—it may be the sound of a sob—pulls his attention back to the benches by the post office nearby. There, hunched over, wilted, and thoroughly deflated, sits the "woman" who had kept him from stumbling to the ground in front of the antique store. Briefly their eyes meet, but

Steve cannot endure the pain and humiliation that radiates from the "woman," who suddenly rises and shuffles off into the shadows of 6th Street, never to return to the Mall.

Reddening up, Steve pulls off his wig, exchanges his heels for the loafers the brothers had been holding for him, and strips off the skirt, top, and pantyhose to the T-shirt and shorts underneath, as the group moves back down the Mall toward Miller's and its canned Dave Matthews Band background music.

Party on today. I've earned it. But the Cat House lady was right. This hazing is cruel and degrading. It's time for a change in the Phi Sig initiation ceremony, and I'm going to be the one to make that change—starting tomorrow—or the next day at the latest. But party on today.

Something to Tell You

She had no idea she could get so out of breath in just the walk this far from Martha Jefferson. She had not had much exercise for some time. She had been so busy, mostly busy immersing herself in family and school, just to try to forget it, or at least not to dwell on it so much. But she had no idea she could grow so weary so fast. She should have just stayed in the lobby over at Martha Jefferson until it was time to meet her aunt and uncle on the Downtown Mall. But she suddenly had to get out of that building and get moving, to do something, anything. Any activity was better than just sitting in that lobby and thinking about what she had discovered. It had been even worse than she had imagined.

She came up to the corner of Park and High Streets and had to hold up for the light that would take her across to the courthouse. And, besides, she thought, as she watched the cars circling the block, she had managed to find a parking place in the Martha Jefferson lot. Who knows whether she could have found one at all over here closer to the Mall at this time of day.

As she waited for the light, Emily looked over at the side of the two-hundred-year-old Albemarle Courthouse. Such history it had. She put her hand up to brush a wisp of fine hair away from her face, only to come away with wet fingers. She hadn't even realized she had been tearing up. History. Such an optimistic word. But the courthouse represented America's history, a proud and noble history. Jefferson, Madison, and Monroe had all trod right here where she was now barely able to drag her 112 pounds of flesh and brittle bone. And the building that these three Founders had known as the local gathering place was still

137

Photo by Rick Britton.

here. It truly could look back on its long history with a sense of pride and awe. What did she have to look back on? Or, for that matter, ahead to? She shuddered at the thought.

The pedestrian light flickered on—and then out again just before she had managed to reach the other side. Good thing this wasn't a busy intersection and that Charlottesville drivers still had some of the manners Southerners were once known for.

The park. The azaleas and the pink dogwood, glorious in their profusion of color at this time of year, beckoned her to rest in the park beside the courthouse a while in the shadow of the bronze equestrian statue of General Stonewall Jackson. She had plenty of time before she was supposed to meet her aunt and uncle for lunch. This was a very good thing, because it never could be a good time to have this discussion with them.

Emily climbed up the short hill to the park and almost collapsed onto a bench, a bench warmed by the springtime sun. It was really nice up here. Sun. That was the ticket. A life in the sun. She began to tear up again and was quite relieved to be the only one in sight at the small park in the very middle of the small city's legal district. But, what was that over on that bench by the corner of Jefferson and 4th? Someone else was in the park. A boy, in the shadows of a stately old oak. But he had not seen her arrive and take possession of her bench. He didn't seem to be paying attention to anyone at all. In fact, he looked even more despondent and withdrawn into himself than she did at this moment. The boy was sitting on the bench. But he was hunched over until only his cupped hands kept him from touching his nose to his knees. He was very still, almost as if he wanted to recede into the worn wood of the bench. She didn't think anyone could be as upset as she was at this moment, but she had been wrong. And for a moment, that seemed to buoy her spirits.

But then Emily discovered she knew the boy, as he slowly sat upright. He briefly stared blankly in the direction of Stonewall, without seeming to see the statue at all. And then, as if gaining the strength he needed from the crafty and stalwart Confederate army officer, he stood up straight. It was Pete Jones. Mary Catherine's son. Emily knew that they had had a rough time of it since Pete Sr.'s death—not financially so much. The death just seemed to rip the family apart. She mustn't think about that. She had to gather her thoughts.

Her own regret—for herself, and her family, and for all that had been and was yet to be—flooded back in and her temporary horror at the reality that she had recently been forced to face overtook her once more.

Still without seeing her, the Jones boy seemed to have reached a decision point and had begun to move to the short flight of steps down to the street corner. He still looked very dejected, and when he had reached the bottom of the steps, he hesitated. Emily got the impression that there was nothing he wanted to do more than to escape to someplace else altogether—a feeling she certainly shared. But he pointed his nose south and started to walk resolutely down 4th Street and toward the Downtown Mall.

It wouldn't be long before Emily herself would need to make that trip. Maybe she had better organize and practice what she had to say. She looked at her watch. There was still time to prepare. Too much time. She laughed a dry little laugh. How could she say that? There could never be too much time. There certainly couldn't be too much time to wait to have this discussion with the aunt and uncle who had raised her. They would be crushed. Her uncle. She couldn't think about him clearly just now. All because of him.

Maybe she could just sort of slip it in. Maybe it wouldn't be such a shock then. Aunt Jane, Uncle Ernest. I have something to tell you. Something good and something bad. Gene got that grant he was working on. Christian's school band was selected to go to C'ville's sister city in Italy. Janey got selected for the varsity soccer team next year. Yes, my grades were good. Very good. I've finished with the classes now. Just have a bit more to do on my dissertation and then I'll be a certified child psychologist. I know it's what we always wanted. But, Jane, Ernest, I have some bad news too. Ernest. Look at me Ernest. Please look at me. You know when we had those special moments when you came home from working at the lab? When I'd perch on your lap and you'd read all of the comics to me? Well, Ernest— —

⋙ ⋘

"I know we're early, but she'll be along any minute, and we never can gauge how long it will take to get into Charlottesville from over at the lake."

Jane had breezed up to and into the Hardware Store's Garden Café on the Downtown Mall a good five paces ahead of her husband and was already looking around for a waiter to place her order before Ernest was even able to decide which chair to sit in. In the end, he picked the one that was as far away from his wife as possible and then looked around to see if there was room to pull it even further from the table.

"The Hardware Store. What a nutty name for a restaurant."

"It doesn't prevent you from coming here whenever we come into town, though, does it, Jane?"

"Oh, button up, you old bastard."

"Let's try not to lose it before she even shows up, shall we, Jane? We really do have to talk to her. And it won't help for you to be doing your Lady MacBeth routine in the background."

"Bastard, bastard, bastard," Jane chanted quietly to herself—although not so quietly that the waiter didn't catch it. Although he had been working his way toward them, he suddenly veered off to another table.

"Now you've done it," Jane hissed through her teeth. "I'm so thirsty, I could drink lake water, and now the waiter probably won't be back until you're gone for good—which couldn't be fast enough now that it's come to this."

"Lake water. That would be fitting." Ernest took up the challenge with a twinkle in his eye. "All those years I worked in the lab over at the nuclear reactor at the end of the lake, and all those jabs you gave me about what we were doing to the environment, and you're now so thirsty you could drink lake water."

Jane pulled a sour face as she built up steam to take a new tack. Ernest took the opportunity to gaze out into the busy walking mall. A toddler had just veered away from an old couple sitting on a bench and was looking directly at Ernest, his attention arrested no doubt by Ernest's magnificent gray-streaked beard. Ernest smiled at the child, and to the little one's delight, started to twist his mouth into a strange shape, setting his beard into motion. The child squealed with laughter, ran off a few paces in mock terror, and then turned and tried to mimic Ernest's mouth movements.

This all provided Jane with the new tack she sought. "Stop making eyes at that little boy, Ernest. People will see you and get ideas. You're always making up to those children. Parents don't like strangers getting too friendly with their children. I think you'd have liked to stay a child yourself. It's not healthy. I might just move to another table and pretend I'm not even with you."

"You'll get your wish soon enough, My Dear. It won't be long before I'm gone. I hope Emily arrives early as well. I'd just as soon get this over, have a last visit with Christian and Janey, and be on my way."

"You bastard," Jane hissed again—again just as the waiter had built up the courage to return for their order. "I don't want you anywhere near Christian and Janey. And after what we have to tell Emily today, I don't think she'll want you near them again before you're gone, either. Bastard, bastard, bastard."

"Um, folks. Are you ready to order yet? Our specials today are really good. For starters, we have broiled lake trout—fresh out of our own Lake Anna, I'm told." Not having seen both Janey and Ernest grimace, the waiter rambled on: "Then we also have a very nice—"

ଓ ଓ

Emily had meant to rise and follow Pete Jones to the Mall, but she found she didn't have the mental strength to do so. She wasn't ready yet. She was ready to tell her parents all the good things that were happening in her life, all the things that anyone would consider to be a joy. But it was the bad thing she had to discuss with them. They had told her over at Martha Jefferson that she just had to confront it, get it over with, and get on with life. Get on with life! Yeah, right.

So, instead of walking south toward the Downtown Mall when she struggled up from the bench, Emily found herself

Something to tell You

walking east three blocks to yet another city park, this one adorned by the bronze equestrian statue of General Lee. *The rebellion lives,* Emily told herself in a wholly unsuccessful attempt to bring a little levity into her day, a day in which she seemed doomed to spend with defeated and dead Confederate Civil War generals. The flowers in Lee Park were even prettier than those in Jackson Park had been. Maybe she would just stay here forever and not meet up with Jane and Ernest on the Mall. Maybe it would be all right if she just pretended nothing was wrong. She had already pretended that for so long that it had become second nature to her. Or maybe she'd just go over to that ornamental cannon and see if it was capable of one more shot—a trip to the moon on gossamer wings.

Oh, lord. Now she was getting hysterical. She mustn't do that. Her aunt was capable of getting sufficiently hysterical for all of them. *Sit on the bench. Pull yourself together. Compose the bad news.*

Jane, Ernest. I have something to tell you. You know when I would perch on Ernest's lap to read the paper with him right after he had come home from his research job at the reactor all those years?

She couldn't do it. It would change their lives forever—all of their lives. Emily thought of her own daughter, Janey, and the hours that she had spent on Ernest's lap, reading the comics—just as she, herself, had done all those years ago. It looked so innocent, but, just below that surface, oh, so cancerous. Innocence was dead.

But she was digressing. The time was getting shorter. Aunt Jane, Uncle Ernest. I have something to tell you. Well, Jane, Ernest, about all that time I spent with Ernest in the early evenings. I've been working with the people over at Martha Jefferson Hospital. We've been doing extensive testing, and ... Jane, Ernest, I have a rare form of cancer. They think I got it, picked it up over a long time, from the clothes Ernest came home in from the reactor lab. They say it's very rare. Only can be picked up by the very young and only through prolonged exposure. But they don't have a cure for it. Not yet, at least. And it moves pretty fast once it gets going. Lies dormant for many years, and then ... They say I should be able to finish my doctorate, but that ... Jane, Ernest. Oh, Ernest, please don't—

Now Emily was sure she couldn't face them. Not just now. When she didn't show up for lunch, they would start getting the idea that something was wrong. Then they'd come out to the house, and having Gene and Christian and Janey there would soften the blow. Then they'd see where they could go from there. She knew they'd be there for her, that they'd both be there and help Gene and the kids get through this. But she couldn't face them now. She was just too low right now. But, Janey would be there. Emily knew she couldn't tell them with Janey there—anywhere in the house.

Something in the way the figure was moving toward her from the direction of the Mall made her look up. It was the Jones boy. He was coming back her way, and he was as different from how he had gone to the Mall as day is from night. He was all smiles now, moving at a good clip, standing up straight, meeting the world straight on. He was bubbling over with a joy that was too much just for himself. Some of it sprang off of him as he passed Emily, this time noticing her, and giving her a cheery "Hi" and a radiant smile. Some of the joy leaped off the boy and started to work at Emily.

She had her family. She had a wonderful husband and two great kids, and an aunt and uncle who would stand by her and see her through this. She had been privileged to have completed her studies. It was spring in Charlottesville, and the azaleas and dogwood were gorgeous. She had seen it and it must be a sign. She had watched Pete Jones crawl off toward the Mall, the lowest of low, and had seen him return from the Mall on a high. She should be able to do whatever Pete Jones had done. Good things must be happening at the Mall. She should get over there as quickly as possible. She needed to latch onto something good.

She looked at her watch. It was time. She rose, squared her shoulders, and started down the street.

ɞ ʚ

"Now, when Emily comes, let me be the one to tell her."

"Not a chance in hell. How about if I just blurt right off when she sits down: 'Emily, we've got something to tell you. Your uncle has got the notion to divorce me and fly off to Phoenix for good.' How about that? Right between the eyes. It's *your* decision to leave me, you bastard. All these years. I gave you my youth and all those years I could have gone off and made something of myself. I gave you Emily, and she always seemed to favor you, no matter what I did. Always there to greet you when you came home from work. Spending the best part of the evenings together, just of the two of you. Smiling your secret smiles and cutting me out. Oh, no, mister. This divorce is *your* decision and it's *your* decision to move across the country. And I'll be damned if I'm going to let you steal Emily's children away from me the way you stole her. I'll be—"

"Shush, Jane. She's coming now. I see her over there. Oh, she looks so weary. And her eyes. Such sad eyes. I'll be glad when she finishes that doctorate. She can really let down and enjoy life if she'll just take a rest after the school work."

"Here we are. Hsst, shush. Now try to be calm about this, Janey. We're over here, Honey."

They both look flushed, Emily observed as she approached. No doubt really enjoying the opportunity to come into Charlottesville for the afternoon. It's terrible to have to lay this on them now. Uncle Ernest's just retired and they just now have the time to do whatever they want with each other and just to enjoy what should be rewards of a long life of work.

"Emily, sit down over here. Your uncle and I have—"

"Aunt Jane, Uncle Ernest, I'm so glad to see you. I have—"

"... something to tell you."

Pork Chops Tonight

Well, Phoebe, shall we have pork chops tonight? But Harley doesn't like pork chops. Her shaking hand fluttered up to smooth her perfectly arranged hair and she dropped a glove. She looked at the glove as it lay there between her mismatched shoes. *Whose is that?* she wondered. *I never wear gloves during the day.*

She gazed at the Williamsburg-fussy glass ornaments in the window of the gift shop on the Downtown Mall. She would have thought them quite clever and cute if she were really seeing them.

What was she doing on the Mall and why had she come into town today? She was sure she didn't know, but for some reason this didn't worry her. Pressing in on her was the nagging thought that there was some important reason she had come downtown.

A passing young man bent down, picked up her glove, and handed it back to her. It was quite dirty and stained. A feeling of indignation flooded in and she was about to admonish the young man, but he was gone before she could say anything.

I should have asked him where the police station was, she thought. But why would she ask him that? It wasn't really his fault her glove was soiled.

I wonder if I left the pork chops out to thaw before I left. But, I. musn't have. Harley doesn't like pork chops. He's really quite nasty about that. About that and so much else. Well, screw Harley. She gave a little giggle, but managed to stifle that because those passing by were giving her strange looks. *Can't look suspicious.*

Harley. It was something about Harley. Whatever she had come here to do concerned Harley. She entered the store and banged the door behind her. A somewhat perturbed shop clerk drifted toward the front of the store.

"Yes, ma'am, can I help you?"

"I think I'm meeting someone here. Maybe for lunch?" She asked the question as if maybe the clerk would know the answer. But then she giggled and let her hand flutter to her hair again. "But, I guess I wouldn't be meeting anyone for lunch here, would I?"

"No, ma'am, the Mole Hole's just for gifts; it doesn't serve lunch. Perhaps you were looking for the Hardware Store just down the block."

"A hardware store? No, I don't think so. Not for lunch, I wouldn't think so. Oh, you mean *the* Hardware Store. Yes, of course, that's a restaurant, isn't it?"

Once again, it seemed as if the saleswoman was supposed to supply all of the answers. But she just smiled and moved back toward the center of the store. You never could tell here in Charlottesville. Some of the looniest people who came into the shop were some of the richest and most famous. She knew enough to be very careful in dealing with any well-dressed woman who wafted in—no matter how wacky she seemed to be and whether or not her shoes matched.

"Yes, I'll just go back to the Hardware Store. I'm sure Janet will be along shortly."

Well, at least that mystery is solved, Phoebe thought, as she went back out onto the shaded bricked walking street. She was meeting Janet here.

Phoebe looked down at her feet and knitted her brow in determined concentration. Her shoes didn't match. Now, wasn't that strange? But not so strange. The image of Harley floated through her mind. She was taking the pork chops out of the freezer, and Harley breezed in, all decked out in his golf togs. But the calendar had clearly said that Harley was leaving this afternoon on a business trip to New York. She had planned to have Janet over tonight. They were going to have the house all to themselves for two days, and then Phoebe was going to tell Harley about Janet and herself when he got back from New York.

On the Downtown Mall

"No, I didn't know your trip had been canceled. Yes, I know you don't like pork chops. I just didn't know you would be here tonight, and I do like pork chops. In fact, I love pork chops. Yes, I do love pork chops so much I was going to have two. Please don't yell at me, stop making those disgusting little piggy noises, and don't be so damned sarcastic. They're just pork chops; they won't kill you. Just go on out on the patio and finish off that bucket of martinis. I'm going upstairs to look for my gloves."

Harley hadn't even asked why she was looking for her gloves. And, if he had, she wouldn't have been able to tell him. She just knew this was a time when people wore gloves.

She managed to find her gloves upstairs and then found Harley out on the patio. Afterward she'd had to throw the shoe away. She regretted that; it was so hard to find spikes anymore. But there weren't any repairmen left who could do a good job of reattaching heels—not ones as dented and scruffed up as that one. Everyone was wearing those flat shoes now that made their calves look fat. At least that's what Harley always said about her own legs whenever she wore anything but those painful spike-heeled shoes.

She had reached the front of the Hardware Store Restaurant, but for the life of her she couldn't remember if she had left the pork chops out to thaw or whether she had put them back in the freezer before going upstairs to find her gloves.

Phoebe looked up and her face was transformed by a radiant smile.

"Phoebe, there you are. I've been looking all over for you. All you said was to meet you on the Downtown Mall. You didn't say where. You sounded so strange over the telephone. Is everything all right?"

"That depends, Janet," responded Phoebe. She paused, her mind momentarily muddled again, and then she stuffed the blood-stained glove in her purse and smiled a secret little smile as she remembered the all-important question. "That depends on whether or not you like pork chops."

Hardship

"Now remember, Mandy, we're not going to ask her straight off when she gets here."

"Why not? She's loaded, and we're going to get a big chunk of it one of these days anyway. Fancy that, an antebellum mansion in the Keswick hunt area. Do you think it's hard to learn to ride a horse?"

"Not for you, I'm sure. You can do anything you set your mind to. We've been over this. We shouldn't ask her for a lot of things at once. The BMW should be enough for now. And don't talk about it not being that long. We can't bank on such things."

"Why forever not? She *is* eighty-two, and she's had several near misses in the last couple of years. And this is important. I can't face life alone just now—especially with a baby coming. Why'd you have to accept that silly old Rhodes scholarship anyway? I've heard it's cold and damp in England. And this is no time for me either to have to cope alone or for us to be separated from our friends at the University."

"Now, don't mope, Mandy. I'm sure everything will turn out all right. We just have to put up with the rocky times every once in a while. Oh, here she comes now. Put on your happy face. This will be hard enough without you pouting about it. You can appear worried and concerned, though, of course. We're in a pretty tight spot on this one, and I don't think she'll be able to grasp the full gravity—not with the cushy life she's led and all."

They both turned in their seats at the Hamilton's outdoor café toward the western end of the Downtown Mall and put on their "So happy to see you" faces for their "dear" Aunt Betty.

They had to hold pose for some time, however, as Aunt Betty, like a majestic ocean liner of the 1930s, was taking her sweet time in sailing out of the afternoon sunbeams and docking at the Hamilton's pier. She wasn't a large woman, by any means, but she had a regal, elegant bearing about her that exuded money and blue blood.

"Good afternoon, My Dears, it's so good to get out in the sunshine for a change, although it's rather a long trudge from where Anthony had to park the car. And it's so good to see you both. I know you must be extremely busy, as I haven't seen either of you since you came by to celebrate Christmas with me and take title on your present. It seems a shame. My only grand-nephew in graduate school right here at UVA for the past two years, and married to such a lovely wife, and I rarely get to see either of you."

"Here, Auntie, let me take that cane and hang it over this chair. I can't believe it's been that long. I'm sure we must have been out to see you more recently. I just told Mandy the other day that it was time we drove out to Keswick to see you. It's a lovely drive out that direction."

"That would be splendid. You could come out in your Christmas present. I presume the car is giving you good service?"

"Yes, of course, Aunt Betty. Of course gasoline prices are going up terribly, you know. And those BMWs take premium gas. Pretty tough on a graduate assistant's stipend. But, yes, of course, we'll drive out to see you soon. My, you're looking well. Isn't Aunt Betty looking great, Mandy? You must have been blessed by an iron constitution or a lucky life. It's great not to have to worry about your health all of the time."

☙ ❧

She was only nineteen. Too young to die, she had thought. It had started out as just a stomachache, but then it got much worse than any stomachache she'd ever known. She hadn't been working in the county assessor's office for more than three months, starting as soon as she had graduated from high school, because every paycheck in a fatherless family counted at the height of the Great Depression. Acute appendicitis, the doctor had said. Little time to act, and, there being no hospital in Craig and the hospital in Hayden refusing to take her because her doctor didn't have privileges there, they had had to operate right there in the clinic under not very sanitary conditions.

"Really too late. It burst. Peritonitis," she'd heard the doctor say, as she drifted off under the effects of the ether. But somehow she didn't care. It was quite peaceful where she was. There was a glowing light and an unexplainable feeling of comfort. She came upon a stone fence and perched there for the longest time, not caring about anything. She understood—without knowing why she should understand—that she was expected to make a choice whether to stay on this side of the fence or to cross over, but she didn't have a particular preference for either side, so she just sat there and enjoyed an extraordinary feeling of peace.

"Are you going to check in on Elizabeth this morning, Dr. Talbot?"

"Elizabeth? Elizabeth Potter? Did she live the night?"

"Yes doctor, she's right here in the hall, where they wheeled her to after the operation. We found she hadn't been stitched up, and the wound has drained and her fever is down."

She drifted off again, but this time when she got to the fence, it had grown to the point where she couldn't look over it, let alone perch on it. Her exhilaration quickly dissipated and she felt a profound sense of loss. But she also thought that there must be a reason she couldn't cross the fence. There must be things she needed to do on this side of the fence first.

"Well, we could stick your sister back in the ward, Homer, but she was brain dead there for a while. I'm not sure how much sense she's got left."

"She hadn't all that much sense before the operation, Dr. Talbot. Guess we'd like to have her back anyway she comes. I'll tell you one thing, though. We're going to get a hospital for Craig out of this. Any time Hayden won't take a Craig girl, we'll just move our support back over here for our own folks."

☙ ❧

"I'm sorry, what was it that you said, Mandy? I'm afraid I was having one of my senior moments. That happens more often these days."

"Oh, how awful!"

"Not really, My Dear. Memories can be pleasantly comforting at my age. In fact, I find the whole concept of death increasingly welcoming."

"Yes, of course," Mandy said, but then she blushed. That could have been taken several ways. But what she actually went on to think was, *how could someone as pampered as you need any comforting? You have no idea how high-pressured life is for those trying to establish themselves these days. There you sit, dripping in gems, all first quality except for that silly little stone in the tarnished ring you keep twisting around your finger. It's going to take several years of hard work by Brad and me even before we can get a half-decent home. Unless, of course, Keswick Hill becomes available before then.*

"Mandy has reminded me that we haven't been able to take that trip to Tahiti you gave us for a wedding present yet. The demands of graduate school are really tough, and Mandy is so new at her job in the bursar's office that we just can't seem to get away. We thought right after finals this year, but, as you know, Mandy—"

03 80

Bradley had called to let us know that he only had two days to get it done—but it turned out to be enough, if only just. He stopped in Denver for a ring on his way home. We'd been engaged for several months, but the army had moved him to Texas for training before he could get me a proper ring. He'd been so apologetic about the ring he'd found in Denver, but I knew that even a lieutenant in those days didn't have money to throw around. It never was about a ring anyway. The poor Minters. They had to put their Christmas tree out on the porch just so there'd be room in the parlor for those we could get to come on Christmas Eve in a snowstorm. Luckily, we could find a minister and enough witnesses at the last minute. We had a few glorious hours, productive ones it turned out, but Bradley wasn't even able to stay the night; they came and told him the unit was shipping out early. To cheer me up, Bradley had said we'd have a fancy honeymoon trip to the South Seas as soon as the Japanese could be cleared out of there. I never held him to that promise, but I vowed that someday someone in our family would get that trip. Just knowing we could get married before the unit was sent off to Europe and having the Denver ring were enough for me.

☙ ❧

"What with her pregnancy and all, I don't know when we're going to be able to make that trip. In fact, we were thinking of cashing the tickets in. Mandy says she'd really prefer going to Cancun. We could manage that in just a week, and then we'd have some money left over. When Mandy's had the baby, she'll want to take some time off from her job, and having some extra cash would help us with that. We'll have to start looking for a house with another bedroom for the baby too. It would be hard to give up a guest room. So many people drop by. We presume that would be fine with you. Aunt Betty, are you all right?"

"Yes, of course, Brad. I'm fine. Just one of those random pains of the heart. Certainly, you can cash the Tahiti trip vouchers in. No reason you should have to go all the way out to the South Seas if you'd prefer something closer. I'd just always dreamed of going there myself some day, so I guess I was just trying to live vicariously. I'm much too old and crippled to go out of town these days, let alone to the other side of the world. I'm so delighted about your pregnancy, Mandy, and I know it will be difficult for you to be home with the baby as long as you'd like. I'd love to help make that possible."

"Well, there's something else we really could use help with, Aunt Betty. Brad, tell your aunt about England."

"England? What about England?"

"We were saving that for a surprise, but I guess now is as good a time as any to tell you about it. I've gotten a Rhodes scholarship for the year after next. Pretty prestigious. It covers a couple of years of study in England."

"Oh, my! That's wonderful for you. I'm so proud. And what a great opportunity. This will make your reputation in your field." Elizabeth was having a hard time smiling. Her only remaining flesh and blood. Now here in Charlottesville, near her, but leaving again so soon. When she'd first heard the baby was coming, she'd been ecstatic. Her family here with her in her final years. They'd hardly had a chance to enjoy each other's company, and now, soon after the baby came, Brad would be leaving for a couple of years. But there were Mandy and the baby. Maybe they could come stay with her. She'd love that.

"Yes, but the problem is," Mandy broke in, "that I simply couldn't exist here alone. Of course I've got to go to England with Brad, but we just can't see how we're going to be able to afford that."

CR ʬ

The call came from Texas through a friend of Bradley's. He'd already been shipped on to upstate New York in preparation for what was to be the landing at Anzio in Italy—although no one was told that until long after the fact, not even the immediate families of the soldiers. The friend told her that Bradley had sent her a check and had obtained permission for her to join him in New York, not knowing how long he'd be stationed there. She had no idea before she reached New York what a privilege this had been; only the officers of the unit had received permission to have their families join them in New York.

The check never arrived, so it was a good thing she hadn't waited for it. Decades later, she found it among the effects of her brother after he died; she had no idea why the letter had gone to him rather than to her, or why he hadn't remembered to give the unopened envelope to her sometime in all these years. But the times were pretty tough and uncertain in those days. When Bradley's friend had gotten to her, she was up at Smither's ranch with Bradley's mother. His mother had signed on to cook with a hay bailing crew that summer, and then most of the men had been ordered down from the mountain on short notice because they were reserves and the unit was being mobilized to go to the war. No bailing, no hay, and no money. Bradley's mother had counted on that paycheck to hold her through the coming winter. Elizabeth had gone to the crew chief and asked him what needed to be done to get the job finished. For two weeks she walked behind the bailer, poking wires and trying to keep from being blinded by the chaff or pierced with a wayward wire. Her hands were stripped raw by the effort. When they were done, the crew chief had handed her a hefty pay envelope. She said she hadn't expected any money; she was just trying to make sure her mother-in-law could make it through the winter. The crew chief said, though, that Elizabeth had turned in as good a job as any of the men who had left could have done. She'd done a man's job, and she deserved a man's pay.

Turns out the money was a godsend, because Elizabeth needed it to get to New York. That was still a problem, though. It was wartime and tires and gas were rationed. Bradley had left her his car, but the tires were bald, and Elizabeth had no idea where New York was, but intuitively knew it was half a world away. Elizabeth asked around and found that two other girls in northwest Colorado had also gotten permission to join the unit in New York but were in no better condition getting that done than she was. Elizabeth had the car, one of the girls had no car but had coupons for four tires, and the other girl was related to someone on the gas board and could get the rations they needed.

By the time Elizabeth and her new life-long friends arrived in New York, it was winter and Elizabeth felt as big as a blimp. Three glorious weeks with Bradley and then he was gone. Elizabeth had no idea where he was when the baby came into the world or whether the army really would get the message to him. She didn't even know if little Annie's father was alive. But she really didn't have much time to dwell on those questions. She could see the street through the chinks in the wall of the only house they were able to find available in Watertown. It had no heat, and Annie's nighttime bottles were freezing before Elizabeth could get them to the baby. And besides, Elizabeth's money was running out and the army wasn't providing much. She'd have to start looking for a job in short order or return to Colorado and beg for her old job with the county assessor.

03 80

"… And they say there are several job possibilities for me at the university in England, but by then I'll have a baby, and I just don't know how I'll be able to cope with both a child and a job. It would be wonderful to have the help you have out at Keswick Hill. Trying to raise a family these days can be so—"

ଓ ଊ

"Lizzie, ho, girl, pull on over for a minute. Some snow we had last week wasn't it? Most of it still on the ground. Don't know what I'm even doing out here. Can't check the fences, when it's hard even to see the tops of the fence posts in all this snow. Hi there, little Annie. Such a sweet little smile—and that's about all I can see in all that bundling. Haven't seen you around in a good bit, Lizzie. See you're coming down from the hills. You aren't still trying to get over the mountain to Denver again, are you?"

"Nope. I'm on my way back to Craig from Denver. Been in Denver all week."

"Been there all week? How'd you get there? When you were lookin around for someone to sit Annie last week, we told you that the snowstorm would surely close Rabbit Ears Pass and that you'd be crazy to try to go. You didn't go on over in all that snow, did you?"

"Yep, had to. Bradley's mother went down with the fever and needed someone to help her out. When Bradley shipped out for Italy, he told his mother and me to look after each other, and we mean to do just that."

"You always were a little crazy, Lizzie—and stubborn as the Clayton's mule. Don't suppose I should be surprised you went on over, though. There's a lot of that kind of stubbornness going around Moffit County. Who took care of Annie for you?"

"Nobody. I took her with me."

"Now, that's downright insane, Lizzie. You both could have frozen up there in the pass and we wouldn't have found you until the spring thaw. That's no way to risk your baby's life."

"Well, when they found us, we'd be frozen together in one family-sized cube, John. I couldn't find anybody to take Annie for me last Tuesday. Sure, everyone I talked to was more than willing in theory, but I didn't need a sitter in theory. I needed one on Tuesday. I saw the way the snow was coming down and was pretty sure I could make it through the pass before it closed if I left right away. And when I found that no one could commit to taking Annie on the fly, it hit me that we've really got no one else to count on except each other—and Bradley's mother over in Denver. I doubt Annie would be much better off in the long run motherless and fatherless down here in Craig than frozen with me up there at Rabbit Ears. So—"

಄ ೲ

"So, we were wondering, Aunt Betty, if you might be able to help float us while I'm at Oxford. You have no idea how worried we are about being apart, especially now that the baby is coming and all. Life is just too tough. We could sell the BMW, of course, but we just received that and I thought you would think us ungrateful if we turned around and sold it. And if we did sell it, we'd only have the Porshe, which, of course, has no room for the baby."

಄ ೲ

It was several years later and she and the children were just about ready to ship out to Korea. Bradley had been there for several months and, although all of his letters sounded like he was profoundly homesick, he had said he really thought the situation in Korea was too volatile for a family to follow him. There now were Elizabeth, Annie, and a son, Brian, who had been born while Bradley had been sent back to Berlin to beef up American troops during the postwar airlift there. Bradley had told them just to stay put in the little house in Denver. Elizabeth wasn't having any of that, however. She was expecting again (for the last time, as it turned out, and the baby had only lived for a couple of months), and she was determined both that Bradley would see *this* baby come into the world and that she would keep her family together. They were actually on the tarmac on the airbase when the message came in, pulling her and the children off the line. She wasn't going to Korea. The North Koreans had come across the DMZ that morning. They were almost to Seoul, and there was no way any more dependents were being shipped to the Far East until the fighting was over. Besides, her husband had been up on the DMZ, as an adviser to a South Korean infantry unit, when the attack had occurred. No one had heard from his unit yet.

Elizabeth had stood there in a daze for a good ten minutes and had only snapped out of it when Brian pulled on her sleeve and asked, "Where's Daddy? You said we were going to go see Daddy," Elizabeth picked her son up, took Annie by the hand, and began reclaiming their baggage. She then asked that their bags be put into a taxi and drove over to the commercial airport. She had just about enough money to get them to Tokyo. They'd work the rest out when they got that far.

☙ ❧

"Yes, of course, children. I've always believed that families needed to stay together at all costs. Of course I'll help support you in England. It will be no hardship for me in the least."

Cruel, Cruel Fate

Not more than halfway through her Tuesday noontime concert at Christ Episcopal Church, Henrietta realized that she would never play the violin in concert again. The church had been packed, and they had given her a standing ovation, but she knew that they knew her violin performances were over for good and that they were just being polite. The realization had actually come as a complete surprise to her—so much so that, rather than going straight home afterward, she wandered the streets of Charlottesville, ultimately finding herself face-to-face with a cup of hot tea at Hamilton's outdoor tables on the Downtown Mall.

She reached over to pick up the teacup, and her hand was shaking so much that she splattered tea on the tablecloth. A concerned waiter rushed over, dabbed at the table cloth, and refilled her cup. She found that if she held the cup with both hands, she could bring it to her lips. It wasn't nerves. She now had to admit that the arthritis was winning the battle. The teacup was hot in her hands, but it was soothing as well. The pain had been terrible, but the heat was helping. She had no idea how she had gotten through the last half of the concert. She leaned over, opened the violin case, and ran a finger down the mellow wood of the fine old instrument, polished with the talented hands of so many violin soloists before her. Her eyes clouded over with tears, and the shape of the violin became hazy.

Her world was coming to an end. Without the violin, she was nothing. So many years of study and preparation, and now, just as she was beginning to get a name for herself as a violinist, she was finished. Cut off in her prime. All of the effort at Julliard and in Paris for nothing.

"Hello, Mrs. S-B. How is life treating you on this beautiful spring day?" Glenda Pauling, manager of Hamilton's, had seen in passing that one of her most valued customers looked down in the mouth, and she slid into a seat at the table in an effort to keep the gloom from spreading to other tables.

"Oh, all right, I suppose." Henrietta valiantly fought to keep Glenda from seeing how despondent she was.

"It was great to hear that William managed to get through the Senate confirmation so quickly for his ambassadorship. One of the youngest ambassadors ever, so I heard."

"Yes, we're happy about that. I'm sure Leonard was able to help with that."

"How many grandchildren do you have now?"

"We're up to twelve." Henrietta tried to flex her bowing hand, but her knuckles seemed to have a mind of their own; they felt like they were pounding on spikes. She picked up the cup again, but the tea had gotten too tepid to help. With a sigh, she took a deep drink, her eyes drifting back to the violin and lovingly—and painfully—tracing the elegant curves of the instrument, an instrument that could never sing for her again.

"But with that many, spread all over the world—mostly doctors, judges, and professors, aren't they?—I guess you don't see much of them."

"Oh, no, no, not as often as I would like. But they always make it home for Christmas and my birthday—and the annual July 4th family reunion . . . and usually for Thanksgiving." She sighed heavily, still staring deeply at her cherished instrument.

"Oh, that's wonderful. I haven't seen my son for more than a year, and he lives just across town." Glenda saw trouble brewing at the serving cart and rose to swing into damage control of a more immediate nature. In parting, she remembered to add, "Oh. We bought your recording of the *Messiah* the other day. Your alto solos were gorgeous. And the National Symphony gave them such a full and rich backing."

"Thank you," Henrietta managed. "I had really wanted to play in the violin section, of course, but—" But Glenda was gone, to be replaced by the waiter, who had noticed that Henrietta's tea had gone cold and who busily brought on a new pot of hot liquid.

"Let me replace that with hot tea, Professor Stowe-Byrd."

"Thank you, Clive. Here, let me hold it a while. Oh, that feels so good."

"I wanted to tell you how much I'd enjoyed your lecture on the Incas, Professor. I try never to miss your lectures, even when I've been scheduled to work. You make history so interesting."

Perhaps Henrietta hadn't heard him, because her response was somewhat distracted. Her attention once more was on her violin. Her hands had regained some of their natural flexibility and the pain had reached a tolerable level, so she reached over and plucked a couple of strings. The sweetness of the tones her stroking produced went straight to her heart like the stab of a dagger.

"Miss Stowe, Miss Stowe, it's so good to see you on the Mall. I'm surprised you are out and about without a scarf, dark sunglasses, and a bulky raincoat. Don't you know there's a mob of readers roaming around and looking for you?" Laura Grace from the bookstore across the Mall and Renata from the art gallery next door had seen Henrietta at Hamilton's and had raced over to greet her.

"Your latest novel is jumping off our shelves like hotcakes," Laura Grace said. "I think I can smell a Pulitzer."

"You think so?" Henrietta asked, only half listening. "I doubt it; I don't think you can get two Pulitzers in the same category."

"Good news from the gallery too," Renata chirped in. "The watercolor you commissioned to us last week went yesterday for five figures. Can't we convince you to do an exhibition with us?"

Henrietta smiled wanly, but the two could quickly see that she was despondent about something, and not wanting to get on her bad side, they quickly said their farewells and drifted back across the Mall.

"Amala," Henrietta said with surprise as she looked up. "What are you doing at the Mall this afternoon?"

"Oh, hello, Mrs. Stowe-Byrd. I came down to pick my husband up from work. I saw Mrs. Potter-Hanson over there at that table and thought I'd ask if she wanted me to bring anything out to Keswick Hill tomorrow morning. I love going by Rivanna's Rest when I go out to the Hill, by the way. You keep the pastures so pretty, and the new white paint on those miles and miles of fences make the area look just like a picture postcard. Oh, and I saw Chester's Chase out in your pasture this afternoon. Congratulations on winning the Preakness last year. Some are saying this may be the year for a triple crown."

"Oh, I don't really have anything to do with the race horses. That's Leonard's hobby. I just stand in the winner's circle with him to give my support like a good senator's wife should. I can't ride the horses. My hands, you know. You can't ride horses and keep the touch for the violin. But I suppose I could learn to ride now."

This brought tears to Henrietta's eyes, and she ran her fingers along the violin's strings.

"Amala, I'm glad you're here. I have something I would like to discusses with— Oh, hello, Henri. I didn't see you sitting over here." Elizabeth Potter-Hanson sank into a chair at Henrietta's table and motioned for Amala to sit as well.

"Hello, Lizzi," Henrietta sniffed. At last someone she could share her grief with. She turned to her friend and neighbor and prepared to throw open the floodgates.

"Meant to tell you I thought that movie about your life was tastefully done, Henri. Meryl Streep is a chameleon. I could have sworn it really was you. Something to talk to the young ladies about when you give the commencement address up at Bryn Mawr in June."

"Oh, Lizzie," Henrietta cried. "I can't play the violin any more. Look at these hands. I'm crippled with arthritis. My life is over. Too soon, too soon. Did you hear me? My hands won't play the violin ever again."

"Good, God, Henri," Elizabeth snorted. "You are eighty-seven years old. Things are bound to start shriveling up and dropping off eventually. Get a grip. If I can even feel my hands when I'm your age, I'll shout Hallelujah."

Henrietta gave one final sniff, reached over and lovingly closed her violin case, turned to the waiter, and said. "Clive, do you think you could find a slug of brandy to go with this cold tea?"

The Appointment

"What a madhouse. It's been one of those days."

"What's the problem, Rafael? It's not threatening to rain and the temperature is good. It didn't seem to me to be 'one of those days.' It seemed like one of those rare days on the Downtown Mall on which you almost wouldn't have to pay me to wait tables out at the outdoor café. Enough customers that the time goes by quickly and everyone feels good enough to think more in terms of 20 percent than 10. You getting stiffed for tips or something? Here, put your tray down over here and put your feet up. We're off duty now."

"No, I agree both the weather and the tips have been great. Today, it's been the customers themselves. There's that raucous crowd at the east end of the café that's been there for more than an hour already and keeps ordering drips and dregs of this and that, and playing some sort of game with the people out on the Mall. Putting their bill together is going to be one big headache—someone else's, I'm happy to say, because they outlasted me. I don't expect a big tip from that group. And there were a man and boy that were so tense and withdrawn in themselves that I couldn't get their attention to get an order—and the same with an old couple near the entrance to the café. Fighting like cats and dogs until they were joined by a younger woman, and now the three of them are all tears and hugging each other. As I say, tough day for just getting the order, delivering the goods, and getting the check paid for. I don't know how much more of this waitering I can take. I'm getting too old for this."

"So, where are you off to now?"

The Appointment

"Nowhere, at least until my wife gets here to pick me up. She's taking me to class and then she'll go on out to pick the kids up for their afternoon activities. Glad she could get the day off today. A lot of work at home to catch up with. Hope Gus doesn't mind if I take one of the empty back booths and study until she gets here."

"How much longer to go before you finish?"

"Just two more years. Then there will be the residency."

"What's that? Four years of undergraduate, four years of med school, and then a couple of years of residency? That's a big chunk of your life. I couldn't lose that much time—and sleep—myself. But I'm sure it will be worth it in the end. Dr. Serrano. Doctor Rafael Serrano. It has a good ring to it. But for now the studies must really be tough, especially with having to hold down a full-time job and raise a family."

"Not as tough the second time around."

☙ ❧

"Doctor Serrano" indeed had sounded quite good. And Rafael had felt proud to be addressed by that name for several years back in Santa Rosa, where he had completed his medical school and started a practice and a family. His family had found itself on the wrong side of a coup attempt more than a decade ago, however, and Rafael had fled Guatemala, and his wife and children had gone into hiding.

Rafael had had little trouble entering the States at Galveston, Texas, as a political refugee, especially since he had a few relatives in California already. His intent was to start up his practice again in the United States and then to send for his family. But he quickly learned that his medical degree had no standing here and that there was much more involved in becoming a citizen of the United States than just having a professional skill and a desire to leave volatile living conditions behind. He had found a job at a pharmaceutical plant in Galveston, which was quite pleased to have a trained medical doctor on line balancing formulas for prescription pills at less than minimum wage.

Eventually, Rafael was able to send for his family, and his wife, who had been a registered nurse in Guatemala, was able to find domestic work up in Austin, where her husband began his climb through the university system again to regain his credentials for his profession. After completing another undergraduate degree, Rafael moved his family first to Birmingham, Alabama, and then to Raleigh, North Carolina, where he worked as a salesman for the Galveston-based pharmaceutical company. His goal was Charlottesville, which had a good medical school at the University of Virginia. There had been no drug sales position in Central Virginia, however, so, upon being accepted at UVA's medical school, Rafael had had to make a leap of faith and take a lesser-paying job that would permit him time to study while supplementing what his wife could make as a maid.

Simultaneously with Rafael's journey back up the academic ladder, the whole family continued a sometimes even more treacherous journey through the hoops of the U.S. Immigration Service en route to U.S. citizenship.

ଓ ଚ

"You must really have thought UVA had the best medical school for you, or you wouldn't have been so focused on getting to Charlottesville," said Rafael's fellow waiter.

But before Rafael could respond to this, the day manger of the Hardware Store Restaurant wafted by and saw them.

"I see you're not wearing the standard shirt yet, Rafael. Thought I'd told you we all had to wear green polos. You're always wearing that white T-shirt with the flag emblem over the pocket."

"Sorry, I'll try to remember to wear the green tomorrow. But can I still wear a flag emblem?"

"Really stuck on this patriotism thing, aren't we Rafael? OK, you can wear a U.S. flag emblem, but keep it small, will you? Some of our patrons get upset at this rah, rah patriotism stuff. We try to stay as neutral as possible."

Rafael looked a little perplexed, not at all sure who could take offense at displaying the American flag, especially in a town as connected with the founding of the country as Charlottesville was. If he lived in the States for the rest of his life, which he fully intended to do, he would never be able to figure out how

The Appointment

North Americans viewed all of these freedoms they took so much for granted.

"You didn't get to answer why you thought the UVA medical school was so important that you had to study here," Rafael's colleague said after the manager had passed by.

"Oh, it wasn't the University of Virginia that brought me here," Rafael answered. "It's a great school and I'm glad it's here, but we had to be here now because of the ceremony."

"The ceremony. What ceremony?"

"The one up at Thomas Jefferson's home, Monticello."

Rafael's friend looked even more confused.

"The citizenship ceremony on the 4th of July. We've worked so hard for our citizenship that we want it to mean something. So we set the goal of receiving our U.S. citizenship up at President Jefferson's Monticello, and here we are. We have a very important appointment this July 4th. Soon after that, I'll have completed my medical degree as well, and we can pick up our lives where we lost them in Guatemala more than a decade ago—but now we'll be in paradise, in freedom."

"Rafael, Rafael, there you are. The manager said I could find you back here."

"Amala. You've come. Good, I can stop off at the library before my class. Tom, this is my wife, Amala. Amala, this is Tom."

"Hello, Tom. Oh Rafael, I have such wonderful news. You know how I told you I was tired of all this moving to new places but that I had no idea where we could settle down? Well, Rafael, I think it may be here. I've just seen Mrs. Potter-Hanson, and she's asked that we move into the south wing out at Keswick Hill. She says she has come to realize that she is too old to live independently but she doesn't want to move into a retirement home yet. She's asked if I'll become her personal assistant and companion—more like a niece the way she described it—and says she'll help get your practice started when you finish school and won't mind the kids treating the house just like their own."

Rafael looked obstinate and not particularly pleased. "I promised you that when I got my medical credentials in order that we wouldn't work like this ever again. This is America, and here someone from Guatemala is just as good as the Virginia blue bloods like Mrs. P-H."

"Oh, no, it's not like that, Rafael. I think I've told it all wrong, and whoever told you Mrs. Potter-Hanson was a Virginia blueblood? She isn't half as aristocratic as your own mother. You should have seen her. She almost made me cry. She said that family had always been very important to her and that she now had lost all of hers. She didn't ask us to move in as servants, Rafael. Why, she showed me books that she'd already bought for our children. She's obviously given this some thought. She said that everything she had was of no importance to her—that all she could hope for now was to somehow regain a sense of family. And Rafael, that's exactly how I feel—and have felt ever since you sent for us. America is wonderful, but our family roots are in Guatemala. We have each other, of course, but I've felt so isolated—at least until I started working out at Keswick Hill. I've grown close to Mrs. Potter-Hanson over the past two years. She's been more like an auntie to me than an employer. Rafael, she and I want the same thing. We want to be family, and she doesn't have a great deal of time left. She's a good woman, and she deserves to die with a family around her. I think we're home now, Rafael. I can feel it. It's not just keeping an appointment for a ceremony and receiving some citizenship papers anymore."

Rafael sighed and picked up his textbook. There was so much to learn about being an American. "You need to get me to the University now. We'll take the kids out to Keswick Hill this evening and see how they like the house."

Honor Violation

Gail had been afraid of receiving the call for more than a month now. The semester was coming to a close and she knew she wasn't doing well. When the call did come, though, it still shocked her. Not only was she to meet with Professor Tremple directly, rather than with one of his graduate assistants, but he wanted to meet her at the Mudhouse on the Downtown Mall for coffee rather than in his office at the University.

She was expecting the worst when she arrived several minutes late at the Mudhouse. But Professor Tremple was there, at one of the outside tables, all smiles and complimentary about how she looked.

"I thought we'd meet here today, Ms. Joyner. It's so much more conducive to a good chat than my office at the University, and the department is in an uproar at the moment—all my fault, I'm sorry to say."

"Listen, I'm so sorry I haven't been doing well this semester, Professor Tremple. The concepts just seem to be getting so much harder. I guess even the name 'molecular biology' makes me feel inadequate. That must be why I saved this course for last."

"Nonsense, My Dear. You are doing fine. Grades don't really show the underlying talent at this level. I can tell that you really have a knack for this subject. Would you like a latte?"

"You can? You mean B's and C's in a graduate-level class don't—?"

The professor waved the menu card in front of Gail's face and gave her a shy boyish smile. "Latte, or would you prefer something else?"

"Oh, yes, of course, that's fine." The professor went for the coffees, leaving Gail to agonize over what kind of academic trouble she was in. She found that it was warmer out on the Downtown Mall than she had thought it would be, so she started pulling her arms out of her sweater.

Returning to the table, Professor Tremple quickly put the coffee cups down, helped her untangle herself, draped the sweater over the back of the chair, and slipped back into his own seat. Under the sweater she was wearing a sleeveless, scoop-necked sundress. A locket on a gold chain was half hidden in the folds of her ample cleavage.

"What a charming locket. Is that cloisonné?"

"Yes, yes it is. My father brought it back to me from a recent business trip to Hong Kong."

"Oh, I would have thought it was from some love-sick young man. You must have simply droves of boyfriends."

"Not really. I really can't manage both boyfriends and studies at the same time, and, as I was saying, this molecular biology seems—"

"Yes, well, I'm happy to see you haven't done what some of the others did. It shows that you really have character. That and your obvious high intelligence show that I'm making the right decision."

"Excuse me? What do you mean that I haven't done something others have, and what decision? I'm so confused. I guess I'm just very nervous meeting you today and all. It's such a big class. I was sure you didn't see me as anything other than that ditz who sits in the second row with that question mark written all over her face."

"Not at all. Not at all. As I said earlier, the department's in quite an uproar, and I have had to make some quick adjustments, and that's what I wanted to talk to you about today." He paused, took a sip of his coffee, and then brought the cup back up to his nose and took a sniff. He then lifted his head and scented the wind. "What *is* that luscious smell? It can't be the coffee. Something delightful and exotic."

"Oh, that must be my perfume. I was in such a hurry to get over here, I'm afraid more of it went on than I had intended. It's called Passion." Gail blushed a bit right after she had given the name. She hadn't given it a thought before blurting it out that the name was a bit racy, and she hoped she hadn't offended her professor. He was such a refined old-world type of gentleman.

"Very nice. Very nice, indeed. As I was saying, I have had to let Doug go as graduate assistant for the molecular biology class, and I have decided—"

"Let Doug go? Whatever for?"

"Honor violation. It's a pity, but it had to be done. I caught him selling papers from last year's class to a couple of the students in this year's class. I've had to turn them all over to the University's Honor Committee. I may not have noticed, but one of the papers was by one of the most brilliant students I've ever had—Rafael Serrano. No one else in my classes this year could have made the connections and reached the conclusions that Rafael made. The student who tried to turn in a slight rework of that is also very smart—in fact he is, or *was*, one of my graduate assistants as well—but he's no Rafael. Mores the pity, because Brad Potter showed such great promise. Just learned that he was awarded a Rhodes scholarship too. This will end all of that, of course."

"Oh, how terrible!" Gail exclaimed. "I hadn't heard anything about all this."

"No, you wouldn't have. I just this morning turned the case over to the Honor Committee. Mr. Potter doesn't even know anything about it yet. Of course, he, Doug, and the other students will all have to leave the University. I just don't know what the honor system here at the University is coming to these days. Today's students just don't know how to comport themselves with integrity and dignity anymore. All the morals of goats. Why, in my day, no one at this university would be so dishonorable. Anyway, My Dear—here a strand of your hair has fallen into your face. Let me fix that. There, that's better—anyway, the reason I wanted to talk to you today is that there are a couple of graduate assistantships on offer now, and I thought I'd just get those pinned down before they get swept up in the controversy of the honor violation case."

171

"Yes, I can see that. Who will be the graduate assistant for the molecular biology class now? I guess I will have to contact them right away for some special help if I'm going to make it through the semester."

"It's you, you silly goose. I assumed you knew you would be up for the post if it became available. As I said earlier, I think you have just the talents for it."

"Me? But, I really don't even understand the topic well enough for my own—"

"Tut, tut, no more false modesty now. So, you'll take the offer, will you?"

"Well, I guess I could. . . . But I really don't—"

"Good then, it's settled. And since the semester is almost over, we'll need to get together right away to put the papers back on schedule. Right away. Can I assume you are free this evening? At my house, say for a little supper at 7:00, and we'll get right to it afterward? Do you prefer white or red wine? I can't concentrate on class schedules without a little fortification myself."

"Tonight? But I wouldn't want to impose on your wife that way. Maybe tomorrow in your office after my morning class is over?"

"No, no, not a bit of it. You'll be no imposition at all. My wife won't even be able to be there tonight. She's gone to her sister's for the next couple of weeks. Always on the fly; hasn't bothered with my needs for years. There'll be no distraction there, unlike at my office—and with this disgraceful honor violation business, there'll be no peace at the office for some time. Let's say 7:00 then, for sure, shall we? Here, that naughty strand of hair is at it again. Let me just fix that for you. There, *very* nice."

The Favor

"Doing you a favor? You must be joking. Judge Hawley hasn't done us a so-called favor since 1983, when he recommended that color-blind interior decorator to us. He just wants to unload some unwanted friends of friends on us. He said they were from South Carolina. They're probably something out of a Snuffy Smith cartoon." *What a weak toad you are.*

"Please promise that you'll be nice to them, Tessa. I have to stay on the judge's good side. I need all the goodwill I can get from him on this sticky murder trial that's coming up. He just asked that we take them for a round of golf—and maybe to dinner. He wasn't real clear on whether that was needed. He has to be at the dedication over at the Paramount Theater at dinnertime. And, the decorator wasn't really color blind; she was just a little more adventuresome with the palette than your Glenmore friends are."

"Dinner? You didn't say anything about dinner. If these people are anything like I suspect they are, Tyler, I'll be developing a splitting headache and will have to leave the course by the sixth hole. And don't say anything derogatory about my friends in Glenmore. If we didn't have such a nice gated community and golf course out there, your good friend Judge Hawley wouldn't be doing you this big favor. What was the favor part of this anyway?"

"He said something about how we might get a couple of passes to the next U.S. Open, and then he laughed."

"I'll just bet he did." *You are* such *an idiot. If you hadn't been born filthy rich—* "And just whose idea was it to meet here at Miller's instead of someplace acceptable, like the Downtown

Photo by Stacey Evans.

The Favor

Grill or Hamilton's—or out at the Boar's Head? Bad enough to have to come down to the Downtown Mall with its afternoon crowds, but a beer joint. Really, Tyler."

"It was their idea, I believe. If they know the judge, I'm sure they are very nice people."

"Oh, yes, I'm just sure it was—and that they are just as well-bred as the judge." *A beer hall. They're probably Hal Hippo and Debbie Dirigible. And rumor has it the judge was abandoned in a gas station bathroom as a baby. Terrific. I think I feel that headache coming on right now.*

"Well, let's just look around and see if we can figure out who they might be. I have no intention of taking a seat at those rusty tables Miller's has in its outdoor area. We'll have to think of something to move them along and get this happy little foursome wrapped up as quickly and painlessly as possible. Look. There is a couple over there who look hefty enough to be them."

"Now, Tessa."

"Oh my G-a-w-d! I think it is them. They're coming this way." *Why hello, Hal and Debbie. George Hawley, I'm going to think of some way to get even for this. Smile, dammit. Get a smile going. That always helps bring on a headache. Migraine, where are you now that I need you the most?*

"Tyler? Tessa? Howdy. We're Al and Avis, George Hawley's friends."

"Yes, I'm Tyler, and this is Tessa. Welcome to Charlottesville. And what do you think of our Downtown Mall here?"

"It's just marvelous, we—

Al the plumber and Avis the second-rate rental car. How simply charming. How can I get these hicks off the Mall before any of our friends can drift by and see us slumming?

"... And we thought we'd meet here at Miller's. We've heard so much about it; it's where the Dave Matthews Band got its start, isn't it? We thought we'd just stop in here for a beer and get acquainted before the round of golf."

"As enticing as that sounds, I'm afraid that Tyler and I got our schedules a little messed up. We forgot that we have an early dinner engagement this evening. At Judge Hawley's, in fact. We have time for the round of golf out at our club, of course, but we really don't have time for drinks before. And such a pity. I really do like Mr. Matthews's, ah——? Yes, he's very good, so I hear."

A slight hesitation and then Al responded: "Oh, that's perfectly fine. Well, lead on to the links, as they say."

Whew. Dodged that nasty little scenario. If I must die of boredom and embarrassment, do let it be out on the golf greens rather than here on the Downtown Mall. I do hope we're taking separate cars. I just got the upholstery in the Jag cleaned. It looks like Little Debbie has brought along a supply of moonpies in that satchel of hers.

○ﾟ ○

"What a beautiful golf course you have out here where you live. If I lived here, I'd be out every morning. And that's probably just what I need to do. Oh, I hope you don't mind. I'm just a beginner. I haven't started learning to hit off the ground yet. I'll have to tee up all my balls on the fairway."

"Oh, no problem, Avis. We're just playing a friendly round today."

Oh, G-a-w-d! I think I'm going to cry. Please, please, please don't put any of my friends out there on the fairways today. Harley had said he might break away from Phoebe if he could—and if I could give Tyler the brush this afternoon—but, please don't let him come looking for me with these bumpkins hanging off my golf cart. If I can just hold out on my migraine until the sixth hole, Tyler, honey, you are going to owe me one humongous diamond bracelet for this favor of the judge's. Oh, look, Tubby Al is going to tee up. Hope the seams in those pants hold. Are you sure you want to take the back tees?

Al Scranton placed the ball at the back of the tee area, straightened up, took a look down the hole one fairway, addressed the ball, and whacked a drive that went up, up, straight as an arrow, and landed what seemed to be several miles away in the middle of the fairway, just shy of the green.

Good G-a-w-d. He must be beside himself with the luck of that one.

Al's shot flustered Tyler a good bit, and, overcompensating on his first swing, he ended up in the rough, far to the right, and short of his usual shot on this hole.

Avis went next. She did a good bit of nervous swinging before finally addressing her ball, and it was all Tessa could do to keep herself from sniggering. When Avis finally hit the ball, though, it too went high and far, landing short, but a very respectable short, of her husband's ball.

Tessa was absolutely livid at the beginner's luck that had graced her guests on the first hole, and she, like her husband, took her frustration out on her own shot, only to find a bunker less than a third of the way down the fairway, where no one else had put a ball since the course had been dedicated.

By the fourth hole, it had become obvious that this was no beginner's luck the duo of Al and Avis were having. Although she, indeed, was teeing up all of her fairway shots, Avis had obviously lied about her golf prowess, and Tessa had become just angry enough to tackle the woman on that point.

"Oh, yes," Avis responded with an open smile. "I've only been playing off and on for a couple of years. I've learned mostly by watching. That's where Al and I met was on a golf course. I was doing some caddying, and I met him when I substituted for his regular caddy. It looked like fun, so after we were married, I started taking it up myself."

By the sixth hole, Tessa's headache had appeared just as scheduled, if not quite in the context she had expected. But Al and Tyler seemed to be getting along together quite well. Tyler had relaxed his swing and had stopped trying to match Al stroke for stroke and thus was doing a lot better than he had when he started. In fact, he was doing a lot better than he normally did; having a natural golfer in the foursome was helping his game.

"Tessa, Al was just telling me that he and Avis met at the U.S. Open a couple of years ago."

"So, I've heard." *Was he a caddy too? A great love story. "I met my match—in tonnage—in the caddy shack." Wait, that's not what she told me.* "Excuse me. That's not what Avis told me. She said she'd first met Al when she caddied for him."

"Yes, that's right," said Avis. "Al was on the pro circuit that year and was playing in the U.S. Open. Did real well too. He's the pro at a couple of the courses down at Myrtle Beach. Well, actually, we own a couple of courses down there, and he serves as the pro to help bring the business in."

"Oh." *So that's what the judge meant about a favor and about passes to the U.S. Open. Think fast, Tessa. There's plenty of beer in the bar fridge and we've got chip and dip.* "What a wonderful 'how we met' story. You must send it into Ann Landers. I'd love to hear more. We live right on the course near the eighteenth hole. We'll all have to go over there after we finish and have some drinks and get better acquainted."

"Oh, that does sound nice. But Al and I'll have to go right back to our suite at the Boar's Head Inn and clean up after we finish here. You see, we've been invited to go to some sort of theater dedication with George Hawley and then to dinner with him at the Metropolitan."

"But, I said *we* were having dinner at … Oh."

A Matter of Weight

The queen had ruled the space in front of Bagby's delicatessen at the eastern end of the Downtown Mall for more than two years. But now she had been, ah . . . , a bit indiscreet, and it looked like her reign was about to come to an end. Having permanent pets roaming around on the Mall was, of course, against city ordinances in the strictest sense, but up until now no one had applied that rule to the Queen of Sheba. All in all, Charlottesville was much more tolerant than most towns, likely because of the spirit of our third president, which watched over the delightful little city from its nearby perch at Monticello. No one knew where the quite regal-looking and acting mixed Persian and Siamese had come from. But suddenly, with no particular decision having been made by anyone, not even by the queen herself, who was quite prepared to make any necessary decisions, Sheba had become an official accepted permanent resident—royal patron, to be more precise—of the Downtown Mall.

What went for the queen, however, did not go for any princes and princesses, and right at the moment Sheba found that she had more than her share of those.

"Beats me how such a sleek, elegant feline could have a litter of six at one time," said Bagby's manager, Reza Mustafa, when Officer Bob Shifflett made his unavoidable appearance on the scene. "We'd prearranged homes for three, but we had no idea that Sheba was going to be so productive. I'm not sure how we're going to place the other three by this evening. I'm somewhat surprised that the three families we recruited to take kittens didn't back out. As finicky as the queen has been with what we feed her and with her personal hygiene, it beats me how indiscriminate she was with her choice of husbands."

"Oh, I don't know," Officer Bob said. "They all look pretty presentable to me. At least they're all healthy."

"Yes, but the Persian-Siamese mix worked out so well with Sheba that we'd assumed she'd want to continue those bloodlines. Some of these are going to turn out pure alley cat."

"If some of them are allowed to turn out at all," said Officer Bob, as he brought the conversation around to the inevitable reason for his visit. "I don't want to be hard hearted about it, Reza, but you know I could get into trouble just for bending the rules for Sheba. If one of the city council people gets a notion of Sheba's productive possibilities, she might be banned from the Mall as well. You've gotten an extension as it is. Come five o'clock tonight, whatever kits haven't disappeared to owners living away from the Mall by then will disappear another way, I'm afraid."

"I know, Bob," a glum Reza replied. "The rule's a good one, I know, and I know you've been great about Sheba and about her little mishap. I just don't know what we can do before five."

The Queen of Sheba quite evidently was well versed in human speak, because her response to this question was to pull her three remaining kits into a corner of the box beside the cash register and give her rebelling human servants an impervious, disapproving stare.

ଘ ଙ

Peggy Danner noticed the woman immediately when she pulled into the piano store next to the vets in her search for piano music that Teddy McAdams couldn't butcher in the fall recital. The woman was just sitting over there in a beat-up old Chevy station wagon and quietly crying. She was staring straight ahead into space, not at anything in particular, with the tears just rolling down her face.

Peggy was somewhat embarrassed. Embarrassed for the woman for such a public display of emotion and embarrassed at herself for having inadvertently intruded on whatever was causing the woman to grieve. Averting her eyes as best she could, Peggy entered the piano store and went about her business.

The business of finding something with a tune that was within Teddy McAdams's grasp took quite a bit longer than Peggy had anticipated. When she had found something that just might do—that would, in fact, just have to do—she came back out into the parking lot and was surprised, and very concerned, to find that the woman was still there, still staring off into space, still drenched in quiet tears.

Peggy couldn't go home and just leave this the way it was; she knew if she did that it would eat away at her for days. So, she slowly walked over to the car, keeping herself within the woman's field of vision so that the approach would not come as a surprise and to give the woman some chance to pull herself together before being approached by a stranger.

"Excuse me, I'm sorry to intrude. But I couldn't help seeing that you were in some distress over here and I wondered if you needed help with anything."

"No, thank you," the woman said in a small voice. "Thank you for offering, but I'll build up to it myself pretty soon."

Build up to what? I haven't gotten myself into a suicide attempt situation, have I? Peggy looked around inside the car, hoping beyond hope that she wouldn't see a firearm of any sort. She didn't. All she saw was a big old dog, laying down on the front seat next to the woman. The woman was stroking the dog with one of her hands and the dog was looking up at her with sad and trusting eyes.

"Oh, I didn't see the dog," Peggy said, as she involuntarily took a short step backward.

"He'll do you no harm," the woman answered. "Too old and sick for that. And he always was a friendly dog anyway. Good old Charlie. So good with the children." Her voice trailed off at that, and her eyes glazed over with tears again.

"I'm sorry," Peggy responded. "Are you sure I can't do anything for you? Are you unable to take your dog into the vets over there by yourself? Can I help with that?"

"I guess that's the problem, all right," the woman said. "He isn't all that heavy anymore, but I guess I just can't face up to that short trip into the vets."

All of a sudden Peggy knew what the problem was. *Oh, Lord, give me strength. I don't know if I can help with this.* And the Lord did give Peggy strength.

The woman dissolved into tears again and brought both hands up to her face to try to shield her grief. The old dog, sensing his mistress's distress, tried to get up and come to her, but he just couldn't manage the effort. Peggy opened the car door and knelt down to where she could cradle the woman in her arms.

"I understand," she said, after a moment. "Are you expected at the vets?"

The woman nodded.

"Would you ... would you like for me to take Charlie into the vets for you and to sit with him?"

The woman looked up with imploring eyes. "You'd do that? You'd do that for a complete stranger?"

"Of course I would," Peggy said with far more assurance than she felt at that moment. *O Lord, please help.* And the strength came to her to carry through with her offer.

"A family friend once offered that help for a member of our family, our Siamese cat, Siam, when his time came, and I'll never forget what he did for us. I'd be happy to be able to do that service for Charlie."

An hour later, when Peggy had sat, holding Charlie's paw to the end, she came back to the woman in the beat-up old Chevy and sat and talked with her about how their separate pets had fit into and enriched their family's lives. After a while, Peggy asked if she might drive the woman over to the Downtown Mall for a cup of coffee, and, to her surprise and delight, the woman had accepted. Peggy knew that she had found a new friend, one with whom she would have a special bond for years to come. This had been quite a day for her. She had had the call and she had responded. Up to now, she'd always been a little hazy on how she'd handle such a call.

☙ ❧

A Matter of Weight

Peggy Danner and her new friend, Susan Strang, were sitting at The Nook's open-air café, working on their second cup of coffee. Susan was looking a lot less pale now and had even managed a weak laugh when describing one of Charlie's antics at a long-ago family Christmas. Peggy was pretty sure it would be safe for her to take Susan back to her car soon.

"I don't know how I can ever thank you enough for this," Susan said. "It's not just taking care of Charlie like that—I just couldn't face anything final, although I didn't want him to suffer any more just because I wasn't ready to let go. But by making me talk about the past and all that he had meant to my family . . . I don't know; it just seems to help, to help a lot. And coming here for coffee. I just couldn't face going home alone to an empty house. The kids are all gone now. The husband's even gone. It's going to be very quiet without Charlie."

"Maybe you need to get a new Charlie right away."

"Oh, I don't know about that. Maybe someday. Maybe another pet someday. But a dog the size of Charlie was pretty much to keep up with. I just don't know."

As she said that, however, Susan felt something wet against her hand. When she looked down, there was the Queen of Sheba. And not just the Queen of Sheba. She had a kit in her mouth that she was trying to hike up onto Susan's lap. Susan looked down at the kitten and found herself helping the queen get the kitten settled on her lap.

"Looks like maybe your plans are being made for you. That is, if you like cats," Peggy offered up with tentative encouragement.

Susan looked down at the kitten and then at the Queen of Sheba, who was staring intently into her eyes. Their eyes locked, and a current of understanding surged between them.

"Oh, I so sorry, Miss," Reza Mustafa called out, as he approached. "Sheba, what are you up to? I hope you're not allergic to cats, Miss. Here, I'll just take that kitten back to the store."

"Is this kitten spoken for?" Susan asked. "Is this yours?"

"No," Reza laughed. "I guess this kitten isn't anyone's but Sheba's. She has her own ideas about who's in charge here. No, the kitten isn't spoken for, and I'm afraid I do need to place it before five this afternoon."

"Well, I guess you can consider it placed, then," Susan said, her eyes dancing with joy for the first time in weeks. "Oh, but what's this?"

The Queen of Sheba had returned, this time with her two remaining princesses, and was working on adding the burden to Susan's lap.

"No, Sheba. Bad cat," Reza admonished. "This is just too much."

"It is, isn't it?" said Peggy, her voice tinged with a mix of regret and hope.

Susan looked down at the squirming mass on her lap and gave the situation a good ponder. "Well I don't know. Charlie weighed a good sixty pounds, and I guess I managed that much weight in a pet pretty well. These kits can't weigh more than a tenth of that altogether. I guess on the weight scale, I'll still be well ahead of the game."

Save the Children

Officer Bob Shifflett attempted to saunter around the 3d Street corner at the Commonwealth Bookstore and onto the Downtown Mall as inconspicuously as possible. This wasn't easy for a heavily muscled, 250-pound, red-haired mountain of a man stuffed into a police uniform to pull off. It was important that he not make a spectacle of himself or cause anyone to panic. But he was no actor and he was sweating profusely from the exertion of not appearing to be concerned or on a mission. He was both.

    The telephone call had been chilling, and he was the first to be able to make it to the scene. He had to remember not to pull his gun—at least not until he had to.

    They had to be here somewhere, somewhere close. Their normal haunts ran from the east down near Chaps, the ice cream parlor, all the way to the Ice Park at the west end of the bricked walking street. He looked east. The Hardware Store Restaurant was packed, mostly with that group of twenty-somethings who spent their evenings at Miller's. There seemed to be a bit of a commotion there with a middle-aged couple and a young woman, but he didn't have time for that now. Further up, in front of the Mole Hole, there was a woman walking around erratically, well-dressed but something wrong with what she was wearing—but right now he didn't want to know what *that* might be about. Ah, another woman had met up with her and she seemed to have calmed down. What he was looking for wasn't in that direction.

    He eased out into the center of the walking mall, using the false columns and palm trees marking the boundaries of Sal's outdoor café as a shield between him and the Central Place. The plaza. That was the most likely place where they'd be hanging out.

Sure enough, now he spotted who he knew would be here, who he had known would have to be at the center of the shocking call they had received on 911. There were two of them there, sitting on the steps beside the central fountain in the plaza, so deep into conversation with each other that Officer Shifflett was sure now that he would be able to approach without alarming them. He had known that the "Save the Children" campaign the mayor and new chief of police had instituted just wasn't going to work. *You just can't coddle kids who let themselves get this screwed up. Where are the parents in these cases? Letting their freaky kids just come down and spend all day hassling other people on the Mall and looking like something out of a zombie movie.*

He was there; the one they called Maggot. *Maggot! Got that right. Something from the bottom of a coffin.* Tall but emaciated thin, with all-black clothes, a skin pallor that must have been enhanced with Halloween makeup, tattoos, every imaginable body part pierced and bristling with chain jewelry, and a teased-up Mohawk haircut that started green in front, turned to orange on top, and ended with a blue pigtail down the back.

Boot camp, that's what that kid needs. Just three weeks with a good drill instructor out in the boonies. But, no, what he's gotten was a "it's just a stage," and "they're not really hurting anyone," and "we just have to relate to them through this 'Save the Children' public campaign and then we'll all be best of friends." True, there's been fewer incidents and complaints since the campaign had a little time to take hold, but there have been some, like this Maggot kid, who have remained hard cases.

Well, all their goody, goody "let's just be friends" stuff is up in smoke now. The phone call had been what they'd all been dreading. A call that some kid down on the Mall was talking about going into his school and blowing everyone away; getting rid of all those other students who had been making fun of him.

Everyone's been saying that couldn't happen here in Charlottesville, but that's what all those other communities told themselves too. Well, it's hard not making fun of what you chose to do to yourself, Maggot, my boy. The police chief was all smiles and public relations announcements last week about how well this "Save the Children" campaign was working. Guess this will change those press releases.

Officer Bob circled around the street vendor tables at the south side of the plaza, trying to get closer to the two boys on the steps before it became obvious he was interested in them. He was glad the fountain was on; he could get pretty close while still being just a blur of blue through the cascading water from where they sat. The relations between these Goths and the policemen on the Downtown Mall beat had once been so bad that the freaks would take off running as soon as a blue suit came in sight. That was at least one good thing the public relations campaign was doing for him. Now the kids knew the police were under instructions not to hassle them, so maybe this one would stay put so that he could be collared without causing a big ruckus on the Mall.

The vendors were getting a little jittery at having a policeman nose around—their presence wasn't strictly legal either, but it had always been tolerated, if kept within bounds, because they provided a sense of spontaneity and color on the Mall that the city council seemed to think would go down well with the tourists. Officer Bob held himself in check as best he could, so that he could smooze some with the vendors and unruffle their feathers a bit. Besides, he figured it would take Maggot off guard as well if he sensed a policeman was in the area but not showing any interest in him.

What Officer Bob couldn't figure out was why Maggot was down here sounding off about blowing his classmates away at all; it was a school day. Why wasn't he in school rather than hanging around down here at the Mall? There wasn't a high school within walking distance of this place. For that matter, why was the kid who was trying to keep him occupied here and not in school? He looked more clean cut, although pretty chubby and short. The skateboard he was rolling around up and down the stairs explained *what* he was doing here. Skateboarding was also illegal on the Mall, but at least it was good exercise and was tolerated as long as the kids were careful about not coming close to the walkers. But it didn't explain *why* he wasn't in school. Oh, well, guess it's a good thing he *was* down here. Otherwise, they wouldn't have gotten that call in time to prevent another one of those tragedies that was spreading across the country like a plague.

The kid was doing fine too. He'd picked a real good spot to settle the Goth down in; lots of ways someone could come in close without being noticed. And the way the kid was rolling that skateboard around and talking softly but intensely, he was really keeping the Goth's attention. Goths weren't known for their long attention spans or for being that interested in anything. It went with the style to be blasé about everything.

Good, kid, you just keep his attention, while I come around the side of this fountain. Just a few more steps and I'll be in position.

"Whoa, guys. Where's the fire?" Both of the boys had jumped up in fright as the bulky Officer Shifflett entered, very closely into their field of vision. They were caught off guard to the point, though, that he only had to lightly lay a hand on a forearm of each of them to hold them in place.

Turning to the skateboarder, Officer Shifflett said, "Thanks, son, I'll take it from here. Shouldn't you be in school, though? Why don't you just take a hike back to school, and we won't mention anything about truancy this time."

The boy gave the police officer a sharp look, as if being disgusted that bringing up the bad in the situation was a typical adult's way of cutting him short for the service he had rendered. Then he dropped his skateboard to the brick pavement, flipped off an insolent, "Yeah, I guess I'll just do that," and shot out of the Mall up 2d Street toward Market Street.

"Aw, why'd you have to do that for, Man?" the Goth whined. "I was holding him here like forever. I sent Rosey off to call you guys. That's one crazy dude. He said he's all set to blow away the jocks who have been hazing him at his school."

"Which school?" Officer Shifflett yelled. "Where's he going?"

"Beats me. I wasn't able to get that out of him before you busted in. Hey, you thought it was me, didn't you? Ah, this is shit, Man. I thought I was doing right by you guys. This 'Save the Children' campaign of yours is just a pile of crap, isn't it? Yeah, just run away. Thanks for nothin, Man."

The Game: Three

"Did you see that cop running up the street?" Shelly asked, as she finished chugging the last of her Coke and started waving at the Garden Café waiter. "He was messing around with those kids over by the fountain, and suddenly one of the kids ran off and the cop wasn't far behind. Moves pretty fast for a man that large."

"Uh huh," responded Tiffany, as she searched around under her lettuce, looking for foreign matter. "Ah hah," she said. She speared a small piece of ham and moved it off her plate with a grimace of distaste.

"Cop? What cop, where?" Dennis said with a slight strangled sound to his voice. He had ducked his head down almost to the level of the tabletop.

"I'm glad Max is gone," Tiffany declared. "He's been such a downer ever since he started mooning over Megan. It was obvious from the beginning that she didn't have any interest in him. Why Jeff was just telling me the other night—"

"What other night?" Shelley asked as her attention refocused on her remaining tablemates. "When did Jeff talk to you the—"

"Let's continue with the story," Dennis broke in. "There are just three of us now, but we can continue with the same rules."

"Oh, all right, but it's *my* turn to pick," said Tiffany. "I haven't had a chance to pick yet."

"Yes, you have, Tiffany," Shelley declared. You were the *first* winner. Don't you remember?"

Tiffany screwed up her eyes in contemplation. It was clear she didn't remember and that she was going to take some time trying to remember.

"Oh, all right. It doesn't matter," Shelley said in exasperation. "Go ahead and take a turn."

Tiffany brightened up and looked around for a few minutes. "There, over there. You can't miss that. There's a woman with a man following along a couple of paces behind her. That woman in the red hat and mink coat and pink pedal pushers. What do you make of them?"

"Ah, das ist the Countess Kremehilde of Geschnorten and her escort," Shelley offered promptly in a broad German accent. She intended to let out all stops on this one. "And let's see. He is mad over his heels for her. He's been a security guard for one of the rich families outside town on one of the big, very private farms where the international jet setters hide out. She's got expensive tastes and he's had a hard time keeping up with her expenses. So, they've just robbed and murdered a local gem dealer and have come down on the Downtown Mall to Snooky's Pawnshop to try to hock the gems before they roar off to Europe on a jet."

"Oh, Shelley," declared Tiffany. "You're so silly. That's really far-fetched. How about you, Dennis? What sort of story do you have? Dennis? Dennis, are you OK?"

Dennis's head had sunk under the table. "That's my former wife," he managed to squeak. "Is she looking the other way? Oh good, she's marching off toward that man in the suit sitting on the bench over there. Sorry, gotta go." And, with that, Dennis backed out of the Garden Café and was gone.

"His former wife?" Tiffany asked, posing the question to no one in particular, when Dennis had slithered out of sight. "She's old enough to be his mother. That's just got to be a story for the game. Isn't it? But why'd he leave?"

"Did you think he was making his former marriage up too?" Shelley responded. "Didn't you know he was living off of older woman? Well, I'll have to admit that his story topped mine. And I was trying so hard. We can't play with just two, and it's getting pretty late." Shelley accepted her replacement Coke from the waiter and turned to Tiffany. "You can go ahead and go now. I'll take care of the check and let you all know later what you owe."

"Go?" Tiffany responded with a blank stare. "But I'm waiting for Jeff to get here. Jeff and Luis are coming. I'll stay and take care of the bill and you can go ahead and leave. I wonder if they have anything interesting for dessert here."

I'd recommend something poisonous, but you'd just pick out all of venom. "I don't know, and you're sitting on all of the menus," Shelley said, barely able to contain herself. "Any ideas on how we can remedy that?"

"We could ask the waiter for another menu," Tiffany answered brightly. "Yes, I think that's just what we should do."

The Chasm between "c" and "C"

"Not so close. I don't want anyone to think we're together. Come here. When we turn the corner onto the Mall, I want you to look down the street at the benches in front of the Kinkade Gallery. See if he's there. Remember. a blue shirt and red-striped tie. No, we can't turn the corner together. Me first. No, you first, and . . . Oh, and he said he'd have a copy of *Southern Living*. H-s-s-s-t. Do you see him?"

"Mother! You've got people looking at us. There are lots of men in blue shirts and red-striped ties. Whose idea was it that those combinations would distinguish anyone in Charlottesville? Yes, I see now. There's one on a bench in front of Kinkade's. Oh, and there's another one on another bench in front of Kinkade's. Hey, you're digging your nails in my arm. Thought you said we shouldn't be anywhere close to each other. And no need to tell me to stay away from you. I wouldn't want to be seen dead with anyone in *that* get-up."

"Well, he caught me off guard, Jamey. I didn't have time to think, and I had to tell him something I'd wear that would set me apart from all the other women."

Jamey laughed. "No contest there. I'm sure it was a safe bet that no one else would be wearing pink pedal pushers under a mink coat and a red straw hat. Trust me, though, you'd have stood out from the crowd in anything you pulled out of your closet."

"You're just mad, young man, that no one's ever thought we were mother and son. Remember that woman at the checkout counter the other day who declared that *you* looked older than I did."

"You were holding up the line, Mother. That checkout woman would have said you were a Shirley Temple look-alike just to get you moving. You led her with so many questions that she knew just what you wanted her to say."

"Pshaw. You're just envious that you got your father's genes instead of mine. And speaking of your father, I wish I had gotten sunglasses myself and didn't have to wear this pair he left behind. Can't see a thing with them. Tell me again whether any of those men over on the benches could be Mr. Blue Eyes."

"Those aren't *my* dad's glasses, Mom. Those are Dennis's glasses. You know. The third one after dad. The one with the motorcycle and the hair in his ears."

"Well, he didn't say anything about the ear hair in his e-mails," Daisy said with a sniff. "And you never really gave Dennis a chance."

"He only stayed three days after the wedding. You only knew him for *five* days *before* the wedding. I was still trying to figure out if he was older than I was and then, poof, he was gone."

"That's a lie. We'd been corresponding by e-mail for *months* before he came roaring in on the Harley and swept me off my feet. It's not my fault I'm able to make deep commitments fast. To some people that's a blessing, not a sin. And that one doesn't count as a wedding, anyway. He was already married, so ours didn't count—and I'm not really sure he was past the age of consent anyway. But, there, you keep walking in that direction. Signal if you see a man on the bench reading a *Southern Living*. There can't be many of those here on the Downtown Mall. He probably has blue eyes. Now, did I ever ask him if that was the case?"

"How I let you rope me into this, I'll never know. You know I don't like you meeting men this way. I wouldn't be here at all if you didn't need some protecting. Anyway, I think that might be him over there."

"Oh, do you think so? No, I don't think it could be him. He looks Hispanic. I don't think anyone who calls himself Mr. Blue Eyes could be Hispanic. And that man's shorter than I was told. And he should have more hair and be a little thinner."

"Ever hear of where the Nazi leaders were said to have gone at the end of World War II? I wouldn't be surprised if you found a lot of South Americans with blue eyes."

"What was that? What did you say?"

"Oh, never mind." Jamey was sure that his mother would meet a Doctor Mengele type this way one of these days, but no use provoking her here out on the Downtown Mall. There was no telling what she might do when she was in the hunt mode. "But I think it could be him. He's got a magazine. Here, I'll try to get a little closer."

As Daisy swung around to pretend like she was window-shopping at the Pear Tree Gift Shop, Jamey walked several steps toward the east end of the Mall. The man was probably in his midthirties, obviously nervous, and also obviously holding a copy of a glossy magazine. Jamey wondered whether it could be a copy of *Southern Living*. Maybe he should have asked his mother what kind of magazine *Southern Living* was before he went off on this errand.

He got close enough to tell that the magazine did seem to have something like *Southern Living* on the cover and turned toward the Pear Tree to signal his mother. But she wasn't there. He scanned the center strip of the bricked-over Downtown Mall almost in panic. There was no telling what his mother would do when she was busy trying to reel in another man. Then he caught sight of her. She had zeroed in on another man on a bench nearby, a man who was wearing the prescribed blue shirt and red-striped tie. But there was no glossy magazine. Just a thick newspaper that was mostly print, probably something like the *New York Times*. Jamey was almost sorry that wasn't the man his mother was looking for. He was very distinguished looking. Probably in his late fifties, tall, thin, graying at the temples. But with such a sad look in his eyes, and just sitting there, staring off into space, a somewhat bored expression on his face. No, Jamey was sure he wasn't the man; he didn't look like he'd even know what an Internet chatroom was.

Jamey signaled to his mother. At first as subtly as he could, but he finally had to do the whole "jet coming in for a landing on an aircraft carrier" routine before he could gain her attention from her concentrated stalking of the dapper elder gentleman. When she did look up and realized that Jamey had found her prey elsewhere, she pretended just not to know him and sauntered around the shop windows on the adjacent block of the Downtown Mall before moving back to the benches in front of the Thomas Kinkade Art Gallery. This was just fine with Jamey, as well. At times like this, he really didn't want to know his mother either.

♋ ☼

"Mr. Blue Eyes? Mr. Blue Eyes? It's me, Daisydo. We arranged to meet here?"

"Oh, excuse me? Are you talking to me? I'm sorry. What was that you said?"

"I asked if you weren't the man who went by the name 'Mr. Blue Eyes.' I had arranged to meet him here near this bench. He was going to be carrying a copy of *Southern Living*. Oh, and isn't *that* a copy of *Southern Living* on the bench beside you? Oh, my goodness. You *do* have blue eyes."

"Yes, yes, I do," the man responded with considerable embarrassment. "My father's side. They say he was German. I'm the only one of the children who got blue eyes, though."

"Do you mind if I sit down? Isn't that your magazine?"

"This? Oh, no. This was on the bench when I sat down, and I was just leafing through it. I like the articles on the houses."

"You do? I do too. Architecture is one of my favorite subjects. I'm Daisy Domant, by the way. Please excuse the way I look. As I said, I was supposed to meet someone here today and we'd agreed I'd wear something conspicuous. I'm normally not a flamboyant type of person."

As if she knew her son was listening to the conversation at a safe distance, Daisy looked up to see Jamey giving a fully animated mime and hearty laugh at her last comment. She gave him a venomous little gaze and moved her hand to behind the man's head, trying to wave her son further down the Mall. The man's blue eyes gave a scared little look, and he leaned away from Daisy.

"Just a bee," Daisy said breezily. "Shoo, shoo. There, it's gone now. Frank Lloyd Wright. He's one of my favorites. That's how I linked up with Mr. Blue Eyes. He was a fan of Wright's."

"Oh, I am too." The man leaned back into the bench again. "My name's Roger. Roger Mengel."

There was a choking noise from the near distance, and Daisy leaned forward in the bench to place her body between Roger's line of vision and where Jamey had collapsed in a pile of mirth onto a bench across the Mall.

"Falling Water," Roger continued. "And the Chicago skyscrapers. I just loved all of the early houses he designed in the Chicago suburb of Oak Park."

"Oh, yes. Just gorgeous. But I've never gotten out to either of the Taliesin complexes."

"I've been out to Taliesin West near Phoenix, but I've never been to Taliesin East in Wisconsin. Of course I'm sure you've seen the Guggenheim in New York. And have you heard about what they have down in Lakeland, Florida—?"

Daisy was enraptured. She took her red straw hat off, crossed her legs, and gave Roger her best profile, as they chatted on and on about their favorite architect.

"... and I did make it to Tokyo once, and went in search of his Imperial Hotel—the only building to have survived the carpet bombing of downtown Tokyo in the war, you know. MacArthur used it as government headquarters during the occupation. But no one had told me that they had knocked the building down some years ago. A great man, Frank Lloyd Wright."

"Well, yes, a great architect," Daisy agreed. "But not a great man, I don't think. Not hardly. Abandoned his wife with all the kids. I just couldn't see doing that. Married again, but just wanted someone to keep his schedule organized. He really wasn't committed to anything but his art, and some of that didn't last either; inadequate support; kept falling down. He never could make a commitment to another human being. I really don't understand that. I, on the other hand, am a person who makes commitments. I can make deep commitments very quickly. That's me. My mother always said I had the big 'C'— and she meant 'commitment,' not 'cancer.' No one even talked about cancer in those days. But I've been so unlucky until now. I always seem to be meeting little 'c' men. But happening upon you here like this—purely by accident—has been so wonderful. I feel like I've known you forever. Isn't this just a beautiful spot for people to meet and get to know each other?" Daisy batted her eyes at Roger and gave him that smile that had served her so well in the past.

Roger departed the Mall soon thereafter, having remembered that he had chatted with Daisy so long that he had forgotten he was supposed to meet friends for dinner. He was just passing through Charlottesville, as a matter of fact. And he wasn't settled anywhere at the moment. He was on his way to take up a new position in Omaha. No address or telephone number yet, and he'd given up his e-mail provider. But if Daisy gave him her e-mail address, he'd be sure to contact her just as soon as he was back on line in Omaha. Yes, he'd felt the connection too. Yes, he'd certainly e-mail—once he'd gotten settled in Omaha.

☙ ❧

Click Welcome to the Artlovers' Chatroom
hotlady: am gng fl and heard its architectural wasteland. help
mrblueyes: hlo hotlady. what part fl?
daisydo: mrblueys? was at Mall today as sched. where were u?
mrblueyes: n or s fl, hotlady? maybe can help.
daisydo: WHERE WERE U?
hotlady: inland tampa? can u help a lonely lady out?
mrblueyes: sure I can. will u be near lakeland?
hotlady: yes. what's to c?
mrblueyes: do u like f l wright? largest grouping of his bldgs at fl sthern colg in
lakeland. must see.
daisydo: roger? roger? that u?
hotlady: sounds good. better not to c alone. u near there? :)
mrblueyes: maybe can do. when will u be in fl? :)
daisydo: R-O-G-E-R????

197

Photo by Rick Britton.

Perspective

"Mr. Crawford, Mr. Crawford. There's an urgent call for you from over at the courthouse. Something about a Ms. Chantel Walker."

"Not now, Freddie. Take a message, and I'll call them back. I'm going to the roof for a few minutes."

"But, Mr. Crawford, your lawyer said—"

"I said not now, Freddie. I *need* to be alone for a few minutes."

"Uh, Clifford. Have you seen the morning's paper yet?"

"Not interested in talking about this morning's paper yet, Sheila. I'm going to the roof."

Nervous laughter. "You're certainly doing well, with it, I must say. Going to the roof. Quite funny."

The steel doors shut decisively between Clifford Crawford and his chaotic work world, and, with glass clinking against chilled champagne bottle, he took the refurbished elevator to the top of the building that was being reconstructed to accommodate his growing financial news service corporation (appropriately named FNS—the Financial News Service). The expansion of his chiefly dot.com financial prediction service had skyrocketed to the point that he, as CEO, had had to take the bold step of taking the firm's departments that had been spread in upper-story cubby holes all around the Charlottesville Downtown Mall and consolidating them in a reconstructed block-long segment of the Mall. He had made this decision without consulting the board of directors, which was to meet next week in its annual session. One or two of the board members were calling for his head over incurring this expense, but he knew something they didn't know. He had a financial backer, a major stockholder, who had agreed to underwrite the expense as long as he, Clifford Crawford, remained at the helm of the company. Insurance against a board of director's fight couldn't get any better than that.

The elevator reached the top, seventh floor, and the door opened onto what had once been a sky-view in-door and patio restaurant of the defunct Miller and Rhoads Department Store. This would be the executive offices. They were now located on the completed second floor. The workers were working up floor by floor and were incorporating the two buildings that shared this block fronting on the Mall, one once a photography studio and the other a women's clothing store. His architects had had to agree to keep the facades of the buildings, but other than that, the two buildings next door were being flattened. He was lucky with this building. Not only was it the most desirable location on the Mall, because it was, by far, the tallest building, with stunning views of Jefferson's home, Monticello, to the east, and the University of Virginia grounds and the Blue Ridge Mountains to the west, but it also was basically of sound construction.

He had been determined that nothing was going to ruin his day. He had gotten up early, played eighteen holes, all by himself, on the Farmington Golf Course, followed by a long massage and sauna. Just some of those perks you could expect by having bought—or at least acquired a gigantic mortgage on—the biggest house in Farmington and being CEO of a highly visible dot.com. He hadn't even read the paper, and he didn't intend to until this evening.

He had always said in his sales pitches that what you saw in life was all a matter of perspective. And from his perspective now, standing out on the patio of his expanding FNS empire and taking in one of the most gorgeous views on the planet, life was all roses. He didn't normally drink at all, but he felt today was worth a special toast, so he'd come into the office with this bottle of champagne. He'd only have one glass of it, he'd do a little inspection of how the construction up here was going, and then he'd go back down and start planning the repopulating of the chairs on his board of directors.

Perspective

"Oops a daisy," he said, as he tripped over a board while filling his glass and spilling most of the champagne. No bother, nothing was going to upset his day. He'd only wanted enough for a silent toast to his good fortune.

He had had quite a session with his beautiful wife, Janet, last night. Phone off the hook and all attention on each other. She had turned him on almost as well as his mistress, Renata, from over at the Raven Art Gallery, could. Janet had said it was a special occasion—and indeed it was—and that she'd have something important to discuss with him this evening. Bet she'd taken the hint about those diamond cuff links he'd admired at Keller and George. Quite a gal, that Janet. Steady and loyal as a rock, and devoted to him. He was one lucky man. With both Janet and Renata readily available, he had all in that department that a husband could want.

As he wandered around the developing office area, he began to wonder whether he was going to get a good view of the Downtown Mall walking street from up here. So, he put his empty glass and nearly empty champagne bottle down near the elevator door and went back out onto the open patio.

Ah, no, he could see now that there was an obstruction. He couldn't get any sort of view straight down, because the third and succeeding floors of this building were set in a bit, and most of what he could see looking down was construction debris on the top of the second-story overhang.

But looking out both east and west, he could see quite a bit of the Mall. In fact, wasn't that? Yes, he thought it was. That looked just like his wife, Janet, coming onto the Mall and walking east. He wondered what she was doing here today. She hadn't said she was coming downtown.

As Clifford watched his wife proceed up the Mall, he had to stretch out over the balustrade. There, she had stopped in front of the Mole Hole Gift Store. She had met up with someone else. Why, from the hairdo, that looked like Phoebe Stewart.

The two women talked briefly and then turned and strode toward the eastern end of the Mall. Clifford followed them with his eyes as best he could, and, unfortunately, he followed them

201

with his body as well, out further beyond the balustrade—much, much too far …

❧ ☙

Dot.com CEO's Death Ruled Market Crash Suicide

by Alfred Dunny
Daily Progress staff reporter

16 April—In the first of several adverse reactions nationwide to Monday's plunge of electronic dot.com stocks, Tuesday's death by five-floor fall from the new Financial News Service building, currently being reconstructed on the Downtown Mall, of FNS CEO Clifford Crawford, 42, has been ruled a suicide at a preliminary inquest at the Albemarle County Courthouse.
Crawford had remained in isolation all Monday evening and Tuesday morning following the announcement that the stocks of his FNS corporation, like those of most other dot.coms, had dropped over 300 points in four hours late Monday afternoon. Of particular concern to FNS, and to Crawford as CEO, was both that FNS, as a major financial reporting organization, had failed to predict the sudden drop in stock values and that FNS was involved in an expensive facilities expansion that was experiencing extreme difficulties. Crawford reportedly faced a board of director's showdown in the next week over his handling of the reconstruction project, and word had reached the FNS headquarters just prior to Crawford's death that FNS did not have clear title to the central building in the FNS construction project.

Joe Tucker, attorney for Chantel Walker, city resident, has been quoted as saying that his client owns the former Regina's women's clothing store and has previously stated her intention to halt construction of the new FNS complex. At press time, Walker was not available for comment.

A spokesperson for FNS, chief information officer Sheila Vestry, has stated that Crawford arrived at the seven-story FNS headquarters building at approximately noon and immediately went to the roof of the building. An FNS employee, Freddie Lindsay, found Crawford's body on top of a second-story setback after employees had grown concerned with Crawford's behavior and had searched the building when he was not found in the nearly complete seventh-floor executive suite. Alcohol is suspected as a factor in the death. The Crawfords had recently purchased a large home in the Farmington Country Club area with, according to neighbors, a minimal down payment.

In a bizarre twist to the story, marital difficulties may also have contributed to Crawford's despondency. His wife, Janet Crawford, has since been named as an accomplice with Mrs. Phoebe Stewart, with whom she allegedly was having an affair, in the bludgeoning death the same day of Mrs. Stewart's husband, Charlottesville businessman Harley Stewart, 45, at their Farmington home. Mrs. Crawford's lawyer has not returned this reporter's calls for more information on a possible connection between these two incidents.

He/She/Them

"Ha, ha, ha ..." wheez. "By geezit, Dr. Stargill, that was a good one." Dwight wiped at his eyes as if to erase tears of mirth and moved a step closer to the newly promoted chief of the Soviet bloc research group for the World Bank. "You know, I'd love to be able to collect Russian jokes like you have. They are just great for double entendre. I'd just die to get to our Moscow office. But I suppose there's always a long line of applicants for all the openings out there. Still, I'll bet it helps to have a degree in Russian studies from a good university, like where I went, the University of Virginia."

The statement just hung in the air, while Clayton Stargill, Ph.D., Harvard, digested something unidentifiable on a Ritz cracker that had momentarily stuck in this throat and then tossed off the last of his martini. Dwight could tell that Stargill had been almost insulted by his claim that the Russian program at UVA was top notch. Well, let him stand there preening himself over his Harvard doctorate. Dwight knew for a fact that Stargill had started out as a good old boy from Morgantown, West Virginia, and he just might use that information one of these days.

"Clayton, there you are." The man who joined them was well tanned and much pampered. "I had been waiting until the congratulatory crowd around you dissipated a bit, but that doesn't seem to be happening. I have something to discuss with you on the staffing of your new group."

The three of them stood there momentarily in a circle of strained silence, but only momentarily, as the young Dwight Pilkington quickly got the point, and with an embarrassed smile departed, weakly saying, "Oh, I think I need to refill my drink. Excuse me a moment." Although all three knew it would be a very long moment, Dr. Stargill half raised his empty martini glass as a signal that he, too, could use another drink.

Juan Perez Caldron, one of the World Bank's vice presidents, rarely bothered to cloak his thoughts. "Hitting you up for a foreign posting already, I suppose. That Dwight Pilkington will go far, but he could go far without really being noticed much, and I doubt he'll go nearly as far as he hopes he will. I wonder, on the other hand, if you've given any consideration to including that bright young woman, Claudia Videla, on the staff you're putting together for—?"

"Congratulations on your well-deserved promotion," European research chief Helmut König offered in passing. "I've got to get back to the grind. Looks like the British are going to give the EU trouble on the euro proposal. I'll be over to talk to you soon, however. We have some projects to go over that involve both of our groups."

Dr. Stargill flashed the obligatory smile and reached for a passing hors d'oeuvre tray, but missed because the waitress had not seen him. The wandering hostess for the promotion party had seen his gesture, however, and snapped her fingers fiercely. Three trays immediately descended on the party's honoree. Alas, the hostess didn't see that the new group chief's glass also was empty.

"And your budget, Clayton," Juan Perez Caldron was saying, "We need to discuss that as well. Your idea to expand operations in key republic capitals is a brilliant one. I think you are quite correct that the Soviet Union will be breaking up soon and that we should position ourselves ahead of the curve by augmenting operations in key locations. But that will require more money in your budget than your group was given, so I thought—"

"Clayton, dear, I just had to speak to you about your recent article in *Foreign Affairs*." The elegant Lu Chan, special assistant to the chief of East Asian operations, wafted in on a cloud of exotic fragrance. She rested a well-manicured hand, with its extensive collection of gigantic jeweled rings, on the forearm that supported Dr. Stargill's empty martini glass and gazed deeply into his eyes. "I think you have the makings of a wonderfully analytical and timely book. The Soviet Union on the brink of breakup. Something of that nature. As you know, I've edited several books for Dr. Fang. I would just love to collaborate with you . . . on a book." A delicate little point of a tongue escaped from a pouting mouth with thick, sensuous lips, and wetted an already sparkling crimson gloss to an even higher shine.

Juan Perez Caldron saw the little squeeze Lu Chan gave Dr. Stargill's forearm with her dazzlingly jeweled fingers, and her impossibly long fingernails directed his gaze on up the arm, where he, at last, caught sight of the empty martini glass.

He turned, and looked around the room. There she was. "Caroline. Caroline, over here. Your husband seems to be high and dry. Perhaps you could get him another martini. I'm sure you know how he likes them."

CB ED

"We'll be sorry to lose you, Clayton," Juan Perez Caldron said privately to Dr. Clayton Stargill after giving the formal toast at the latter's retirement reception. "The Soviet Union is very much a front-burner issue at the World Bank just now, and your insights into what is happening there and, more important, what the trends are, have been extremely helpful. You're a bit young to be retiring, you know."

"I appreciate that, Juan. But there's this book in me that is screaming to get out. And the situation in the Soviet Union is moving so fast that I've found it very difficult to keep ahead of events when I have only been able to snatch an hour or two here and there for writing. I've thoroughly enjoyed working with the World Bank, but I believe it's time for me to be moving on."

The Balkans research section chief, Dwight Pilkington, joined the group. "That was a very nice retirement speech, Clayton. If you compose your book half as elegantly as you speak, I think we'll have a best-seller on our hands. I understand that Nikolai Bunin is in line for your position. Is there anything you can tell me about him? I've heard he's quite smart, but that he also has some buttons one wouldn't want to push. What does he—?"

"Here, I see you've drained your glass, Clayton," Juan Perez Caldron interjected. "Excuse me, young lady, over here. Ah, I see she doesn't have a martini on her tray. Do you want to switch to something else, perhaps? No. Well, we'll have to watch for another tray of drinks, won't we. Or, I think there's a bar over there in the corner. Mrs. Stargill. Caroline. Did you perhaps see a bar over in the corner? Clayton's glass is empty. Oh, no, don't bother yourself, there don't seem to be many people pressing about him at this point. I'm sure he'd just as soon get his own refill."

Lu Chan floated in on her heady fragrance. "Such a shock that you are retiring already, Dr. Stargill. You have helped Soviet research here so much. And I hear you are leaving us for the countryside. That has such dreary connotations in my own country."

"Just down to Charlottesville," Stargill responded with a laugh. "And there's nothing dreary about Charlottesville. The location's beautiful and the research facilities are quite good. I can't concentrate nearly as well here in the Washington environment. Too frenetic; too much going on; too many people making demands on my time."

"Well, I suppose that will change," said Juan Perez Caldron.

Dr. Stargill looked a little bemused.

"But, won't that be a long commute for Dr. Stargill?" Lu Chan asked. Clayton Stargill gave her a confused look. "Excuse me, I mean for your wife, Caroline. Interesting. Two Dr. Stargills working for the same organization."

"Well, Charlottesville is only a bit over two hours away, but Caroline thinks she'll keep the apartment here in Foggy Bottom for a while. She'll be a bit busier at work now."

"Yes, she certainly will be," Dwight Pilkington agreed. "She's really done well this past year. Imagine having fallen into the Canadian research section chief position."

"I wouldn't necessarily refer to it as 'having fallen into' the position," Juan Perez Caldron quickly said, a slight irritation showing in his voice. "As a matter of fact, Dr. Hutton's talents

207

have been shining forth even better than that. We didn't want to make the announcement yet so as not to overshadow your retirement reception, Clayton, but the decision has been made for Caroline to move up to the vacant North American research group deputy slot."

"Oh... that's wonderful," Dr. Stargill managed after a slight pause. "But what was that you called her? Dr. Hutton? Hutton is Caroline's maiden name. She's always gone by Stargill."

"Oh, I thought she'd discussed this with you already. Lu Chan noted the problem just now, it's become very confusing to have two Dr. Stargills on senior staff. I know you're leaving, but people will remember you and will be mixing up your theories and practices with Caroline's if we don't make a change as she moves into a policymaking position. She agreed that it would be best all around if she struck off entirely on her own now. Hence, in the office she'll be referring to herself with her maiden name. Many professional women do that."

"Excuse me, I think I'll find that bar," a pale Dr. Clayton Stargill managed. "I couldn't face another cheese puff without a martini."

Lu Chan's tinkling laughter drew Dr. Stargill's attention as he was turning.

"Oh, about your offer to help me by editing my book, Lu Chan—"

"I just know your book is going to make a significant contribution, Clayton. I just wish I could be a part of its creation. Unfortunately, I see from the planning schedule that Dr. Fang is doing extensive traveling throughout the Far East this year. And you know what that means. Wherever Dr. Fang goes, there must I go also."

ॐ ॐ

"Welcome to the executive suite, Dr. Hutton," Juan Perez Caldron congratulated Caroline. "I usually have to say something about it being a long, hard climb, but in your case, it has been a zip to the top. And most deserved, too, I might add. It is not often we have someone with such a fine analytical mind who can also plan and guide complex projects and motivate people to do excellent work."

"Thank you, Juan. And thank you so much for having this promotion party for me. This is really the first breather I've had in several months. I agree that it's been a real whirlwind. I can hardly believe it is happening."

"Well, it *is* happening, and I'm afraid you won't have much time to yourself for the next couple of months. With Rodney's illness over the last couple of months, we have allowed your group to get very much shorthanded. I think I can help you with that. I know of a very talented woman, a brilliant economist, who would be just right for the executive officer position. You do know Claudia Videla, don't you? She used to work with your husband. Well, I think, ...uff." Someone had knocked Juan Perez Caldron's arm, and he had dropped a biscuit with caviar, which had been slowly making its way to his mouth.

Caroline looked away momentarily and saw Helmut König and Dr. Fang in conversation across the room. They looked over and saw her at the same time. She waved to her colleagues, whereupon Helmut König gave her a smart military salute and Dr. Fang bowed deeply. Those around them looked to see who they were saluting and then broke out in wide smiles. A few even contributed to a short burst of clapping. Caroline Hutton had been a popular choice for ascension into the World Bank's front line of officers.

"Congratulations, Dr. Hutton. Here, let me help you to the hors d'oeuvres." Dwight Pilkington had appeared at Caroline's elbow from nowhere. "The first woman group chief, and arguably of the most prestigious research group. Follow the money they say, and where could most of the money be if not in the North American group? I've always wanted to serve there. I hear there will be some openings at the section chief—"

"Go away and leave Dr. Hutton alone for a while, Dwight. You can suck up to her tomorrow morning when she's on the office clock again. I need to talk to her about that extremely insightful exposé she's written on the Costa Rican loan repayment plan." Lu Chan had glided up to Caroline's side. She placed her sensuous, heavily ringed hand lightly on Caroline's forearm and gave her a dazzling pouty smile.

"Ah, Caroline, dear. I see you are completely out of bubbly." Juan Perez Caldron took the champagne flute and looked around the room. "Clay. I say, Clay. You are close to that man with the tray of champagne. Be a good husband and bring another glass over for our new group chief."

ଔ ଓ

"I'm sorry, Clay. You're the one who wanted to run off to Charlottesville as soon as you retired, you know. Now that I'm a World Bank vice president, I just can't promise in advance that I'll be able to come down every weekend. I'm really sorry."

Clayton gripped the telephone receiver hard and tried not to betray the panic in his voice. "Retiring to Charlottesville was your choice as well, Caroline."

"But you're the one who up and decided to retire early. I didn't. I'm only forty-three. I've still got a career ahead of me."

Silence.

"Clay. Look, I'm sorry. There's a conference on the Mexican debt repayment plan up in New York on Saturday. It just came up. I wrote up much of the reporting on corruption in their debt restructuring maneuvering. I just can't fail to show up. I'll take off Friday of the next week and we'll have a long weekend." And then to change the subject. "How's the book coming?"

Silence. The wrong new subject to choose.

"I know, how about if I ask Maria and Juan to come through Charlottesville on their way down to Atlanta to see their twin granddaughters next weekend. Wouldn't that be nice? You haven't seen Juan in a while, have you?"

"Not since your promotion party to group chief more than a year ago. What twin granddaughters?" The knuckles of the hand Clayton was using to hold the telephone receiver had turned white much earlier in the conversation and now had a blue tinge to them.

"Surely you know their daughter had twins. We got an announcement, you know. It was a very fancy announcement. I'm sure you remember it. It almost didn't fit through the slot of the ... apartment door. The Washington apartment door." A moment of tense silence. "I'm sorry, Clay. I've just been so busy. I'll go through all the mail I have here before I come down next week and will bring anything I think you might like to see. I presume you've heard about the Königs going back to Austria?"

"No, I haven't," Clayton answered through clinched teeth.

"Well, surely you knew he'd retired very suddenly. Very sad. Cancer, and there doesn't seem to be anything they can do about it. I had assumed that one of your friends from work would have told you about it when they called to check up on you."

"No one's called me from work in more than a year. It would have been nice to have been able to talk to Helmut again before he left."

"I am still exchanging e-mails with him. He took the diagnosis hard and seemed to appreciate our conversations about what he plans to do with the rest of his life. I'll pass on your regards. But, about the Perez Caldrons stopping over for a night next weekend. You'll need to get in some provisions. You do a nice roast, so how about planning something around that? And you'll have to be sure the cleaning lady comes in to do an especially good job on the house. I guess you'd best make a trip up to the Barboursville winery for—"

After disconnecting with his wife, Clayton just sat there for several minutes in his dimly lighted living room. After a while, he got up and went to his study. He really should get cracking on the book. But what was the point? Every time he figured out what was happening in what now was a Russian island surrounded by a whole gaggle of volatile Central Asian states, the situation changed before he could get the manuscript to his publisher. He had written the equivalent of four books in the last four years, and none of what he had written had any relevance anymore. Clayton took another of numerous trips around the large house. The oppressive silence was only relieved by the loud ticking of mantle clocks in the breakfast room and the den. He turned on the computer and checked his e-mail. Nothing.

He walked down to the street and checked the mail box. Three charity solicitations and a coupon for 20 percent off at Bed Bath and Beyond. He came back up to the house and turned on the television. He'd already seen this segment of *Judge Judy*.

After a solitary lunch sitting next to the ticking clock in the breakfast room, Clayton went back to his computer and sat looking at the screen. He checked the e-mail again. Still nothing. The telephone rang, and he snatched up the receiver. No, he didn't want to change his long-distance provider (but he was willing to hear the telemarketer's entire spiel just to hear another human's voice). He checked the e-mail again. He lifted his eyes to the wall behind the computer. His framed masters degrees and doctorate, several exceptional performance awards, an overhead shot of the World Bank headquarters, a signed photograph of him standing with presidents Clinton and Yeltsin at an economic summit, the framed cover of his first book—they all stared back at him, reminding him that he had once been somebody, that he had once had a life worth living, that he had once had a function in this world.

He stood up, went into his dressing room, and began to dress in a finely tailored pin stripe suit, a blue shirt with white cuffs and collar, and a blood-red striped silk tie. He left the house, got into his car, and drove off. Just like all the other men on the block. Just another executive from a well-to-do neighborhood in a wealthy university town, home to several former presidents and many fine research institutions, going to work to attend meetings, give advice, and lead a large group of respectful, attentive employees in solving real world problems.

A half hour later, Clayton walked onto the Charlottesville Downtown Mall. He stopped at the newspaper vending machines and bought copies of the *Washington Post* and the *Financial Times*, and, having found that his usual bench in front the Thomas Kinkade Art Gallery was free, he sat and turned his mind over to the minutia of self-congratulatory press reporting until he had drained the last drop of opinion and trivia from the pages of the two newspapers. He then neatly folded the newspapers and lined them up beside him and just sat there, his mind drifting where it would. It wasn't as if he had any place he needed to be or anything he needed to do. He didn't really have to tell the cleaning lady what she needed to do to prepare for house guests, and there was nothing on his agenda before he had to prepare a roast beef dinner for four with wine from the Barboursville winery nine days from tomorrow.

He liked the Downtown Mall. There were people here, but it was also easy to be alone. Today nothing was happening to hassle him. He briefly had thought that a strange woman who went by wearing a short mink coat, pink pedal pushers, and a red wide-brimmed straw hat was going to stop and talk to him, but she then saw someone else sitting nearby who also was wearing a blue shirt and red tie and went and sat by him. So, that obviously had just been a case of mistaken identity. Sort of a pity. Even being approached by a woman so bizarrely dressed would have been the highlight of his week.

Where had he gone wrong? He'd planned his retirement for years and everything had worked out just as he had planned. He should be walking on the clouds. He and Caroline were comfortably solvent. Charlottesville was a paradise. They'd been able to afford a much nicer house down here than they could have dreamed of owning in the Washington area. There were entertainment and intellectually stimulating events in abundance, and he had all the time in the world to pursue his writing. Everything he had wanted in life was here, just as he had planned it. But was that true? Had he planned on becoming an instantaneous nonperson after years of responsible and meaningful work on real world problems? He had been able to foresee the fast-rolling breakup of the Soviet Union. So, then, why hadn't he been able to see how difficult it would be to publish relevant analytical books on such volatile events?

And Caroline. He had been completely blindsided by her success and their involuntary separation. But was that her fault? No, certainly not. If he'd paid half the attention to her that he'd paid to himself those last years at the World Bank, he would have seen the great talent she had. He would have known that she would be capable of rising even higher than he had. And knowing his own ambitions, he should have realized that she would want to make the most she could of her career. No, he couldn't blame Caroline for what had befallen him. She was right. He had been the one to retire, and he hadn't even bothered to discuss his plans with her or to give her a say in what he'd do.

He opened his eyes and looked around the Downtown Mall. The afternoon sun was keeping the early spring chill out of the air, while the gently swaying trees down the center of the Mall provided a mottled pattern of shade to those sitting and strolling on the walking street. A group of university-age young people were sitting over at the Hardware Store's open-air Garden Café and pointing to various people walking by and chatting and laughing amiably among themselves. Oh to be young and relatively innocent again. But Clayton knew these young people were looking at the others around them and imagining the better lives they were leading. Was there to be no time of life that one could feel total contentment? No, perhaps not. Perhaps that would somehow take the edge off life and demean it. Somewhat like not being able to truly appreciate joy without having known a modicum of pain and despair.

An attractive brunette in her mid-forties, but very well preserved, and with a great deal of self-assurance, strode by and approached a woman standing in the doorway of the Mole Hole Gift Shop. *Funny that,* Clayton thought. The woman in the doorway, although very expensively turned out, was wearing mismatched shoes. Was there yet another trend in women's clothing that he had missed? The brunette, however, had made Clayton's thoughts return to Caroline.

Why had he married Caroline in the first place? Had he been so self-centered that he had mistaken the aging executive's classic vanity of wanting an attractive younger woman on his arm for something else? Had he fallen into the trap of being attracted to and flattered by a young, ambitious office colleague in search of an older mentor, someone to give her a leg up in the business? No, he wouldn't admit just wanting to collect a sweet young thing for himself, and he couldn't bring himself to seeing such brutal motivations in Caroline. The sparks that had sizzled between them from the beginning of their relationship were unmistakable. And, although he *had* immensely enjoyed discussing foreign policy issues with his brilliant wife, there had been so much more in their relationship as well. They had enjoyed the same music, had both delighted in attending concerts, and were equally comfortable with each other on mountain hiking trails. Then why was he suddenly questioning his relationship with his wife?

He had lied to Caroline on the telephone this morning. He *had* recently talked with someone from the office. The young brownnoser, Dwight Pilkington, had called him a few days earlier and had mentioned, in the course of the conversation, that Caroline had been asked to move to head the World Bank's London operations. Pilkington had, of course, called assuming that Clayton knew of the offer and might help him with a transfer to a cushy assignment in London. But Clayton had not known about the offer—and much of the tension that had ruined his phone conversation with Caroline earlier today had been because she hadn't mentioned a word about the offer to him. Was she planning a break? Had she had enough of this relationship? Where had this gone so far wrong, and what could he do about it?

Clayton was beside himself with worry and with despondency about how quickly his fairytale retirement had crumbled into dust. As he sat there on the Downtown Mall, blindly watching the sun begin to set over the Omni Hotel at the western end and the twinkling lights in the trees begin to fight to keep away the creeping shadows, Clayton resolved to let Caroline determine where they went from here. If she still wanted him, he would return to Washington or even follow her to London. He'd make roast beef dinners for her colleagues whenever she asked. And, if he had become an encumbrance to her, he'd let her go without rancor and willingly sink ever deeper into the frustrating nonperson status that he had found that his retirement had become.

Clayton had always tried to take an optimistic view, though. So, while he continued to sit on his bench on the Downtown Mall in the gathering gloom and listened to the tinkling of a piano from the direction of the Central Place, he started to plan what he would serve with the roast beef when—and if—Maria and Juan arrived the weekend after next.

Having made this resolve, Clayton became more aware of the activities swirling around him on the Mall. Or was it an incongruous noise he had heard that had brought him back from his deep thoughts? Where had it come from? A sound like something falling from a rooftop. He looked around and noticed the construction over at the nearby FNS building, where workmen were refurbishing the old department store building. Dust was rising in the air from on top of where the building inset at the third floor. He assumed it was just part of the construction process. He'd be glad when that construction was finished. He stood up to leave. If he was going to be serving roast beef, he needed to stop by Foods of All Nations for the roast.

☙ ❧

Lu Chan slapped her Tivoli Restaurant menu down on the tablecloth and lit up a cigarette in a long holder, completely oblivious to the disapproving stares she received both from the maître d' and from Caroline. "I assume you've heard about Juan Perez Caldron and Claudia Videla?"

"Yes, I have," Caroline answered in her best I-don't-want-to-talk-about-it tone.

"I'll bet Maria is on the warpath. This despite the fact that this is exactly how *she* landed Juan."

No response from Caroline.

"But do you think Juan has heard about Claudia and Dwight Pilkington? I'll bet that's a twist he didn't foresee."

Caroline colored. "I don't really think we should be—"

"Well, please give me *some* nugget of juicy gossip that will make ingesting all of these extra Tivoli calories worthwhile. Have you accepted the London offer?"

Caroline blanched. "How did you know about that offer?"

"What do you think being Dr. Fang's very, very close special assistant entails, My Dear? Trust me, I am about as 'special' to Dr. Fang as you can get. There's nothing that goes on at the World Bank board meetings that I don't know about."

"Well, I don't know," answered Caroline, resigned to Lu Chan's inner circle status, no matter how lurid it might be. There were a lot of things Caroline had learned about the Bank's inner circle in the last few months that she would have preferred not knowing. "I'm really not thinking that much about the London offer at the moment. I'm worried about my husband. He hasn't been himself of late. He seems so distant."

"Yes, he's about two and a half hours distant at the moment. And let's see. When you move to London, he'll be about—"

"Lu Chan!" Caroline said in exasperation. "My marriage is important to me."

"I'm quite sure it was. But why is it still? Have you been completely oblivious to the attentions the Colombian ambassador has been pouring on you? Now, there's the catch of the season. Your marriage was quite useful when Clayton was still a powerhouse at the Bank. But he's gone, and he can't help you a bit more with your career. You've eclipsed where he was on his best day. I don't see the problem. Have you lost touch with why you married him in the first place?"

Caroline sat and stared at Lu Chan for some time. The woman was brutally blunt, but she was quite right. It was high time that Caroline thought of why she had married Clayton and where she wanted to go from here. When she had first asked Lu Chan to go to lunch with her, she had no idea herself why she had done so. But now she knew why. Lu Chan always said exactly what she thought and provided a clear, objective assessment of the situation.

"Yes, Lu Chan, I think that perhaps I had lost touch with why I married Clayton. Thank you, you've helped put it back in perspective for me. I somehow knew you would do that for me."

Lu Chan's bright-red lips formed into a false pout. "And I thought you had asked me to lunch because I was fascinating and mysterious."

"Oh, yes, of course, for those reasons as well," Caroline responded with a broad smile and a laugh. Lu Chan returned the smile, but her smile was rooted in a far darker and more complicate world than Caroline's smile was.

"Here's to foggy old London town." Lu Chan toasted as she lifted the wine glass that had arrived at the table at last. "Dr. Fang and I are scheduled to visit there shortly after you should be taking up your post. We'll have to meet, and . . . compare notes while I'm there."

"Yes, here's to the lifting of that old London town fog," responded Caroline, as she raised her wine glass high.

03 80

"Hello, I'm home. Anybody here? Are you decent?"

Clayton closed his unproductive e-mail link and rushed from the den. At the door, though, he slowed down and tried to look nonchalant. No use letting her know that he was starved for human contact.

"But you're a day earlier than I thought. My God, I hope the Perez Caldrons aren't right behind you. The roast is still in the freezer."

"Nope. No Perez Caldrons lurking in the driveway and no need to thaw the roast. Last I knew, Maria had flown down on her own to Atlanta and Juan won't be welcome there until Maria has departed."

Clayton looked totally confused. It was an attitude Caroline had never seen her husband take before. He looked just like a vulnerable little boy. She wanted to reach out and give him a hug, but now wasn't the time for that.

"The Perez Caldrons are on the outs. I'm sure it will all blow over in time. I'll tell you about that later, but right now, why don't you grab a bottle of wine and meet me out on the patio. We have something serious to discuss."

Uh, oh, Clayton thought. *Here it comes.* He almost felt a surge of relief. He knew he couldn't get on with a new life until all vestiges of the old one had been stripped away. He hadn't been idle in the last week. He had contacted some friends at his undergraduate college, West Virginia University, and they'd be delighted for him to join the faculty there. It would be a clean break with everything that went before, and he'd be back at work again.

When they were settled on the patio, Caroline opened the conversation. "I've been asked to move to London."

"So I've heard."

Caroline gave her husband a sharp look, but she continued on. "I've told them that will be difficult to do, since I won't be working for the World Bank anymore."

"Excuse me?"

"I've told them I'm leaving the bank at the end of May. I've found that the attractions Charlottesville has to offer are just too tempting, so I'm moving home. Home to Charlottesville, to this house, to you."

"Oh, Caroline. I don't think . . . You have a brilliant career. You're still young. Our marriage probably was just a mistake. It's all my fault. I don't think you have any idea what it means to give up your professional identity. God knows I now do, and it isn't pretty. I can't let you throw yourself—"

"Hush, now. Just be quiet and hear me out. I didn't say I was going to stop working, did I? More on that in a minute, but close your eyes. Yes, I'm serious, close your eyes, and I'll close mine too. Hush, hush. Listen to that. Birds, the rustle of air coming down off the Blue Ridge and ruffling the new-born leaves in our trees—*our* trees, in *our* yard. Smell. Do you smell the exhaust from the cars crossing the Potomac bridges into Foggy Bottom from the Northern Virginia suburbs? Neither do I. Sit, be still. How many memos marked 'Urgent' and 'Top Secret' have been slapped down in front of you in the last two minutes? None? Me neither. Isn't that just marvelous? Now, try to remember why we bought this place in Charlottesville. Think of all those things we were going to do when we were able to break away and live here. Now, open your eyes."

Clayton didn't want to open his eyes. And he didn't want Caroline to open her eyes, either. He didn't want her to see the tears in his eyes. He had never wanted Caroline—or anyone else—to see that he could cry. Yes, he'd had those dreams. But they were all dust now. Swept away by brutal reality.

"I want to do those things now, Clayton. I don't want to wait until I have to struggle with arthritic legs and arms just to make it to the breakfast table. And I want to do these things with you. If I took the job and went to London, I wouldn't have time to do what I really want to do even if you came with me."

"You don't really understand," Clayton said, his voice heavy with regret. "You just don't know what it means for people like you and me to retire and to try to build a new life."

"I'm not talking about building an entirely new life. We always enjoyed concerts, travel, reading, and being in the outdoors. They've always been a treasured part of our life together. I'm talking about just letting them be a greater part of our life. And I'm not talking about full retirement. I know trying to publish a book on fast-moving events in Russia has been frustrating for you. That doesn't mean you have to give up analysis of Russian affairs based on your rich background, however."

Clayton looked skeptical. "I've tried. For the past four years, I've tried. But it isn't working."

"It's just a matter of the right packaging, Clay. Look at me. Meet the new editor of the Walker Institution's *Western Hemisphere Security Policies Yearbook*. Every year, I'll be responsible for producing an updated version of security issues facing the nations of this half of the world. It's not a full-time job, but it's challenging, will build on my background, will challenge me to keep current in my field, and I can do it from here."

"That sounds wonderful for you, but—"

"And go over and look in the mirror. There you will see the editor of the companion *Russia and Central Asia Security Policies Yearbook*, if you want the job. The people at the Walker Institution were delighted at the prospect you might accept the position, and they were simply ecstatic when I told them you already had four books worth of notes on the stages the Russians and their former republics had gone through to get to where they are today. They say there's a way to publish all of that so the academic community will have the historical texture it needs. Let's not mess up the life we've chosen, Clayton, let's just rearrange it a bit."

There was that vulnerable little boy look again. Clayton worked hard to try to remember just why he thought he'd be better off returning to Morgantown, West Virginia, as Caroline indulged herself in that hug she had wanted to give him ever since she returned home and saw how lonely and forlorn—and bravely resigned to his perceived fate—he had looked.

The Game: Four

The shadows were beginning to lengthen on the trees at the Charlottesville Downtown Mall and were also contributing to the gloomy mood forming at Shelley and Tiffany's table at the Hardware Store's open-air Garden Café. Shelley was searching the adjacent area of the Mall for any sign of the long-anticipated appearance of Jeff and Luis. Tiffany was digging around in the hot fudge sundae she had ordered, trying to separate out some vanilla ice cream that hadn't been polluted by fudge topping.

"Why didn't you just order plain vanilla ice cream to start with?" Shelley asked, her voice dripping with irritation.

"I wanted some nuts with it, and they don't have vanilla ice cream with nuts on the menu."

"Then why are you pushing the nuts off to the side too?"

"These are pecans. I thought they might be macadamia nuts. I love macadamia nuts. Don't you?"

"Yeah, right. They always serve their hot fudge sundaes with macadamia nuts. That's a real American institution," Shelley said. Her eyes rolled. She wasn't sure how much more of Tiffany she could take. Shelley hoped Tiffany would split soon after Jeff arrived. Maybe she'd go off with Luis. That would be just great.

"Well, you never know. Macadamia nuts are getting quite popular, you know." Tiffany pushed her ice cream around a while longer. She was really bored. If she weren't waiting for Jeff to arrive, she wouldn't stay around here another minute. Shelley was such a shrew. Just a shop girl type. Maybe when Jeff did get here, she and he could go off by themselves. Luis liked Shelley. He was always after the blowsy type. Maybe they'd be happy

The Game: Four

being by themselves. But, boy was Tiffany bored now. She looked around, but Jeff wasn't anywhere in sight. Boy she was bored. "Let's do something. Let's start playing the game again. Make up a story for that man loitering around the newspaper machines over by the carousel. He's been moving around over there for a long time."

"The game's no fun with just two," Shelley answered. And especially not with someone who's half brain dead.

Shelley did take another look around the Mall, however, and her inspection now was rewarded. "There's Luis. I don't see Jeff, but Luis is headed in this direction."

"Oh, goodie," Tiffany squealed with delight. She flipped her purse open and grabbed at a mirror to determine whether lunch had done any damage to her face.

"Luis. Luis, we're over here. Where's Jeff?"

Luis slowed up, but he didn't stop altogether. He gave Shelley a very guarded look as he approached the table.

"Where's Jeff?" Tiffany asked him as he walked up, apparently thinking he would give her the response he hadn't given to Shelley.

"Didn't you hear?" he asked. "Didn't Max tell you?"

"What do you mean? What was Max supposed to tell us?"

"Max called our place more than a half hour ago. I told him and he was supposed to tell you. He said you were all here at the Hardware Store. He said he'd go and tell you right away."

"Tell us? Tell us what?" Tiffany was still smiling, not yet having gotten any vibes that anything could be wrong.

"Jeff came out last night. We were at a party and he and Tim announced that they were a couple. They left for Virginia Beach this morning to celebrate."

Photo by Rick Britton.

Another Day

He had only come down to the Downtown Mall to pick up the latest issue of *C'ville Weekly*. He hadn't come for any other reason. But once he'd gotten his paper from the newspaper machines in the covered walkway below the parking garage, he'd stayed around and looked at what all of the other newspaper machines had to offer. He was in front of the post office at the eastern end of the Mall. His staying around the machines in the passageway had nothing at all to do with the pretty little refurbished carousel. The ornately painted wooden merry-go-round had recently taken up position out on the walking street between here and the Discovery Museum on the other side of the Mall. No connection at all. Just came down to the Mall, same as every week, to pick up his copy of *C'ville*.

As he was reading through a real estate guide for the second time, leaning up against the brick pillar with his *C'ville* under his arm and nodding his head in a neighborly way at those coming in and out of the post office, his attention was suddenly arrested by a flash of red and the squeals of delight. A small convoy of children with two mothers in escort had burst forth from the Discovery Museum and were swarming around and onto the little carousel.

"OK, children. Off the carousel for a minute. We'll pay the man, and then you can all have a ride before we go home." This announcement was met with renewed squeals of delight.

The red flash. Follow the red flash. Red was one of his favorite colors. A stimulating color; an exciting color. There. Over there, just jumping off the carousel and running up and hugging the legs of one of the women. He closed the real estate guide and let it drop to the ground. He also went over and carefully returned the copy of *C'ville* in the newspaper machine. Another day. He'd pick the *C'ville* up another day. Saliva was rising in his mouth. The old feeling was gripping him. He was mesmerized by the dancing red sandals on the little girl.

He forced his eyes away from the sandals. Good, very good. She was wearing a yellow sundress with white trim and some sort of red-colored cartoon character on the bodice. A white sweater. Yellow and red. Very good colors. Very attractive—and attracting.

The little girl broke away from the woman and ran back to the carousel, as money had exchanged hands and the other children were beginning to load up. The woman raised her head, like a she wolf sniffing the air, and started looking around the east end of the Mall, as if she sensed some faint incongruity. He ducked back into the passageway and strode into the post office, where he spent a minute or two deciding whether he needed an express or a priority mailing packet.

Having decided he needed neither, he looked out of the window. Beyond the covered passageway. The children were settling on the wooden figures of the carousel now, and the women had moved to a park bench nearby and were talking. The calliope started its tinny tinkling, and the carousel began to move in a circular motion.

Where was she? He was drawn back into the passageway, where he tried to stay in the shadows as much as possible as, in panic, he tried to pick her out. She wasn't there. She wasn't there! He began to feel deflated and angry. But no, he caught a flash of red and picked her out once more by her dancing sandals. She had just managed to climb up on a giraffe. A yellow giraffe. The old feeling was rising in him once more. He tore his attention away from the sandals and looked into her face. A pretty blonde. Maybe four or five. Nice chubby legs, and a sweet smile. Couldn't tell the eye color from here, but no bother. She was the right type. He just knew she was the right type. He had no idea why he preferred a particular type. Just about the same age as his daughter, before he had had to go away.

Hazel eyes. His daughter had had hazel eyes. Even though he couldn't see this little girl's eyes, he was sure they were hazel. They'd better be hazel. He was drawn out of the shadows of the passageway and out onto the bricked Mall by the sudden need to verify that her eyes were hazel.

The mother abruptly interrupted her conversation and looked over to the carousel to check on the children. Just in time, he realized he had already been drawn out into the open and had the presence of mind to put a determined and purposeful air about him and to stroll over to the other side of the Mall, past the carousel. Just a businessman on his afternoon coffee break.

Damn! He'd gotten the carousel between him and the park bench where the two mothers sat, but the girl with the sandals was on the other side as well when he passed by. No way of checking the eye color. In panic, he continued on to the other side and walked up to the Discovery Museum. No windows to gaze into. No excuse for a businessman on a coffee break to be loitering here. The next couple of doors down, there was a delicatessen made up like a country store. A front window here. He hadn't had lunch today. Surely he needed something to eat, something that took more time to pick out than an afternoon coffee. Stand and look into the window, deciding what was good to eat. Stand and look and plan another pass.

After several snatched looks out to the Mall, he'd figured out the timing. He'd also had a stab of consciousness. What in the hell was he doing? After all of the therapy, why was he out here again? He'd just come down to the Mall for a copy of the *C'ville Weekly*. But she was perfect. Or she was perfect if she had those hazel eyes. He was sure of it. She had those hazel eyes. And the dancing red sandals. It was all just so . . . right. It was preordained, meant to be. Nothing to do with him at all.

Just about now. One, two, three. Shove off. No, don't walk too fast. Will get there too soon and that she wolf will notice. Ah, yes, it's working. Just about where the carousel will blot out the park bench. There's the giraffe. There's the giraffe, but panic. Where's the girl? Is there more than one giraffe on the carousel? She was there when I pushed off.

His steps had carried him past the carousel, and then he saw them. The little girl was standing there with her mother between the carousel and the park bench, looking pretty pouty.

"That's enough for today, honey. We have to get home and fix supper. Your dad will be home soon. You'll want to tell him about your day at the Mall. We'll be back. There's always another day. Listen. There is some piano music up the Mall a bit. We'll check that out on the way to the car."

The little girl brightened up and the two of them walked, hand in hand, west down the tree-lined Mall and into the late afternoon sun. The little girl's red sandals sparkled and danced in the dappled sunlight.

Another day. His momentum had carried him back to the passageway outside the post office. He stopped long enough to open the newspaper machine and retrieve a copy of *C'ville Weekly*. That's what he had come down to the Mall to get. He continued on around the corner and up the hill, away from the Downtown Mall, calmer now and his breathing less ragged. Yes, he was sure they must be hazel. And, indeed, there always would be another day.

Tug of War

"Ouch. Just look at those prices. High tea at the hoity-toity Downtown Grill. *High* tea is right. Why I could get a full three-course meal, *plus* a bucket of tea, up at The Nook Restaurant for less than this. Why, I could feed a whole Lao village—for two days."

"I didn't really realize that you would be coming along with Cemal for this outing, Jenny, or I certainly *would* have picked someplace where you might be a bit, ahh, more comfortable. I wanted to talk to Cemal about what he planned to do now that he'd retired."

"I figured that's what you wanted to do," responded Jenny with a jangle of her bangle bracelets and a flick of her brightly flowered cotton skirt across crossed legs. "Cemal and I have already decided what he's going to do. He's going to come over and help me manage the Innisfree store, that's what he's going to do. That's right, isn't it Cemal?"

"This is the first time I've been to the Downtown Grill," said Cemal Hoolagu. "It's got a very nice outdoor café area. It's great out here at sunset, the lights in the trees on the center of the Mall starting to come on. Good tea, Sami. Thanks. I had no idea we could get a Turkish blend like this in Charlottesville. Brings back some good memories."

Sami Attakun looked across the Downtown Mall at the sliver of the Innisfree Gift Shop on the southern flank of buildings. The colorful handicrafts spilled out of the door and onto the bricked walking street. "The Innisfree store," he said, turning a baleful look on Cemal's girlfriend, Jenny Martin, who was busy adjusting a strap on one of her sandals. "I don't think I've quite figured out exactly what you sell there. Some sort of knick knacks, isn't it?" He straightened the bejeweled cuffs of his starched white shirt and consulted a gold watch at the end of a long gold chain before putting it back in his silk vest pocket.

"Knick knacks!" Jenny declared with a hurt inflection to her voice. "We sell fine handicrafts from around the world. We're supplied by a consortium of self-help projects in the poorer regions, projects that help get money and supplies to remote villages in exchange for lovely handicrafts we can sell in such wealthy and socially conscious places as here in Charlottesville. Most of our employees are from local projects as well. Our goal is to take as little money as possible from the producer in the marketing process. It's just perfect now that Cemal has retired with a good pension. He doesn't need much additional income."

"*My* goal is to put an oriental carpet on every floor in Farmington, Keswick, and Glenmore." said Sami, looking straight at Cemal. "With your experience in working and traveling abroad, you could make a fortune as a buyer for Orientals Limited. We want to expand; we have our eyes on one of the large two-floor shops being built in the new FNS complex up the Mall. There's a great market for Turkish and Persian carpets in this region, and we'd like you to join our family. There are so few Turks here. We need to stick together like family."

"Don't talk to Cemal about family and Turks sticking together. It's just too painful for him to think about. What mainland Turks were sticking together with Cemal's family when it was wiped out in their village in Cyprus by the Greeks?" Jenny asked.

"We were marshaling our military forces—and we swept in and helped create and preserve a Turkish state on Cyprus for Cemal's people," Sami responded quietly.

"And don't talk to Cemal about traveling the world to buy your carpets, either," Jenny went on, with a toss of her long, straight, blonde hair, oblivious to the not-at-all-friendly tone of Sami Attakun's previous response. "That's why he retired from international journalism. Haven't you heard him tell people he was tired of checking his car for bombs before he drove it anywhere? Didn't he tell you about those children by the New Gate in Jerusalem who were good-naturedly following along and begging him for candy and coins in one minute and then blown away by a Palestinian bomb in the next?"

"Isn't that piano music coming down on the breeze from the Central Place?" asked Cemal. "Isn't that a wonderful sound? Not too loud, just a kiss on the breeze. So restful and calm. I think I could sit out here, sipping Turkish tea and listening to the music, forever."

"It's perfectly safe in the areas where you would have to go, Cemal. And you could check in on all of those people you've known in your travels around the world. You would be making a substantial contribution to Orientals Limited and to the city's economy."

"Safe? Checking up on the people he's known? Just to line the pockets of the Attakun brothers at Orientals Limited? How can you say you're a friend of his and still want him to travel abroad again? And bringing up the people he's known in this context. How insensitive can you get? Have you forgotten about Kaduna, where he was once assigned in northern Nigeria? About those he cared for there? How can one feel safe ever again when on one night half of your servants are taken away and slaughtered simply because they are Ibos—and the next night they come back for your new wife because they've discovered that she is also a quarter Ibo? No," Jenny continued in a loud voice, causing all activity at the tables in their vicinity to come to an embarrassed, but, at the same time, deliciously curious halt. "No, Cemal has put in his dues when it comes to world travel and in covering world crises. Isn't that right, Honey? He knows he can do even more meaningful work now. He can help enrich the impoverished lives of those in all the isolated villages around the world—to have a key role in helping them help themselves to a better life. Tell him, Cemal. Tell him that you've decided to do something more creative and important in your life than to peddle oriental carpets to the filthy rich out at Ednam."

All eyes in the vicinity were on Cemal, who cleared his throat—twice—and quietly said, "Those pastries certainly do look good. I think I'll have just one more of those and finish this cup of tea. And then I might wander on up the Mall to listen to the piano music for a while. Certainly does soothe the weary soul. Maybe I'll stop and pick up a good biography at the Blue Whale to start while I listening to some Gershwin. Great idea spending an evening on the Downtown Mall, Sami. Must do it again real soon. Lots of time for that now."

Ain't Whistlin Dixie

It was approaching that secret time on the Downtown Mall. That time that only a few of the locals knew about and were not about to tell anyone else who wouldn't appreciate it at least as much as they did—the hours between when dads and mothers went home to their wives, husbands, and children and when the sophisticated diners and lonely-hearts bar flies began their night prowl on the Mall.

The almost-daily event was signaled along about 4 P.M., marked by the emergence from the Moondance Café on Central Place of a wrinkled old black man in a worn shiny black suit. Amid the bustle of the Mall's day people rushing to finish up their business and get to someplace else, the man took off his bowler hat and laid it gently and precisely on the top of the battered upright piano that huddled under the green awning of the Moondance. The piano sat between the windows of the café and the restaurant's twenty-some tables that were roped off on the Mall's bricked central courtyard. He placed a large tumbler of amber-colored liquid on a low table beside the piano, sank onto the piano stool, and closed his eyes in momentary contemplation. A twittering ran through the gathering regulars that, thankfully to those "in the know," didn't seem to faze the disappearing crowds of the Mall's "sunshine shift." As the day activity folks moved toward the streets running away from the Mall, those who remained stealthily crept to the tables of the cafés near Central Place, many of which had closed down their service for the day.

A jolt of pleasure ran through the settlers, as Sylvester cracked his knuckles and started to help the day people on their

Photo by Stacey Evans.

way with a few Irving Berlin ditties, first saluting the beautiful spring day they had all enjoyed with "Blue Skies," moving on to "Cheek to Cheek," and eventually trying to push the season with "Heat Wave."

As always, some of those who had really intended to go on to somewhere else—those with a particularly good ear for music—slowed their steps, momentarily weighed their schedules and responsibilities, and then sank into one of the decreasing number of available patio chairs. Sylvester was that good.

The regulars didn't need clocks to determine that it was now past 4:30, because, with only a brief pause to sip on his drink and to have a passing word with the Moondance's patio waitress, Sylvester segued into Gershwin with another season-pushing rendition of "Summertime." This was followed by a surprise performance of "Rhapsody in Blue" that the nearby renovated Paramount Theater would have been proud to have sponsored on its concert stage, "Embraceable You," and as the shadows lengthened on the bricked walking street, a wistful "The Way You Looked Tonight."

By now the bustle part of the day's activity was pretty much finished on the Downtown Mall. The bakery and art street vendors were packing up their wares and giving way to the Indian jewelry and classic CD street vendors. People were arriving for the next round of Mall activities, of course, but most of these were day workers who considered the Mall only a pathway to the beer at Miller's or the beer and pool at Rapture. However, there were some folks who drifted into the area, sensed that the real show was outside, and, even though they had intended to hit the bars, joined the secret society near Central Place. One such group this evening consisted of several out-of-town businessmen who had drifted down from their temporary digs at the Omni Hotel on the west end of the Mall and who, after ferreting out the drinks of their choice in Miller's, brought their booty back out into the open and plopped down on the steps near the central fountain.

The musicians in the vicinity knew the Gershwin half hour was over when Sylvester transitioned into Johnny Mercer's "Laura." The regulars knew better what this meant, however. As

235

Sylvester teased out "Laura is the face in the misty light. . . . That was Laura, but she's only a dream," many gathered about turned their eyes west in delightful anticipation. On cue, the compact little lady with the big voice appeared on the scene from the doorway of the classic book resale shop, Read It Again Sam, several doors up the Mall, and slowly made her way to Sylvester's side.

Laura Grace had worked the dayshift at the book store for several years. Once, on the way home from Sam's to a dreary, empty house that she no longer particularly wanted to face, Laura Grace had been drawn to Central Place by the sound of an old man tinkering on the keys of a piano. Before she knew what she was doing, she was humming a few bars. She was so much into the tune that she hadn't even realized that Sylvester had stopped his playing and was giving her a very sharp look. Since then, he wouldn't have let her leave the bookstore at the end of the working day without stopping off and doing a set. Truth be known, thanks to Sylvester, Laura Grace's house was no longer dreary and empty, either.

Laura Grace did a breathtaking Billie Holiday, and this very special transitional hour on the Mall was taken over by such as "Mean to Me," "Lover Man," "Ain't Nobody's Business if I Do," "My Old Flame," and "Them There Eyes." Before anyone knew it, an hour had gone by. And although the mood was briefly pricked when one of the now well-lubricated out-of-town businessmen chirped in with a loud "Why that's where I'm from" after the first few bars of "Georgia on My Mind" were played, the time had sped by without anyone present realizing that the magical transition had arrived on the Mall.

The natural light had now dissipated enough that the twinkling white fairy lights in the trees running down the Mall were taking control of the mood. The shadows from these danced as a gentle breeze played through brand-new leaves. Sylvester reached over and turned on the small light on the piano, and the string of colored lights that outlined the Moondance's awning also began to glow. A distant squealing sound drifted down from the east end of the Mall, where, much to the delight of the last group of children leaving the Discovery Museum and to the consternation of their frazzled parents, the fantasy lights of the newly installed carousel also burst forth.

It was this time of the evening that the awareness of the Downtown Mall as a living organism hit. The lights were also beginning to come on in the upper stories of the eclectic, but strangely harmonious buildings that lined what had once been a typical small southern town main street. These weren't just pretty refurbished facades for daytime businesses. People lived on the Mall. It knew life in every facet. Here could be seen a bosomy matron, hanging out of her window to gather in every note Sylvester produced. Next door to her, a lonely widower sat glued to his bedroom window and his bottle of Jack Daniels, pretending that he was still alive. Over there was an actor at the nearby Live Arts Theater, pacing in his living room and across two windows opening out onto the Mall and trying to memorize his lines for a Tom Stoppard farce. And up there were two young lovers, coming together at the end of their separate work days and oblivious to and uncaring about what the rest of the world could see or might think.

Laura Grace had faded away as the lights had flickered on, but Sylvester continued, starting with the gentle rhythm of "Ebb Tide's" waves—"First the tide rushes in, plants a kiss on the shore"—and building up the tension toward the climax of the secret time. The music had become richer and had acquired a stereo quality. Maurice, finished with his tea-time gig at Hamilton's, had temporarily set up near the fountain, and Sylvester deftly moved into songs that showcased his friend's sweet saxophone. "I'm in the Mood for Love," changed into "Red Sails in the Sunset" and "Stardust," and all too soon Maurice was having to close up to get over to his next shift at the Metropolitan.

Sylvester started warming up the crowd with Scott Joplin rags. "The Entertainer" led to the "Maple Leaf Rag," and then Archie started putting in his two cents worth from where he had set his drums up down by Sal's Caffé Italian.

The whole works started going over the top when they got to the "Coconut Conga," and some of the newcomers, including the businessmen from up at the Omni, started to form a Conga line.

The businessman from Georgia was flipped off the end of the line too near Sylvester and almost landed in his lap. Wrapping one arm around the piano player, he patted his captive on the head with his free hand, dug around in his pocket and came up with a money clip, extracted a torn dollar bill, and looked around for a tin can. Not seeing any, he stuffed the bill into Sylvester's shirt pocket.

"Ya take requests, don't cha? Be a good boy and play 'Dixie' for me. I'm just a good ole Georgia boy a long way from home."

Sylvester extricated himself from the drunk with a little help from Louise, the Moondance's patio waitress, stood up from the piano in indignation, clapped the bowler on his head, picked up his iced tea, and snapped off the light over the piano, before disappearing through the Moondance's doorway. The awning lights and the front bank of lights inside the restaurant also switched off and the north end of Central Place was plunged into night.

"What'd he do *that* for? Mr. Uppity, ain't he? Where's the manager? He can't just stiff me. I want to hear 'Dixie.' N'fac I want you to get that, that ... get him out here, and I want to hear him *whistle* 'Dixie.' Where's the manager?"

"The manager won't do you a bit of good, Sugar," Louise snapped, as she turned the drunk back toward the fountain and his gaggle of buddies. "Sylvester trumps the manager, Mister. Sylvester Turner *owns* the Moondance. Hell, Honey, he owns the whole damn block. And if he doesn't feel like whistling 'Dixie,' he ain't whistling 'Dixie.'"

None of the regulars moved. They just sat there in the dark for the longest time. Just waiting for the Philistines to leave, slightly ashamed they hadn't all rushed to Sylvester's aid. Eventually, the interlopers got the message, nosily gathered themselves together, and started back up toward the Omni.

Several moments of silence, and then, out of the darkness below the Moondance's awning came the requested whistling. A strong, clear, rich baritone. But it wasn't "Dixie." It was the "High and the Mighty." As the last strains of the song echoed off the walls of buildings along the Downtown Mall, a great release of bated breath escaped from the gathered regulars. The lights came on at the Moondance again. Sylvester was at the piano, gently coaxing the strains of "Deep Purple" from the battered, but mellow-toned instrument. "Thru the mist of a memory, you wander back to me, breathing my name with a sigh."

All was well with the world. Sylvester was in the blue indigo mood once more, and the night owls had not yet started coming in for the night shift. The magical secret time on the Downtown Mall spun out and down the Mall once again.

The Spotlight

"This is just great. You would have loved this, Lil."

Joyce Donnell couldn't have looked more radiant if she had been decked out and dripping in diamonds like the partygoers swirling around her rather than in her simple black dress and carrying a service tray. She couldn't help murmuring this comment to her long-dead grandmother, even as she offered hors d'oeuvres to the Charlottesville city and Albemarle county glitterati, who had gathered this evening for the reopening of the restored lower and upper lobbies of the Downtown Mall's Paramount Theater.

She needn't have worried that her comments would be overheard in this packed and expressive crowd gathered just inside the front doors out onto the Mall, however. Judge Hawley dove for two dough-wrapped sausages and Mrs. Stowe-Byrd dismissed the tray with a vague wave of her hand without missing a beat in their discussion of what a boost the reopening of the Paramount would be to the cultural life in the town center or a hint of acknowledgment of Joyce's presence.

As Joyce turned, however, she almost delivered the contents of the tray down the décolletage of the imposing Mrs. Potter-Hanson.

"Oh, sorry, Mrs. P-H. There's really not enough room in this lobby for trays this size."

"Agreed. The lower lobby wasn't designed for cocktail parties. When the dedication is over and we can move to the upper lobby, there will be less danger of hand-to-hand combat. You look quite sparkly tonight, Joyce. You must really be proud of what's been done here."

"Yes, Mrs. P-H, thanks to you and other generous sponsors, we've been able to afford to refurbish this much of the theater. Just a few more years and the stage will be alive again as well."

"Humph," was Elizabeth Potter-Hanson's only response. "Tell me. Do you recommend these little caviar crimpets or that gooey thing over there with the walnut hat?"

☙ ❧

As Joyce moved on toward other guests, she was thinking that Mrs. Potter-Hanson didn't know the half of her pride—and awe—in what had already been accomplished in the restoration of the Paramount. Tonight had been her grandmother's dream. It was just too bad that she had died before anyone had gotten the idea of helping the revitalization of Charlottesville's downtown by restoring rather than knocking down the finely decorated theater house that had once graced the town's main street, now turned into a bricked walking street.

Her grandmother, Lillian, had blown into town at the height of Vaudeville. Her own specialty at the time, such as it was, was to be her tempestuous husband's target in a knife-throwing act—quite literally. Charlottesville had once been on the backend travel schedule of the Barnum and Bailey Circus, which stopped over here for two nights in the fall while en route to winter quarters in Sarasota, Florida. Lillian and her husband hadn't been getting along very well all the way from Wabash, Indiana. As they got ever closer to Florida, his knifes were coming ever closer to Lillian's then-pretty neck with each passing performance. It was here in the Charlottesville stopover that first blood had been let, albeit it was only a prick, and Lillian, having run in panic from the big tent, had found herself spilling her life's troubles out to a very presentable, but quiet and sympathetic young man behind the fortune-teller's booth. The circus—and the mad knife thrower—had gone on to Florida, but Lillian had stayed behind.

Her young man had turned out to be a conscientious teacher, soon to be principal, at a junior high school in what was then the wrong-side-of-the-tracks community of Belmont. Once her first husband had been thrown out of the picture, Lillian's second marriage had been a blissful one in which opposites got along quite well, thank you very much. Although Joyce's grandfather had gotten his principalship and had recorded a sterling, if somewhat dull, career in education, his wife was never really accepted by the community, even the community on the wrong side of the tracks. She was entirely too loud, too heavily decorated, too opinionated. In short, she was having a lot of fun that the rest of the community envied, and she could manufacture a good time out of a pittance.

Having received the cold shoulder in Belmont, Lillian had crossed the tracks and gone to work at the old Jefferson Theater on Main Street, then the venue for all of the live entertainment passing through Charlottesville, which was quite a bit. The historical and intellectual center known as Charlottesville has always enjoyed a regard that far outstrips its natural due as a result of population or location. As a girl, Joyce had been regaled by Lillian's stories of being a dresser for the likes of George and Gracie Allen and Jimmy Durante, and even for that woman who Stanford White got shot over up in New York, although Joyce always suspected that her grandmother had stretched her years of experience with the Jefferson Theater. Once, Lillian had started talking in personal terms about her backstage brush with Sarah Bernhardt but had clammed up real quick when her granddaughter had started to giggle.

The opening of the Paramount Theater on Thanksgiving Day, 1931, should have been observed by Lillian as the death knell for the world of the theater as she knew and loved it, but Lillian hadn't been anything if not resilient. As the motion picture era that the Paramount Theater ushered into Charlottesville slowly choked out the Vaudeville era represented by the Jefferson Theater across Main Street and a few block west, Lillian gathered her skirts about her and transferred to the box office at the Paramount. Here she held sway for the next twenty years, offering her own unique and succinct reviews for the shows people were paying to see. Eventually some people came and paid their money less to see the movie than to hear Lillian's pithy commentary on it.

All of those years, however, Lillian dreamed of the Paramount becoming what she called a "real" theater. She had been instrumental in seeing to it that the dressing rooms that had been included, along with a proper stage, in the original design as a hedge against the possible failure of the newfangled motion picture technology were kept available and clean for the real live actors who never showed up. By the time Lillian had retired to spend more time with her pursed-lipped neighbors in Belmont, the first-rate movies had moved out to the suburbs, and the Paramount closed its doors.

When it came time for Joyce to go to work, she crossed the tracks from Belmont, just as her grandmother had, and started working at Timberlake's Drug Store, across the street from the boarded-up Paramount. Timberlake's was even more of a historical fixture on Main Street than the Paramount had been and was one of the few businesses that survived the transition of the area to an open-air walking mall. Joyce loved tradition just as her grandfather did, and she thoroughly enjoyed working at Timberlake's, with its customer-friendly ambiance and its real-life soda bar. But the Lillian in her kept pulling her attention across the street to the moldering Paramount.

When the rumors started circulating that a cultural consortium was going to start restoring the Paramount to be reopened as a movie theater, Lillian's theatrical juices started acting up in her granddaughter's veins, and Joyce volunteered to help. She couldn't help much with the massive amounts of money that would be needed, but she wasn't afraid of hard work and she had the spirit—or rather she had Lillian sitting on her shoulder and yakking directions in her ear.

First thing Joyce had done when they had fought their way through forty years of cobwebs in the outer lobbies was to work her way back to the dressing rooms her grandmother had told her about. She helped a great deal with all the cleaning, polishing, renailing, regilding, and so forth basic work. But she always made an effort to ensure that those dressing rooms were free of debris and construction material and just a little cleaner than the rest of the theater. Somewhere along the line the members of the board, through their infrequent visits and inspections of the laborious work of bringing the old theater back to life, had gotten the message that the Paramount had been built with a regular stage, proscenium, and dressing rooms and started changing their basic concept of the building's use. The Downtown Mall already had movie theaters. The old Jefferson Theater had reopened and a new Regal multiplex had established itself out on the western flank of the Mall. What the downtown really needed, they declared, was a theater that could be used for live performances—for plays and concerts.

At that point, the plans and funding for the reborn Paramount had really taken off, and here they all were, at last, standing in the restored lower lobby and facing a thick red ribbon cordoning off the grand staircase that led to the equally well-refurbished upper lobby. With these visible signs of progress, it would be a matter of only a few short years before the entire theater project would be completed and the sounds of Neil Simon comedies on some nights and Mozart on others would be wafting down the staircase from the main auditorium. And here also was Joyce, just busting with pride and glowing with a connection to her grandmother's dream, delighted to have been able to sign up with the serving volunteers and thus to be here this night.

ଓଃ ଓଡ

The mayor gave a short speech in front of the ribbon and then called the project's most generous patron, Mrs. Elizabeth Potter-Hanson, up to cut the ribbon. Mrs. P-H sailed forth, firmly gripped the oversized scissors, mugged for the photographer from the *Daily Progress,* and looked around the room, surveying the crowd. Her gaze fell upon Joyce, who was standing at the back of the crowd, transfixed, savoring every precious moment of the experience.

"Just a minute, Walt," Mrs. P-H said to the newspaper photographer as he started to turn away. "I don't much like this photo. We've only got a very small part of the picture. Joyce, Dear, could you come up and help me cut this here ribbon? I'm just a weak old woman, and I'm not sure I have the strength to get it done on my own."

Little Joyce from Belmont could only manage a squeaky, "Me?" as the spotlight gyrated around the room and came to rest on the object of Mrs. Potter-Hanson's questionable attention.

"Yes, you, Joyce. I haven't been blind. All I gave to this project was my money, something I can very well do without. I've been watching. You have given this project the very spirit of what this Downtown Mall concept is all about. You have brought to it your many volunteered hours of hard work, a healthy appreciation for living and reinventing history, and, certainly not least, a flair for fun and adventure. And all you've taken away is a sense of pride and of place and of connectedness with the people of this community. Get yourself up here right now. These scissors are getting heavy."

As Joyce broke out of her trance and started to move to the front, the mayor whispered something in Mrs. Potter-Hanson's ear.

"Appropriate? Not even an invited guest?" Mrs. P-H barked, and then declared, loudly enough for all to hear. "Why, Matt, Joyce has probably put more thought and effort into getting this project to where it is than the rest of us here together. And as far as 'appropriate,' I let loose of that a long time ago. When I was this girl's age, I found myself married to an army lieutenant without having any idea what an officer's wife was or what they were supposed to do. When I was called on the carpet by the major's wife for fraternizing with an enlisted man's wife, a girl who had shared four tires with me so we could get across the country to see our husbands off to war, I caved in—for the good of my husband's career. That was the biggest mistake I made in my life—and the last one I remember making, incidentally. Here, Joyce, you come on up and cut this ribbon on your own so we can make use of all that space at the top of the stairs. And give me that damn hors d'oeuvre tray. I'll give it its next ride around the room. Let's get this here party back on the road."

PART TWO

THE HISTORY

West Main Street, Charlottesville, looking east from the foot of Vinegar Hill, circa 1885. Photographer unknown. Special Collections Department, University of Virginia Library.

Reflection of American Resilience:
The Charlottesville Downtown Mall

Many city and town centers across America were successfully revitalized in the urban renewal initiatives of the 1970s and 1980s. In this vein, the creation of the Charlottesville, Virginia, Downtown Mall started with considerable hope and faith in the nation's bicentennial year of 1976. This center city revitalization project stands out as a particularly successful reflection of how many American small cities have managed to reinvent themselves over the past three hundred years. Charlottesville's efforts have well served the fulfillment of the current needs of the diverse peoples the city encompasses as well as the social and economic progress of the greater central Virginia region.

Charlottesville, and what was once its seven-block central main street, have been touched by significant American history more often than have most locales. This section of road was born as a ridgetop Native American hunting trail. In the years preceding American independence, it became a major gateway to the West and the starting place for some of America's most famous Western explorers, George Rogers Clark, Merriwether Lewis, and William Clark. The Lewis and Clark Expedition, long credited with signaling the opening of the American West and celebrating its bicentennial in 2003, started from the western edge of what is now the Charlottesville Downtown Mall. It was home ground to three founding presidents, Thomas Jefferson, James Madison, and James Monroe, as well as frequently traveled by several other presidents, including Zachary Taylor, Woodrow Wilson, and Franklin D. Roosevelt. It was a literal "main street" embodiment of America's mercantile and industrial revolutions. And, in its present incarnation, it serves as the centerpiece of one of America's most celebrated model small cities and as the stomping ground for a long list of current literary giants and internationally renowned entertainers.

Even the regular activities and the individual buildings making up the Charlottesville Downtown Mall reflect the trends and controversies that have run through American history and attest to the vibrancy of the Mall's lifestyle. The eclectic collection of mostly Victorian-period facades and several blocks of tree-lined bricked pedestrian mall provide a focal point for several regional festivals. These include First Night Virginia, one of the nation's first community-based New Year's festivals; the summertime Friday's After Five celebration of the end of the workweek; the Virginia Festival of the Book; and the Virginia Film Festival. Some of the Downtown Mall's businesses have been present for more than a century, although not always in the same building; some businesses have retained an identity that has survived long after they left the Mall; and some buildings appeared on the street to national acclaim. The changing face of the street was in the thick of such national testings as the use of urban renewal to obliterate vital African-American communities. And it has most recently made national news with its plan to place a "freedom of expression" blackboard monument opposite the city hall building at the eastern end of the Mall.

The Charlottesville Downtown Mall lives at the foot of the small mountain crowned by Monticello, the home of Thomas Jefferson, author of many of the founding principles of the American nation and father of the nearby University of Virginia. On the whole, the beauty, creativity, and vibrant intellectual life nurturing this model for the progress of the nation's small city main street are truly reflective of the best of Jeffersonian principles. The success of the Mall has been recognized by the Pew Partnership for Civic Change, which has selected the project as one of the nineteen "Solutions for America."

From Three Notch'd Road to Downtown Mall

The first-recorded habitation of the Charlottesville region was that of the Monasukapanough Native Americans, who settled

East Main Street, Charlottesville, looking east. Parade by Monticello Guard, World War I, 24 September 1917. Photo by Holsinger. The Holsinger Studio Collection, Special Collections Department, University of Virginia Library.

some five miles north of the Charlottesville downtown area and who established trails across the area. Settlers of European origin traveled the east-west segment of these trails in the early eighteenth century in their move up from the Virginia Tidewater area. This trail took them through Richmond and out to the frontier beyond the Blue Ridge Mountains, located some thirty miles to the west of what was to become Charlottesville.

By the 1730s the Native American east-west ridgetop pathway had been improved into a surface suitable for supporting wheeled vehicles all the way into the Shenandoah Valley. The road, which passed through what became the Charlottesville downtown area where the Downtown Mall is now located, had become established enough by this time to have acquired a name, variously given as the Mountain Road or Mountain Ridge Road. In the spring of 1734, Peter Jefferson, father of Thomas Jefferson, was appointed as surveyor of the road, and organized settlement of the region started in earnest.

By 1737 the elder Jefferson had marked the road off in segments east to Richmond and through the Woolen Mills area of current Charlottesville from a zero-mile marker located a few miles west of Charlottesville at the D. S. Tavern. This building, which was owned by U.S. Supreme Court chief justice John Marshall from 1809 to 1813, still stands on Route 250 West. By 1742 the Charlottesville end of the road became known as the Three Notch'd Road. It had acquired this name from the notches axed into trees at intervals along the route of the now-surveyed road to mark the way for travelers and road builders. The Richmond end of the road was (and still is) known by the variant name of Three Chopt Road.

With an established road available as a reliable transportation route to support the plantations that dotted the area, including Peter Jefferson's Shadwell, the incentive was now there for settlements to grow at strategic locations, usually where navigable water and a road intersected. The county of Albemarle was established in 1744. Charlottesville, even though its river, the Rivanna, was not navigable at this point, was established as the county seat on 23 December 1762. The city was unpropitiously named for Charlotte Sophia of Mecklenburg-Strelitz, who the previous year had become the queen of the English king George III, the monarch some of Charlottesville's leading citizens later helped depose as sovereign over Virginia and twelve other colonies on the American continent.

Like most county seats in Virginia, Charlottesville's legal and mercantile center formed around the courthouse on Court Square. The 1803 portion of this building still stands as part of the Albemarle County courthouse complex. It was not until the early nineteenth century that the mercantile center moved two blocks to the south to Three Notch'd Road, which became Main Street for its Charlottesville segment and later transcended into what is now the Downtown Mall.

Three Notch'd Road can claim a couple of footnotes in the winning of the Revolutionary War. This was the road that was traversed during the major portion of the 1781 ride by the patriot Jack Jouett to warn then Virginia governor Thomas Jefferson of the approach of British Colonel Banastre Tarleton and a company of Dragoons, bent on capturing Jefferson and his cabinet, which was in session at the Charlottesville Courthouse. And near war's end, forces under the Marquis de Lafayette held a position on the road near Giles Allegre's Tavern on Mechunk Creek to thwart Earl Cornwallis's attempt to reach munitions stored at the old Albemarle Courthouse near the town of Scottsville. This action eventually helped lead to Cornwallis's surrender at Yorktown.

By 1840 Charlottesville's business center was slowly moved away from the Court Square area to just north of a branch of the new lifeline of the nation, the east-west railroad line. The Louisa Railroad Company, eventually to become the Chesapeake and Ohio, arrived in Charlottesville in 1850. The city's business community developed quickly through the nineteenth century. The city was occupied by Union forces under Major General George Custer and Colonel Philip Sheridan in 1865, and these troops burned the Woolen Mills, the main supplier of uniforms for Confederate troops. In spite of this, Charlottesville was largely untouched by the Civil War, reportedly in deference to the memory of Thomas Jefferson, and thus did not suffer many of the ravishes from war that were experienced by other southern communities.

In 1895 the city macadamized the in-town segment of Three Notch'd Road, now renamed Main Street, and Charlottesville's downtown business area became quite prosperous. The city's African-American community also was flourishing during this period in which many African-American-owned businesses became established in the Vinegar Hill area just to the west of the Main Street shops.

In the 1930s the east-west Route 250, which was built to straighten the old Three Notch'd Road route from Richmond to the Blue Ridge Mountains, traversed Charlottesville via Main Street. To relieve the burgeoning of automobile traffic into and through the town center after World War II, a bypass was built around Charlottesville in the late 1950s and early 1960s. But this move, along with the rise of suburban strip shopping malls, resulted in economic depression for the inner city area, just as was occurring under similar circumstances elsewhere in the nation.

In the 1960s Charlottesville was just one of many towns and cities across the United States that suffered deteriorating inner cities. Like some of these other communities, Charlottesville took advantage of the Federal urban renewal program that had been included in the Housing Act of 1949. In 1965 it started its own urban renewal project by leveling the Vinegar Hill neighborhood, located at the western end of Main Street, for future new development. The first five blocks of the pedestrian mall that transformed the Charlottesville Main Street business district into the current Downtown Mall was completed in 1976. Extensions to the Mall were completed in 1980 and then again, along with the completion of a large hotel and conference center at the western end, in 1985. An indoor ice park later joined the hotel at the western end of the Mall, and an open-air amphitheater was added at the eastern end in 1995.

The area now covers seven city blocks of bricked shopping and restaurant mall that include a central plaza with a large fountain and maturing trees down the center. This is not a "finished" project, as construction plans were recently announced on the extension of the pedestrian mall concept to nearby streets in the

Charlottesville downtown area. The mall's open-air cafés, boutiques, and numerous book stores combine to form a favorite meeting ground for city residents. But they also attract visitors to the region who are searching for an oasis of informal ambience after a day of visiting one of the nearby historical or recreational attractions. These include the presidential estates, Monticello, Ashlawn-Highlands, and Montpelier; the historic University of Virginia; the Michie Tavern, originally constructed on land once owned by Patrick Henry's father; the Blue Ridge Parkway, Shenandoah National Park, and Skyline Drive; and the many wineries dotting the beautiful rolling hills of central Virginia.

Timberlake's Drug Store

Unquestionably the longest surviving business on the Charlottesville Downtown Mall is Timberlake's Drug Store, which has been at its present location since 1917, but which has had a presence on Main Street since 1890. The drugstore's current building was constructed in 1895 as the People's National Bank. However, the site had originally been occupied by the town's tinner, who built a wooden building there in 1828. The tinner was replaced by the offices of the *Chronicle Newspaper*, run by Nancy West, a free African-American who lived above the shop with a prominent Jewish merchant, David Isaacs. The first brick building was erected on the site in 1848 on a much wider foundation. There were three shops downstairs, including Nancy West's new enterprise, a millinery, and the upstairs was occupied by the *Jefferson* newspaper. This building was torn down for the construction of the current building.

The only changes initially made by Timberlake's when it moved into the building in 1917 was the construction of display

Timberlake Drugstore (left) and the Charlottesville Hardware Store (second from right), 22 January 1918. Photo by Holsinger. The Holsinger Studio Collection, Special Collections Department, University of Virginia Library.

windows for the front. Adjustments to these display cases constituted the only restructuring of the facade for the next forty years. In 1956 the storefront was remodeled to return its facade to its 1917 look.

Almost from the beginning, the store's soda fountain, initially located at the street end of the building, became its most popular feature. Because of the soda fountain's increasing popularity over the years, the store was remodeled in 1960 to switch the luncheonette to the rear of the building. By this time, people who were visiting the pharmacy for drug items and prescriptions were finding it almost impossible to get through the crowded soda fountain to the back of the store. Then, as now, the soda fountain featured ammonia-infused Cokes and egg salad sandwiches. The drugstore itself was well known for delivering prescriptions and for stocking hard-to-find items. In the 1960 remodeling, the original mahogany cabinets and a rolling ladder to aid access to upper shelves were also removed.

Timberlake's, now in its third generation of ownership by the Plantz family, received yet another remodeling in 2000. But its longtime patrons have been delighted to discover after work was completed that the old-time ambience of Timberlake's has been preserved, that the soda fountain still serves its ammonia-infused Cokes and egg salad sandwiches, and that the pharmacy still delivers prescriptions.

The Hardware Store

When is a hardware store not a hardware store? When it has been serving meals in its storefront restaurant and its open-air Garden Café on the center of the Charlottesville Downtown Mall for more that twenty-five years.

For even longer than that, however, the store on the Mall that now goes by the name of the Hardware Store Restaurant did sell everything from china and crystal and household items to hog oilers and Ford automobiles. You could buy a Ford Runabout there in 1909 for $359.75 that was just as fully equipped as was anyone else's Runabout—except that it came unassembled because the store did not have access to space to assemble the vehicles.

Charlottesville's Paramount Theater, circa 1936. Photo by George C. Seward. The George C. Seward Collection, Special Collections Department, University of Virginia.

The Charlottesville Hardware Co., Inc., was built on Main Street in 1895. The store's owner and proprietor was Charles H. Walker, who had served with the audacious and legendary Confederate cavalry colonel, John S. Mosby, during the Civil War. The original building was destroyed by a fire that leveled the entire block on 5 February 1909, reportedly set to cover up a robbery. But the hardware business was booming and Walker rebuilt immediately. Typical of the elaborately decorated Victorian buildings being constructed on Charlottesville's Main Street in the early twentieth century, the new building was tall and narrow, extending the entire block back to Water Street. Its face was embellished with tan pressed brick laid in stretcher bond on the three-bay facade.

Business continued to be so prosperous for the hardware store that it relocated to a larger building in 1969, where it promptly went out of business. Apparently even then location was the key to success. The store's Main Street location was occupied in late 1975 by a restaurant in the main part of the building with shops at the front, on the mezzanine, and in the basement. The restaurant, the first to open on the newly created Downtown Mall, retained the Hardware Store motif. It continues as a major attraction in and of itself in Charlottesville and on the Downtown Mall, because the original wall shelving, the rolling shelf ladders, and much original hardware store merchandise have been left intact as decoration.

The Paramount Theater

Charlottesville made a national splash on 25 November 1931 by opening an ultraluxurious new-style motion picture house on as big a scale as those being opened in major cities across the nation on the wager that the motion picture would replace live entertainment. The Paramount Theater that was constructed at the center of Charlottesville's Main Street hedged its own bets by including facilities to accommodate live performances. But from the beginning, the 1,200-seat gilded palace concentrated on presenting first-run movies.

In deference to the theater's location in Thomas Jefferson country, the Chicago architectural firm of C. W. and George L.

Rapp rendered the Paramount in the eighteenth-century Georgian style. Most of the firm's theater designs at the time were being rendered in the then very popular art deco style. In contrast, Georgian chandeliers and a mural of Monticello predominated in the Paramount's plush interior.

The theater was opened in style. According to the *Daily Progress* report on 27 November 1931, "Throngs had to be turned away from the doors." The line of those who could not be accommodated wound around the block. The account reported that congratulatory baskets of flowers were sent by Marlene Dietrich, George Bancroft, Maurice Chevalier, Joan Crawford, Norma Shearer, and Clark Gable. Those attending the opening were entertained by Brownie, the celebrated single-monikered theater's organist at the console of the "mighty three manual Wurlitzer." They also viewed the theater's first feature, *Touchdown*, a "thrilling football drama," starring Richard Arlen, Peggy Shannon, Jackie Oakie, and Regis Toomey.

The Paramount closed its doors in 1974, a few years after a string of suburban movie houses opened on the city's northern periphery. The later years had not been kind to the theater. Alleged years of neglect by the theater management resulted in a celebrated lawsuit between the building's owners and the theater company. The last movie shown was *Thomasene and Bushrod*, which closed its run on 30 June 1974.

Twenty years later, a preservation foundation was formed to restore and reopen the Paramount for films, live entertainment, and center-city social gatherings. Painstaking restoration continues. A neighboring storefront was recently purchased by the foundation to enlarge the streetfront lobby space for the theater. In time, the rejuvenated Paramount will become yet another jewel in the crown of and will increase the opportunities for entertainment venues on the Charlottesville Downtown Mall.

Urban Renewing the African-American Community

Charlottesville was not morally or intellectually superior to any other American city or town in its move to employ the post–World War II urban renewal and housing programs to "beautify and revitalize" its downtown area by demolishing a flourishing inner-city African-American community. The clearing of the Vinegar Hill neighborhood just to the west of the Downtown Mall project was an integral part of the city's downtown refurbishment planning.

Most of the displacement of African-American homes and businesses occurred on the periphery of the Downtown Mall project. However, at least one construction project attached to the program, the construction of the current Charlottesville city hall at the eastern end of the Mall, displaced the only then African-American–owned outdoor sign advertising business in the nation.

The Vinegar Hill community had originally been established as a cohesive neighborhood in the early nineteenth century by Irish building construction artisans. These specialists and their families had fled reprisals for involvement in the United Irishmen cause in Ireland and ended up in central Virginia to work on ongoing construction in the region. Projects they worked on included Jefferson's home, Monticello; Madison's home, Montpelier; and the lawn pavilions at the University of Virginia, which is located two miles west of downtown Charlottesville. The name for the community is said to have come either from a fighting ground in Ireland or from the questionable quality of the whiskey produced within the community.

As the nineteenth century progressed and as slavery came to an end in Virginia, the Irish residents became displaced by African-Americans, who established a viable neighborhood of their own on Vinegar Hill. During the early part of the twentieth century, Vinegar Hill became a busy commercial district, with tailor shops, thrift stores, grocery stores, and restaurants, all of which were owned and operated by members of the community.

In 1965 the provisions of the 1949 Housing Act were used to evict the residents of Vinegar Hill and to rehouse many of them in cookie-cutter public housing projects on the fringes of the town. When this occurred, there were six hundred residents of the neighborhood, 92 percent of whom were African-Americans. The subsequent demolition destroyed 130 buildings, which included 29 African-American–owned businesses and 2 churches.

In a visual indictment of the city's quick-fingered urban renewal planning, in 1982, twenty-three years after the massive demolition of the neighborhood, seven acres of Vinegar Hill still remained empty. The first major construction project in the area, near the western end of the Downtown Mall, was the Federal Court Building, completed in 1983. The second, the Omni Hotel, anchoring the western end of the Downtown Mall and completed with vast infusions of city money on more than one occasion, was finished in 1985.

References

Bacque, Peter. "Hardware Building to Become a Restaurant." *Daily Progress*, 24 June 1975.

Cross-White, Agnes. *Images of America: Charlottesville, the African-American Community.* Dover, N.H.: Arcadia Publishing, 1998.

"Historic Landmark Study." Charlottesville, Va.: Landmarks Commission, Department of Community Development, 1976.

Johnson, Chris. "Timberlake Drug Store." Available on Internet website "Charlottesville and Albemarle, Virginia, Then and Now: Articles and Interviews of Local People and Places" <http://xroads.virginia.edu/~PUBLIC/AHS/AREA>, accessed 30 June 2001.

Landmark Survey. Charlottesville, Va.: Department of Community Development Landmark Commission, September 1974.

Lay, Edward K. *The Architecture of Jefferson Country: Charlottesville and Albemarle County, Virginia.* Charlottesville, Va.: University Press of Virginia, 2000.

Martin, Mary Sproles. "The Paramount: Creating a New Venue from a Landmark Building." *Charlottesville Area Real Estate Weekly*, 8–14 June 2000.

Maurer, David A. "Timberlake's Preserves the Past for Those Who Want to Go Back." *Daily Progress*, 18 February 1990.

McGrath, Ray. "Old Hardware Store Gone Forever." *Daily Progress,* 28 May 1978.
Meeks, Steven G. "Tracing the Trail of the Three Notch'd Road." Charlottesville *Bulletin* 8, no. 20 (26 February 1986).
"Paramount Opens with Gala Show." *Daily Progress,* 27 November 1931.
Pawlett, Nathaniel Mason. "Three Notch'd Road." *Bulletin of the Albemarle County Historical Society* 14, no. 3 (Summer 1994): 6–7.
Pawlett, Nathaniel Mason, and Howard Newlon Jr. "Historic Roads of Virginia: The Route of the Three Notch'd Road. A Preliminary Report." Charlottesville, Va.: Virginia Highway and Transportation Research Council, January 1976.
Pettitt, James. "The Hardware Store." Available on Internet website "Charlottesville and Albemarle, Virginia, Then and Now: Articles and Interviews of Local People and Places" <http://xroads.virginia.edu/~PUBLIC/AHS/AREA>, accessed 30 June 2001.
Rose, Deborah. "Make a Date for Paramount Benefit Gala." *Daily Progress,* 28 June 1999.
Schwartz, Ken. "Charlottesville: A Brief Urban History." Available on Internet website <http://www.avenue.org/achs/links.html>, accessed 30 June 2001.
"Theater News Promising," *Daily Progress,* 16 August 1999.
Theater program for Teresa Dowell-Vest's *Vinegar Hill,* presented by the Live Arts Theatre Ensemble, 5–20 May, 2000.
"Timberlake's, Downtown-on-the-Mall." 1990 centennial brochure. Charlottesville, Va.

About the Author

Having fallen in love with the foothills of central Virginia while both were attending the University of Virginia, author Gary Kessler and his wife, Evelyn, vowed that someday they would return to Charlottesville, Virginia, to live. Following diplomatic careers of nearly three decades that took them around the world twice, they did just that. During their period of foreign service, the author served in the U.S. government's foreign media news agency in postings that included senior editor at the East Asia bureau, deputy chief at the Mideast and Southeast Asia bureaus, chief of the Mideast bureau, chief analyst for China and the Third World, and managing editor. While living abroad, the author also served as a drama critic and entertainment columnist for four national-level English-language newspapers, the *Bangkok Post*, the *Bangkok Nation Review*, the *Cyprus Daily Mail*, and the *Cyprus Sun*. He also produced plays and concerts and worked on movie productions that included *The Deerhunter*, *The Killing Fields*, *Good Morning Vietnam*, and *Volunteers*. Since retiring early to the Charlottesville area, he has worked as a freelance book editor and novelist. The first book of his Cyprus Intrigue espionage thriller series, *Laughter Down the Mountain*, was released as an e-book in 2001, and a second in the series, *Retired with Prejudice*, is forthcoming. For more information on his writing, visit his web site at www.editsbooks.com.

About the Photographers

Contemporary Photographs

Rick Britton is a Charlottesville-based professional writer and photographer. He has regularly provided the "Archives" article for *Albemarle* magazine for several years and is a book reviewer for the *Washington Times*.

Stacey Evans, an art photographer for seven of the twelve years she has been practicing the craft, focuses mostly on the impact of time and humans on the environment surrounding her. A native Virginian who has lived in Georgia, she received her Bachelor of Fine Arts in Photography from the Savannah College of Art and Design. She has steeped herself in the culture of the Charlottesville Downtown Mall by living and working there for the past several years. Her business, Evans Imaging, is located below the Jefferson Theater on the Mall and focuses on creating and reproducing images for commercial and fine art sales.

Vintage Photographs

Rufus W. Holsinger's amazing collection of 9,000 dry-plate glass negatives and 500 celluloid negatives of Charlottesville locations and people of the early nineteenth century is housed in the University of Virginia's Special Collections library and exists as a major repository of central Virginia history of the period. An extensive database of this collection is available on the Internet at http://www.lib.virginia.edu/speccol/holsinger/holsinger.

Holsinger came to Charlottesville from Pennsylvania in the late 1880s and established a photographic business on West Main street. During a prolific career of capturing Charlottesville life on film, he also served at various times as president and treasurer of the Photographic Association of Virginia and the Carolinas and as treasurer of the Photographic Association of America. When he died in 1930, his photography studio passed to the family; his surviving collection of negatives was acquired by the University of Virginia in 1978. The collection is especially notable for its nearly 500 portraits of African-American citizens of Charlottesville, and many of his photographs have been published in Cecile Wendover Clover, F. T. Heslich, and Rufus W. Holsinger's *Holsinger's Charlottesville: A Collection of Photographs* (Charlottesville, Va.: Art Restorations Services, 1985).

George C. Seward's photographs captured life at the University of Virginia and in downtown Charlottesville during the 1930s and are contained in a special collection at that university's Alderman Library. Mr. Seward received a B.A., Phi Beta Kappa, from the University of Virginia in 1933 and later received an LL.B., Order of the Coif, in 1936. He joined the leading New York law firm of Seward and Kissel, LLP, in 1953, where he is senior council. He is a former president of the Arts and Sciences Council of the University of Virginia.